An Unexpected Complication

Book 1 of Keeper and His Tiger

A Novel by **Aidan Red**

Copyright

Keeper and His Tiger: Book 1, An Unexpected Complication
Copyright © 2018 by Aidan Red
All Rights Reserved
Revision Date 3/1/19

Published by Red's Ink and Quill, Wichita, KS

For information on other works by Aidan Red, Science Fiction and Fiction, published or forthcoming, visit RedsInkandQuill.com or AidanRedBooks.com

eBook ISBNs:
978-1-946039-33-0
1-946039-33-0
Softcover ISBNs:
978-1-946039-32-3
1-946039-32-2

To my family and friends that have supported me and have made the challenge of creating and bringing life to my stories so rewarding.

◻-◻-◻-◻-◻

My many thanks to my editors and cover designer.

Content Editing by Trenda London,
http://ItsYourStoryContentEditing.com

Copy Editing by Amy Jackson,
Copy Editing and Proofreading, http://AmyJacksonEditing.com

Cover by Amy Queau,
Q Design Covers and Premades, www.QCoverDesign.com

Things seldom go as planned, especially when you're chasing a murderer.

Contents

One

Young William, in the back seat of his parents' car, reminisced over the most enjoyable Labor Day weekend he could remember. His family's friends were always welcoming and put great effort into making each visit wonderful. The meals were lavish, as his mother called them, and the nights around the fire pit on the back patio were memorable, especially when their younger daughter snuggled beside him as they listened to the adults in the evenings.

Smiling, he was remembering when he had first met them and their two daughters, Sandra and Wilhelmina. *Oh, how she hates that name!* He chuckled, remembering how, eyes blazing, she would punch him on the arm every time he teasingly called her that. Then he smiled and squeezed himself; they had been invited for an overnight visit so both of their fathers could discuss some business project. His mother eagerly looked forward to what she called "one-on-one woman time" while the men would ponder their higher business goals. He was nine and the daughters were five and eight when they met.

He grinned contently as he unbuckled his seat belt, stretched out across the back seat, and closed his eyes. During the five years after he met them, it was the younger of their two daughters that had caught his attention and it was obvious to him that he had caught hers too. He knew she was a bit of a show-off, but she showed off more when he came to visit.

Tonight, when they left their friends' place, his dad asked why he did not favor Sandra more, since she was only a year younger than him, similar in maturity. William shrugged, unable to explain. He remembered smiling at his dad and asking the only thing that came to his mind: why did he favor Mom over someone else? His dad gave a wide, understanding smile in

1

response. William was not certain at first why she had caught his attention, nor why she became the one he thought of most of the time, but as their visits continued, he knew it was her spirit—the way she looked at him, singling him out, choosing him to share in everything she did while he was there. She seemed to only see him when he was around, eager to do things he suggested and to show him new things she had discovered between their visits and that she wanted to do. It was strange, but he was reluctant to tell his father how he felt about her. It was not that he could keep it secret, but it was the first time he felt something he did not want to explain. She was the first thing he had ever experienced that he wanted to keep private, to himself.

Why, he did not know, but he remembered the day three years past that he and Wilhelmina were riding; she was seven and her horse slid on a muddy spot and slammed against a tree. His mind cringed in his intense mutual feeling of pain, the sickening sound of her hitting the unyielding trunk, pinned by her horse as it fell.

Her pained scream echoing in his mind blurred into his father's startled yell! The car suddenly dropped out from under him and began to tumble. He slammed against the roof and then against a door, and suddenly everything was dark.

William heard the soft, unfamiliar crackling sounds and tried to twist around, but his body writhed in pain. Unable to tell how long he had lain there, he tried to open his eyes only to realize they were already open. Everything was dark, topsy-turvy and mashed against his face. He tried to push himself upright, but searing pains shot up his arms and across his chest and torso. Suddenly he saw the dancing yellow reflections in the visible trees, saplings, and brush all crammed tightly around him. Confused but determined, he gritted his teeth against the pain in his arm and stomach and slowly turned toward the flickering light. He saw a car engulfed in a raging fire and his heart stopped.

He could not move or yell, his mind frozen as he recognized details and absorbed the reality. He tried to move, to go, to see if they had gotten out, to—

A searing pain across his belly just above his waist stopped him, doubling him up, and one arm felt like it was on fire. Gasping for breath, he caught a movement beyond the flames: a man carrying a gas can climbed the other bank of the ditch and got into the back of a pickup truck.

Disoriented with pain, grief, and fear, William held his breath and tightened his guts against the horrific pain as he watched another man collect things from the road, toss them in the bed of the truck, and then get into the cab. The man glanced back at the burning car and drove away as a wave of nausea swept over William.

William gritted his teeth and tried to hold the spew back, fearing he would tear his stomach open if he heaved. The tears came and William tried to look for signs of his mother or his father, but he saw nothing except the torrent of flames gushing out through the shattered windows, bright fingers curling up into an angry fist and disappearing in the thick, oily cloud of smoke, swallowed by the darkness of the night.

He wiped feebly at the unrelenting tears streaking his face and stared at the burning hulk, knowing it was too late to help them. Despair and emptiness overwhelmed him and the unceasing tears poured from his eyes, stinging his lacerations.

He looked at his stomach and tried to understand why the end of a broken tree branch was poking out of his shirt. Desperately he gripped the stub, and his touch confirmed it had pierced him, ripping the flesh from one side to the other as it gored him.

William took a deep breath, clenched his teeth, closed his eyes, and jerked. He screamed, the pain leaving him breathless and lightheaded as he bunched his shirt up around the gash and held it tight, his fingers holding the edges of the tear together.

He looked up at the road where the truck had gone and sudden fear engulfed him; they might come back and look for survivors. It was just him now, and he knew he could not stay where he was. Somehow, he would find out who did this and make them pay. Somehow.

William did not know how long he lay there after the men

left, but finally he forced himself to move, crawling the best he could until he could pull himself up beside a tree. Appraising his condition, he figured one arm was broken and he stuffed that hand in the shirt to hold it wadded against the rent across his stomach, thankful his fingers still worked. When he put his weight on his legs, he knew something was wrong with his opposite hip, but he could make himself stand. With short steps, he hobbled through the trees and brush until he could cross the ditch to the bridge. Against his body's demands to stop and rest he pushed himself, squeezing the long gash shut with his fingers and holding the wadded shirttail tight against the bleeding with his good hand, knowing he had to get into the city. It was closer than home, and maybe he could find his mother's sister. He had to tell her what had happened, and he knew she could help him. He glanced over his shoulder where the fire still raged, and he hurried to get away before the men came back.

¤-¤-¤-¤-¤

William stumbled into the haphazard suburb of displaced people on the northwest side of Chesterfield just before noon the next day, dazed and exhausted. The last of his energy finally spent, he reached out to steady himself and collapsed against the first cardboard hovel.

-¤-

An angry man jumped out of the collapsed refuge, profusely shouting profanities at whoever was so vile as to decimate his dwelling. He turned with his fist cocked to confront the intruder, but stopped suddenly when he saw the blood-covered slight of a boy, gritting his teeth and groaning in pain as he tried to push himself up.

"What in...Owl! Help me!" the man shouted as he knelt down and slowly rolled William onto his back.

The woman stopped as he looked up at her.

"Get old man Crutches. This boy's hurt somethin' bad, I

4

think."

The woman hurried up the alley, zigging between and around the makeshift shelters.

The man leaned closer and started looking the boy over. "What's your name, son? Where did you come from? What happened?"

Before William could answer, the woman came back, stopping beside the first man as Crutches knelt beside William. Crutches looked at his arm, then his leg and finally pulled his bloodstained shirt up and scowled at the tear across his stomach.

"This boy needs a hospital," Crutches said, pushing as gently as he could around the boy's torso.

William tried to hold his scream, but it slipped out with a vengeance.

"I'm Cutter, my wife Owl, and this is Crutches, son," the younger man said. "He's had some medical training and he knows what to do."

"No," William said softly. "No hospital. Find Mary. She'll help me. Find Mary. Please."

"Okay." Owl grimaced, looking over the men's shoulders, and asked softly, "Who's Mary? Where can we find her?"

"Mary Butler. Restaurant," he said softly, barely more than a whisper as the pain and continued effort to stay awake drained the last of his energy. "Please. Find Mary Butler..."

"I'm afraid he's out for a while," Crutches said as he sat back on his heels and stared at the unconscious lad. "Please find some clean cloths and some warm, clean water, Owl. I'll see if I can at least clean him up a little." Crutches shook his head and looked at Cutter. "If you don't find this Mary Butler, I'm afraid this lad will bleed out before we can help him."

"How bad is it?" Owl asked.

"Broken upper arm, possibly a hip, and a very bad goring. It isn't good," Crutches said, and felt the boy's forehead. "And a fever."

Cutter got up and turned to the faces that had gathered

around them. "Has anyone seen Ferret?"

"I'm here," a skinny boy of ten said as he shouldered his way between the adults.

"You have a knack fer finding things out," Cutter said. "Find this Mary Butler he's asking for. She's somewhere in town and has something to do with a restaurant. And hurry! He doesn't have much time."

"Okay," Ferret said, and turned back into the crowd. "Hey, Mouse," Ferret hollered as he disappeared. "Come and help me."

Two

Tuesday, April 12

Seventeen Years Later

Billie Mattis absently swept a vagrant lock of her bright red hair aside and focused on the contract's development concept and proposal options. Slowly she flipped through the pages of the Boster, Lange and Hammersmith Architectural Design firm's real estate development project definition, carefully comparing the contract to the project details.

She came to the design consulting firm shortly after graduating college with a Master's Degree in Business and was very happy when the firm's junior partner, "The" Mr. Boster, interviewed her and decided she had a place with them. Of course, fact checker and file corrector was not a great position, but it did have its perks. Billie knew the work was important; someone had to do it, and she was happy that someone was her.

"He didn't call, did he?" the blonde from the next office asked as she stopped in the doorway.

"No, thank God," Billie said without looking up. "Thanks for bringing him up and adding those cheerful memories to my morning, Sue."

"Just checkin' to be sure you're standin' your ground," she said. "It's been what—two, three weeks now?" Sue smiled and then went into her office.

"A month."

Billie stopped her scanning and looked up, absently staring out through the large, westerly facing window with open blinds. The rolling Midwestern countryside and farmland stretched out across the horizon beyond the city buildings. The bright, clear, almost cheerful sky belied the cold of the north winds. Sue's questions stirred unwanted memories and Billie frowned.

She had only known Blake Lawrence a week before he had barged into her life, making the next three months the worst she had ever experienced. The first couple of weeks had started normally, but quickly degenerated into barely tolerable. At first it was simply meeting for lunch or dinner, some quiet venue, a light meal going Dutch. Then the venues became larger, the dinners more elaborate, and the bars more frequent. He had invaded her girls' nights out, and the rift between her and her girlfriends was just beginning to heal.

Billie relaxed her clenched fist and thought back, wondering what it was that had attracted her to him in the first place. If that was even the word. He was not overly attractive—only marginally handsome—and seldom had a kind word to say about anyone, and she could not remember ever inviting him to join her in anything. Damn! She was pathetic! She hated the way he had just moved in and demanded her attention. And shit! She had let him.

Then, the arguing began.

She had been caught completely off guard the first time he "forgot" his wallet and credit cards, further perpetuating the uneasiness in their association; dinner at a new high-end steakhouse out by the airport. It was late and they had imbibed more than they should have, and without thinking it through she had paid, explaining that he owed her, but outside he had turned abusive "helping" her into his car. He had made sure she knew he expected her to pay once in a while. The incidents had come more and more often, and he had become more physical each time she had argued or refused to succumb to his demands. Each time she had tried to fight back, but he had always overpowered her. She was not certain which had angered her more—his increasingly insensitive and abusive demands or that she was such weak and easy prey for him. Whichever it was, somehow her rage had begun to break through the shroud of despair that had held her captive ever since Willum. Finally, she had even started watching streaming martial arts videos, looking for and hoping to find some way to defend herself.

Billie could not remember why it had happened when it had. No matter how much she had told herself to end it, she had known there was no way to force it. She had not planned to tell him when she had, but finally tired of the demands and the abuse, she had seized the moment when it came. They had been in the hallway just outside her apartment when he had announced that he expected their relationship to rise to a higher level.

She had exploded! Shouting and shrieking that intimacy with him was the last thing she would ever do!

She should have been more afraid, knowing her continued denial of intimacy was one of his biggest triggers.

Blake had smirked at her as if she were jesting, and she had quickly opened her apartment door and tried to slip inside. He was quick and had shoved the door open before she could latch it.

Her hand involuntarily jumped to her face and she inhaled sharply, shaking, a squeak slipping past her lips, suddenly remembering Blake's fist when he had pushed the door open and slammed it into her face.

She had screamed as she hit the floor, knocked nearly halfway across her apartment. She had scampered back to her feet, cursing and screaming as loud as she could. She had tried to push him out of her apartment, but her efforts had been futile; he had refused to leave and had the mass to enforce it. She had even tried a boxing kick and a jab to his face.

Finally, she had resorted to punching his stomach and chest, screaming for him to leave, and somewhere during the commotion one of her neighbors had called the building's security. The guards had arrived in time to see Blake swing and hit her in the face again.

The security guard had held him until the local police had come and escorted him out. Billie had filed a report and the immediate tension evaporated. She had curled up on her sofa with a pillow, crying herself out until she finally fell asleep.

But now she was shaking; Sue's casual inquiry had plunged

her back into the nightmare of memories, and the old worry of Blake coming back to find her had reawakened.

Each day of the past month had started without anxiety or remorse and she had felt extremely relieved, free. Even the bruises were fading, but she knew she still did not know what she could do if he came back.

Billie shivered and tried to shake off her growing depression, forcing herself to stop thinking about Blake. She sipped her tepid tea and suddenly a happier thought crossed her mind. She picked up the phone's handset and keyed a sequence.

"Lori," she said when the connection made. "Are you up for a burger at the Streetcar?"

Lori's voice answered, "Sure. Eleven thirty? I'll call Stacy and Becky."

"Okay. Meet you there," Billie said, and glanced at the clock as she hung up.

She turned back to the folder and scrolled the computer display to a new page, wondering if she could finish the section of the customer order she was on in time. She had forty-five minutes before she had to leave.

¤-¤-¤-¤-¤

The Streetcar Diner sat on the northeast corner of St. Anne and Duberry, west of Chesterfield's city center. Its exterior was in the character of an old St. Charles trolley car, with wide windows along its length overlooking St. Anne and the two-step-up, raised platform on the west end, emulating a streetcar's covered platform.

Billy Carson, the oldest of the Streetcar Diner's staff, finished wiping down the stack of plastic laminated menus Angie had dropped off on her way to the powder room. "They're all clean, Angie," he said, turning back to the dishwasher when she passed through the kitchen.

"Thanks," she said, and grabbed the menus as she hurried back to the hostess' station. Angie, dark hair, taller than normal for a young woman in her mid-twenties, was the head waitress and hostess. She managed the dining room. Her very attractive figure, attention to her appearances, and her assertiveness made her perfect for being the first person customers met when they passed through the double set of front doors and entered the diner.

Billy stepped up to the swinging saloon-style doors in the archway between the kitchen area and the dining room, and leaned out looking for Ned, the youngest of the Streetcar staff. Ned helped Billy clear the tables, wash the dishes, mop the floor, and about anything that did not involve preparing food. Ned was filling his tub with dirty dishes and glanced up to see Billy at the kitchen door. With a nod, he gathered his tub and hurried to the kitchen and the waiting dishwasher.

"Gotta get the two tables by the front door," Ned said, and grabbed a tub that Billy had emptied moments before. "They're running me ragged today."

He turned and rushed back into the dining room, almost running over the attractive blond woman on her way to take the order at a table near the kitchen door. "Sorry, Carole," Ned said softly as he dodged around her and kept going.

"Slow down," Carole absently answered.

Carole was also in her mid-twenties and their second waitress. She assisted Angie when the rush got demanding, hustling the trays of orders from the long back counter to the various tables, and taking orders from new customers once they were seated. She also set the place settings on the tables after Ned bussed them.

At the long back counter under the kitchen pass-through window, Melony, a thin brunette of average height, quietly and quickly organized the plates from the kitchen onto the trays matching the order tickets.

"Order sixteen up. Seventeen up," she said as Angie stopped and looked over her shoulder, picking up the first ready tray.

"Thanks, Mel," Angie said, and turned with the tray. "I'll be right back for that one."

Between the long back counter and the diners, another attractive brunette, Julie, the second youngest of the dining room staff, served the customers seated at the drugstore-style counter, handled the drink portions of everyone's orders, and helped when the rush demanded more than two waitresses.

Billy finished loading the dishwasher, closed the doors, and switched the cycle on. He glanced across the kitchen from his sanitary station to see the flare-up on the grill and Niles jump back. Niles dropped a domed lid over the steak flare-up and scolded Kevin, telling him to watch where he splashed the cooking oil next time; the order was not flambé.

Niles, a spindly young man just in his twenties and Kevin, a heavier version of Niles, though shorter in stature, helped Sid, the owner and head cook, with food preparation and occasionally cooking.

Billy chuckled but smiled at knowing the staff. Together, the nine of them, under Sid's guidance, were the backbone and the lifeblood of the diner. Except for himself, they were young in years and yet very much professionals when it came to the daily demands of a top-rated casual eating establishment.

Billy was the "elder" of the staff at just over thirty, and had been employed at the diner in his sanitary technician capacity longer than any of the other employees, save Sid. It was also his job to come in early, before any of the others, and start preparing the diner for Sid every weekday morning.

Billy thought about the steadily growing lunch business as he grabbed an empty tub and stepped into the dining room to help Ned with bussing. He was pleased with the happy, almost jovial sounds of the customers and their conversations.

Billy cleared a table under the middle front window, wiped the booth's benches and the bright steel support rail across the back of each of them. When he picked up his tub, he absently noticed four women waiting by the front door. They looked younger than himself. Regulars, he thought, knowing he had seen them before; but today for some reason, the redhead with her long curls caught his attention. Something seemed oddly familiar about her, but he shook his head, unable to think what it was as his dry towel made one last swipe across the table before he turned to the back room. Angie had seated the four in the booth before he reached the sinks.

◻-◻-◻-◻-◻

Bundled against the sharp wind in her heavy jacket, Billie hurried up the sidewalk and met her friends as they reached the steps to the Streetcar's front doors. Becky pushed their way through the entrance and they stopped just inside to survey the nearly full dining room. The hostess met them quickly, pulled four menus from the rack by the door, and led them to a booth at the front of the room. She asked for their drink orders and adjusted the blinds; the sun was brilliant and the sky cloudless, though the weather was still cold. The sun could be hot through the huge glass windows.

Billie enjoyed the normal banter with her friends, and dodged most of the questions about her recently exed boyfriend—a subject she did *not* want to get into. Their conversation drifted to work: Lori's accounting job at the drugstore, Becky's assistant curator job at the museum, and Stacy's job at the bookstore. Billie was about to mention the project she was reviewing when the elderly man at the table across the aisle from them moved a plate and accidently pushed his soup bowl off the edge of the table.

◻-◻-◻-◻-◻

Billy had just finished rinsing and stacking the dishware and glasses in the dishwasher tray when the unmistakable sound of a dish falling on the linoleum floor resounded from the dining room. In reflex, he grabbed his tub, extra rags, and the bottle of cleaner, and turned and hurried into the dining room. There, in the aisle between the front row of tables and booths, he spotted the soup bowl, split into two pieces lying on the floor, bits of meat and vegetables swimming in the puddle of thick broth between them. As he knelt down and picked up the pieces amid the old man's profuse apologies, Angie was already straightening the customer's place setting, assuring him that everything was all right and placing a new bowl of soup in front of him.

Nice, Billy thought to himself. *The customers sure can't complain about Angie's service.*

Billy had the dish fragments collected and floor wiped clean when he noticed the red boots on long slender legs covered by dark leggings under the adjacent booth. Soup spatters of varying sizes dotted the red boots.

Suddenly, triggered by the appearance, a long-sequestered, almost-forgotten memory slipped back into his mind. He pulled a small bottle of sparkling water from his apron pocket and wet the corner of a clean rag. He looked up past the thigh-length skirt and smiled into the redhead's beautiful, lightly freckled face, remembering a twelve-year-old, green-eyed redheaded girl that wore a similar pair of red boots and a spiky, cone-shaped renaissance hat. The remembered words in a heavy, informal Old English accent unexpectedly spilled out. "M'lady, may I wipe this dreadful soil from your pretty boots?"

She looked down at him, stunned, and before she could utter a word he gently took her foot and began cleaning the soup spots.

Silently he released her boot, gently setting it down, and then took the other one. As he cleaned the second, he looked up and the rest of the remembered phrase flowed out. "M'lady, may I say that red distracts frightfully from the beautiful color of your hair."

Her expression completely blank, her mouth moving in confusion, her beautiful, piercing green eyes said it all.

Shit! Billy suddenly thought to himself. *What did you just do, Billy? You shouldn't have done that! You really shouldn't have done that!*

Quickly, realizing the situation had caught him up and the

discomfort he was causing her, he dropped his rags into his tub and hurried to the back room. He barely heard one of the women asking the redhead, "Billie, what did he do? Billie? Billie, are you listening?"

He glanced back with a flick of his eyes as he turned through the swinging doors and saw that she was watching him, her confused expression still filling her perfectly proportioned face.

"Billy!" Sid said, blocking Billy's path. "What was that?"

"Just...cleaning up a spill," he said as he pushed past Sid and went to the sink and the dirty dishes.

❑-❑-❑-❑-❑

Sitting next to the aisle, Billie jumped when the bowl fell, broke, and splashed the soup. She stared at the broken bowl in stunned silence until a man in a white shirt, pants, and apron bent over the spill and began cleaning up the mess. She was startled when he looked up at her and asked if he could clean her "pretty boots." His accented words made her thoughts stumble, but his actions were so surprising that she found herself unable to react.

Strangely frozen in place, she watched the man as he took her foot, gently wiped the boot clean, and then cleaned her other boot. She barely heard him when he said something about how her red boots distracted frightfully from the beautiful color of her hair. She stared at the man's strong, square facial features and bright, light brown eyes smiling up at her, repeating the "distracts frightfully" and "beautiful color of your hair" phrases in her mind. She knew she needed to respond, say something about his unwarranted actions, but when she tried to mouth a suitable reprimand, she had no words to say.

She watched, unable to take her eyes off him, unable to turn back to her friends as he scooped up his tub and rags and hurried to the back room.

He glanced back at her as he turned in the doorway and Lori's voice interrupted, breaking the spell the man seemed to have cast over her. Lori asked from the opposite corner of the table, "Billie, what did he do? Billie? Billie, are you listening?"

"Of all the opinionated, pretentious..." Billie muttered quickly and looked at Lori, still unsure she had heard what she thought she had heard. She was surprised she had words to say now, but not during the moment before. Her eyes flicked back to the archway and then back to Lori.

"What happened?" Lori persisted. "What did he do?"

"He cleaned her boot," Stacy said from her place beside Lori and across from Billie. "He just cleaned her boot and said something about the color red or something. Honestly, it was so inappropriate. He was so weird."

Lori just stared at Billie. Bewildered, Becky said she did not understand.

"What would possess someone to do something like that?" Billie asked half out loud, and looked down at her menu, befuddled. "That was so pompous and rude."

When the waitress stopped with their drinks, she apologized for the disturbance and offered Billie an appetizer or a dessert for her inconvenience. Billie chose a rain check on a dessert and then the waitress took their lunch orders, entered the items on a handheld digital pad, and turned with a smile to a table out of Billie's view.

"So, what does Old Man Boster have you working on these days?" Stacy asked, and took a draw on the straw in her soda.

"Someone has an interest in that old building on Second and Baker Street, the old Duckard's Department Store," Billie said, shaking the surprise from her mind and taking a sip of her cola. "Mr. Boster and his associates have worked up a proposal for the renovation designs and cost estimates, and I'm doing the detail crosschecks."

"Sounds simply tedious," Lori said.

"Could be interesting," Becky said. "Do you know who owns it now?"

"You know, I don't," Billie admitted. "I will after I get to that part of the proposal this afternoon. But the work is actually interesting. Especially seeing how they look at the designs."

"Has to be in arrears by now," Stacy said, and took another long draw on her straw. "It's old and looks run-down."

Their orders came, and over lunch, Billie watched the tables as people finished and left, but to her disappointment, a different, much younger fellow cleared and reset the tables. When they had paid the waitress and left, Stacy caught Billie's arm at the bottom of the platform steps.

"You should report that guy to the owner, manager or whoever," she said, and glanced back at the door.

"Yes. I want to know what he was thinking," Billie said. "But I think he did actually ask if he could clean the spatters from my boot."

"Whatever," Stacy continued to push. "It was inappropriate, if you ask me. Unprofessional and very, very inappropriate."

"Yes. It was certainly a surprise," Billie said, and noticed Lori and Becky had stopped to listen.

"Drinks after dinner?" Lori asked.

"Probably," Billie said, and started back to her car. "Call me about seven. I'll know by then." She waved and hurried. The wind had picked up and it was not the least bit warmer.

Three

Billie stopped in Mr. Boster's office later in the afternoon to ask if he had a moment and he said he did. She stepped in and laid a folder in front of him.

"Sir," she began, "I think there may be a problem with the ownership details on the Duckard's Department Store property."

"Shouldn't be," he replied, and pulled the folder closer. "The client said the property was available for back taxes from the city and made an Offer to Pay. His representative indicated they would have the title by the end of the month. That's…" He looked at the calendar on his computer monitor. "…in nineteen days. Plenty of time for him to finish working things out."

"I agree there probably is time. And some parts of these files agree with the client's claim," Billie said. "But I did a quick tax roll check and that property is not on the city's delinquent tax rolls. It never has been, as far as I can tell."

"Hmm. Really?" he muttered softly to himself. "Don't worry yourself over it. I'll have our contracts department look into it. Leave it to them to worry about the details and you just continue looking for discrepancies. Thank you, Billie." He looked up at her, held her in his gaze for a moment, and then smiled. "I'm certain Mr. Hammersmith will not let anything happen to jeopardize the project."

"Yes, sir," she said, and picked up the folder. "Thank you, sir."

She turned and left his office, wondering if this sort of discrepancy happened often. Puzzled and curious by what Mr. Boster did not say, she returned to her office and decided to do a few checks of her own. She laid the folder on her desk, closed her blinds against the afternoon sun, dropped back into her chair, and keyed for a search of municipal records.

It was after six when she heard Mr. Boster close his office door at the end of the hall, and suddenly she felt uneasy. He knew she normally left work around five and would certainly ask why she was staying late if he saw her. She did not want to explain that she was researching the very things he had told her to ignore, and from what little she had found in her searching, her curiosity was piqued more than ever.

She asked herself if this client had a history of letting projects fall through as she switched her monitor off, grabbed the folder, and quickly crossed the room and closed her office door. *Is there a money issue? How can Hammersmith keep the client from jeopardizing a project?* She had more questions than answers, but that would not help if Mr. Boster caught her searching instead of moving on like he had told her to.

With her chair neatly pushed up to the desk it looked like she was gone, and if he did open the door to check on her, she felt it would be an indication that he was concerned that she was not following his instructions. Of course, if he did not, she would not know any more than she already did.

Damn! she thought suddenly. *What do I say if he does come in and he finds me behind the door? I guess I'll just say I had a few personal things to do before I left and time got away from me. Maybe he'll accept that.*

She felt silly and started to take a step back to her desk when the doorknob turned and the door swung inward. She inhaled and held her breath as Mr. Boster stepped into the opening and glanced around the office. Then slowly he stepped back, closed the door, and she heard him walk down the aisle to the elevator.

◻-◻-◻-◻-◻

"Billy," Sid said as Billy finished loading another dishwasher tray. "What really happened in the dining room? Angie said you were holding some woman's foot?"

"Yeah." Billy smiled as he looked sideways at Sid. "Some of

that spilled soup splattered on her boots and I didn't think she would want the leather stained."

"Sure, sure. And you just happen to notice soiled boots and not the long, shapely legs?" Sid chuckled and started to turn. "Wait a minute. Didn't something like that happen—?"

"Yeah. I'd been here almost two years." Billy smiled.

"Riiight," Sid said, stretching the word, and smiled. "A redhead then too."

Billy just smiled, and slowly Sid caught his drift.

"Nah. Couldn't be."

"I'm not completely sure," Billy said, "but I think it's the same girl. By the way she reacted, though, I don't think she remembers."

"So you think that's her, all grown up." Sid smiled and rubbed his chin as he glanced at the clock. "It's nearly six. Are you working late or you off at your regular time?"

"I need to go at the regular time, Sid," Billy said. "Mr. Filton said he'd meet me around six fifteen at that kiosk by the bank."

"Better get a hustle on, then," Sid said with a smile. "Here," he added, holding a rumpled letter envelope out to him. "You didn't pick up your pay last Friday."

"Thanks," Billy said as he wiped his hands and untied his apron.

"Thirty well-circulated ones, just like usual," Sid said, still smiling. "I deposited the rest like I always do."

Billy nodded with a knowing smile as he stepped into the bathroom off the kitchen. When he came out, he wore threadbare jeans, worn-out boots, and an old, soiled jacket. He took the bills from the envelope and handed the envelope back to Sid.

"Thank Mary for doing my laundry," he said, and pocketed the money.

"I will," Sid said. "Thanks for thinking about her, Billy."

"How can I not think about her? And you, for that matter?" Billy glanced at the floor. "I appreciate everything you've done

21

for me." He suddenly looked up at the clock. "I've got to run. See you in the morning."

"Here," Sid said, and hefted a stuffed canvas bag by its straps. "Don't forget this."

"Thanks," Billy said, and took the bag.

He ducked out the back door and looked up the alley in both directions before he turned south toward his meeting.

¤-¤-¤-¤-¤

After lunch, Billie had dropped her SUV off at her apartment, having persuaded herself that a walk would be good for her. Now, however, as she slipped out of the office building and faced the north wind, she instantly wished she had driven back from lunch instead. She chided herself; with both of her parking spots paid for, it did not make any economic sense to do one thing instead of the other. But the walk to the office gave her time to think about the incident in the diner and calm her irritation a little. She also admitted there was something about the words he had said that was confusing, something that kept her from bursting out in protest. She could not believe she had just sat there, dumbly watching him take her foot and clean her boots, one at a time. With everyone in the diner watching!

Three blocks up, she stopped at the traffic light, still puzzling over his actions. Billie absently glanced around as she waited for the pedestrian crossing signal to change. She noticed the florist was closing and the few people on the streets were scurrying from one place to another, huddled against the cold breeze, but two people caught her attention. They were not doing anything to make them noticeable, except they were casually talking at the street vendor's kiosk across the street to her left, drinking coffee, completely oblivious to the cold and the breeze. She thought it was odd that a well-dressed man wearing a long, black London Fog was in earnest conversation with a very disheveled-looking man in worn jeans, horribly worn boots, and a soiled and stained brown jacket. Put off by his looks, she suddenly thought she had seen him somewhere.

The light changed and she quickly turned her thoughts to reaching her apartment and going for a drink with her friends.

◻-◻-◻-◻-◻

"Hey, Lori," Billie greeted as she slid onto the stool at the corner of the long, *L*-shaped bar in the Library, a beer and wine bar across the street from the Chesterfield Junior College. "Where's everyone?"

"Running late," Lori said as she set her purse in her lap. "I just got here and Stacy and Becky said they would catch up as quickly as they could."

Billie pulled the ordering pad to her and scrolled down the list. "I can't believe—"

"What happened today?" Lori asked, as if filling in the words for Billie.

"What?" Billie stopped and looked at her. "No. I was saying I can't believe I'm thinking of ordering a beer." She tapped a selection and inserted her card. When the pad released it, she slid the pad to Lori. "I'm in a rut with my wine choices and need something different."

"Well, I can't believe it happened again," Lori said as she took the pad and began scrolling the list.

"Again? What are you talking about?" Billie stared at her and waited.

"Having soup spilled on your boot and someone coming quickly and cleaning it off," Lori said, and looked up. "Don't you remember? A long time ago—your mom and sister were with us. We stopped for lunch and the same thing happened. We must've been about twelve."

Billie stared at Lori. "It did?"

"Yeah. It did," Lori said. She tapped a selection and slipped her card in and out of the pad. "Honestly, I can't believe you don't remember. An older boy—I don't know how old he was…

sixteen, maybe—cleaned up the mess and then your boots. Like today, he said something about your hair and the color of your boots not going together."

"And you think it's the same man?"

"How odd would it be if he wasn't, and they both said the same thing about your red boots and your red hair?"

Billie sat and thought a long moment as a memory slowly came back to her. "Yeah. I think I do remember something. Did I follow him around the diner after we ate, asking questions?"

"You sure did," Lori said, and smiled. "You were so taken with him that I was certain you'd remember. Your mother had to literally go fetch you and drag you out of the diner when it was time to go."

"Now that I think about it, it does seem like it was a bright spot in my gloomy years," Billie admitted as the bartender set their brews in front of them.

"I know the loss of your friend really had you down for a long time," Lori said, "but I am still surprised you don't remember. Are you going to go tell his boss what he did?"

"I...don't know. He deserves a reprimand, but why should I deal with the discomfort all over again? Besides, who knows what he might be. He could be seriously deranged, trying to start something to entice me into a private place so he could do who knows what."

"Well." Lori smiled. "You're certainly pretty enough that if I were a man, I'd try to entice you into a private place and do who knows what."

"Stop it," Billie said sharply. "You're not helping one bit."

"Maybe he could explain—"

"What? What can he possibly say that makes it all right to grab someone's foot and fondle it in public?"

"Fondle? I don't think—"

"He was gentle though. Careful, almost caressing in the way he..." Billie stopped and looked up at Lori's startled expression, watching it slowly turn into a smile.

"I think you, Miss Mattis," Lori said brightly, "must go and find out more about this guy."

Four

Wednesday, April 13

It was still dark and cold when Billy rolled over on the thin mat, pulled the tattered blanket tight under his neck, and opened his eyes. He listened, as he always did, for the stirring of the others who were huddled in bedrolls or on mats like his on the concrete floor along the walls. He knew what time it was, always waking up at this same hour out of habit, ever since he first came to live here. Back…when was that? He remembered he was fourteen when he came to the city that September. He had to make himself remember, and slowly the memories of those first days and the many days after drifted back into his awareness. He sighed, realizing the past was getting hazy and he was beginning to lose hope of finding any more evidence. It was many years ago that he had given up his youthful wondering of why this happened to him.

Billy sat up and stretched, absently staring at the soft glow seeping in from another area of the basement. He had come to this basement a year after he had first arrived in the city, and within a few nights he had found insulated wire, lightbulb sockets, and some bulbs. He had brought them into the dark hovel and an older fellow, Lloyd, that lived there at that time, wired the cord into the electrical panel Billy had pointed out, and by the next evening they had electric lights.

Finally able to see in the dark basement, and with a little finagling and persistence, Billy had gotten the water running in the bathrooms and Lloyd had gotten some of the regular overhead fixtures working. By the time Billy had gotten back to the basement that night, the women in their homeless group had mopped and wiped the bathrooms into decent facsimiles of their previous lives. Billy had smiled; suddenly their refuge from the weather had taken on a feel of relative luxury, though it took another month before he could get the hot water functional.

Billy rolled up onto his knees and dug the small flashlight out of his backpack. Using its dim beam, he folded his blanket, rolled it up inside his mat, and tied it with a thin rope. He stood it in the corner where he always did and switched the flashlight off. The woman and her husband stirred a few feet away, just beyond the fabric curtain he had helped them hang to partition off their small space for what privacy one could get under the circumstances.

"It's early," the woman's soft voice said. "You up already, Billy?"

"Yeah," he answered softly. "Sorry to wake you, Cat."

She said something he could not understand as she snuggled back under her blanket and closer to her husband. Billy stood up, picked up his backpack, and stopped in the bathroom. Refreshed, he went up the stairs and through the door opening onto the alley behind the vacant store.

Out on the street, bundled in his soiled-but-decent coat, Billy braced for the cold spring breeze and the dark predawn morning as he stepped around the corner onto Second Street. He stopped at Simmy's newsstand a block west, in the pool of a streetlight at the bottom of the concrete-and-glass canyons, like he did every weekday.

"Morning, Simmy," Billy greeted as the aged man lifted the panel that sealed the front of the kiosk.

"Morning, Billy," he answered, pushing the panel up in place and setting the two long poles that held it open as an awning. "The usual?"

"Yeah. Sid likes the *Beacon*," he said, and passed Simmy a bill.

"You'd think he'd just subscribe," Simmy said as he set the papers out and opened his cash box to get change, "instead of gettin' the *Herald*."

"His customers like the *Herald,* and if he did subscribe, you wouldn't get my business," Billy said with a chuckle.

"Yeah, I guess that's right," Simmy said, and handed Billy the coins.

"Thanks. See ya in the morning." Billy tucked the paper under his arm and turned back into the wind.

After another block, he turned south and followed the curving street to the block square park hidden in the darkness, visualizing the tall elms and maples and dozens of conifers dotted around its green lawn. Billy stopped at the small flower stand snuggled between two buildings and two streetlights across St. Charles Street on the north.

"How's Maxie this morning?" he asked as she opened one of the two panels that hid her narrow stall.

"Good morning, Master Billy," she said with a wide, toothy smile as she opened the second panel. He smiled in return; she had always called him "Master Billy."

"Good morning, ma'am," he said with a mock bow. "You do remember that I'm now over thirty, or is your memory failing you also? What do you have that's good this morning?"

"You know you'll always be that pretentious but courteous runny-nosed kid that showed up one day about seventeen years ago. And you know everything I have is always good, Master Billy," she said playfully, and then turned serious. "And I think I have somethin' Mrs. Butler will like very much." Maxie turned to her unopened bins and baskets, and after a few minutes found the basket she was looking for. "Here it is," she said, and handed him the large bunch of spring blooms and some greens.

"That's nice," he said, and looked at the bundle. "How much more is this gonna cost me?"

"What?" Maxie said, feigning surprise. "You know I wouldn't ask a penny more than they're worth." She looked aside and flicked her eyes back at him. "Ten? For Ms. Butler's?"

"Oh! Maxie, how could you?" he said, grabbing his chest. "Ten? And me, barely making ends meet."

"Okay, five," she said, and faced him, holding his usual

29

order.

"Three," he said, looking hurt and disappointed.

"Damn you, Billy! Okay, three!" She shoved her hand out and handed him the flowers.

"Thanks," Billy said with a smile as he took the flowers and handed Maxie a number of folded bills. He turned to leave and glanced back and saw her smile as she unfolded the money; he had given her the extra ten anyway.

Three blocks farther west, Billy ducked into a dark alley, passed the numerous trash bins, and stopped at the locked metal door. He retrieved the key from his boot, unlocked the door, slipped in, and snapped the light on. He relocked the door and reset the alarm system.

Billy laid the newspaper on the counter in the kitchen, the same place he did every morning when he came to work. Then he took a tall vase from the shelf in the dry storage area, filled it half full, added a little sugar, and gently settled the large bunch of flowers into it. Smiling at Maxie's taste, he wrapped a ribbon around the neck and tied a bow on the vase and placed it on the counter beside the paper.

The usual bunch of short-stemmed flowers he pushed to one side on the counter; he would fill the table vases when he prepared the tables.

After he hung his coat on the rack next to the back door, he made a quick walk through the dining room and checked the front door. Satisfied everything was as it should be, he returned to the separate bathroom that Sid had built when he had started work there. And as usual, Billy took his clean clothes from the backpack, straightened them best he could, and hung them on the two hangers in the narrow closet in the bathroom. As much by habit as by necessity, Billy undressed, showered, and cleaned up for the day. He placed yesterday's clothes in the white laundry sack that Mary hung in the bath for him and dressed in his clean work clothes.

He thought about the day before: the absurdity of suddenly remembering the redhead Billie, especially after seeing her often and not realizing who she was. He smiled. *Man, she grew up looking nice,* he told himself. *I knew she'd grown up, but man! She's a real knockout, drop-dead gorgeous!*

But quickly, regretfully, he thought about how upsetting his bringing attention to her must have been. He really did not mean to make her feel bad, but the memory was so vivid and the words and actions just took hold of him, suddenly overpowering his common sense, taking him back to a pleasant memory of the life he once had.

Billy donned his apron and his low-topped rubber boots, added water and detergent to his bucket, and started mopping the dining room floor, thinking about his conversation with Mr. Filton. As he suspected, his almost rash actions had set something into motion. Westman Associates had risen to the bait, a name forever etched in his mind and recalled whenever he remembered his parents' deaths. It was a name he would never forget.

He had just finished repositioning the tables and setting the chairs when Sid came in through the door from his living quarters.

"Hey, Billy," Sid said absently as he checked the coffee urn. Timed to come on an hour before Billy arrived, the coffee was always ready by the time Sid came in to prep the kitchen. "Cup?"

"Sure, Sid. How's Mary this morning?" Billy asked as he pushed the mop bucket back to the back room.

"Good this morning," Sid said as he set a mug of coffee on the counter and sipped from his. He double-checked the alarm. "She'll sure like the flowers. Maxie again?"

"Of course," Billy said as he dried his hands and took the mug from the counter. "Maxie knows who I get the flowers for and she had something special this morning. Word about Mary is getting around."

"Take the extra out of the till," Sid said as he unfolded the paper.

"Nah," Billy said. "I got it. It's the least I can do for Mary."

"That won't leave you enough for the rest of the week," Sid

argued. "Let me know if you run short."

Billy shook his head and waved the notion aside, and when he finished his coffee he went from table to table and booth to booth checking the shakers, straightening the menus, and setting out the table vases with the fresh flowers. He straightened the chairs and then the stations along the seating counter. Behind the counter, he arranged the clean glassware and replenished the napkin supplies and silverware trays.

As he wiped Melony's prep shelf behind the counter for the last time, he heard the rap at the front door. When he peeked around the edge of the shade pulled down over the door, he saw Angie, Carole, Melony, Julie, Kevin, and Niles waiting. He let them in and Sid reset the alarm.

"Morning," Billy said as he relocked the door. "You look cold. Where's Ned?"

"Ya think, Billy?" Angie snipped, and unwound her scarf. "It is and I am."

"Haven't seen Ned," Julie said as she took her coat off. "He still has a half an hour."

Angie and the others went to the back room to hang up their coats, and Billy stopped and filled six cups with coffee and refilled his. He stirred two packs of sugar and one of creamer into one and handed it to Angie as she came back into the dining room, pressing the front of her apron with her hands.

"Thanks," Angie said as she stopped at the end of the counter and looked at him. Julie started the second coffee urn and checked everything behind the counter, and Carole and Melony picked up a cup. "What did you do this last weekend?"

"Oh the usual," Billy said, and sipped his coffee as Julie passed Nile's and Kevin's cups through the serving window. "Went to a big rock concert. Hooked up with a real shapely bombshell and spent all day Sunday in a drunken stupor trying to find my way back home. How about you?"

"Shit, Billy. I know you didn't go to any rock concert, much less get laid," she said, and turned to the kitchen. "Hey, Sid? Can I get a sweet roll, warmed?"

"Sure," Sid said without looking out.

"You're in fine spirits for having two extra days off." Billy smiled at Angie. "You and your brother must've had words for you to be this happy."

Angie stuck her tongue out at him and picked up the sweet roll Sid placed in the pass-through.

"I think Billy goes down on the south side and peeks in windows," Julie said with a giggle. "Otherwise he wouldn't have any nightlife at all."

"Really Billy," Angie said in a more serious tone. "What do you really do on your weekends?"

"Leave the poor guy alone," Niles said from the kitchen.

"Heck, Angie," Billy inhaled and said. "I dabble in real estate deals, and in my spare time I walk dogs for the wealthy and feed the geese along the river."

"Someday," she said, shaking her finger at him, "you'll tell me what you do. You've never even said where you live—not in the seven years I've been here."

Billy smiled and rinsed his cup, then set it in the sink. With Angie still staring at him, half blocking the archway, he eased around her and went back to his chores.

Billy pulled the blinds and shades open and Sid opened the diner at seven and the day started uneventfully. Even Ned snuck in five minutes late, as usual.

Five

Thursday, April 14

It was a cold, overcast morning. Carl Boster came to work about nine and stopped at Robert Lange's open office door before going to his own office.

"Bob?" he asked, his brow furrowed with concern, unbuttoning his long coat as he stood in the doorway. "What do you know about the purchase of the Duckard Property? Billie noticed Tuesday that the property title was still an outstanding issue for the contracts."

Robert looked up from his desk. "Frederick said he'd have all of the purchase details finalized and completed by Friday the twenty-ninth," Robert said as he called something up on his computer. "It's here in the contracts that he agreed to the end of the month. The twenty-ninth is early, but it's the last banking day."

"What does the contract say if he fails to close?" Carl asked, and folded his coat over his arm, his expression still showing his discomfort.

"I'll have to look," Robert said. "I don't have that section on my computer. He still has plenty of time, but I'll check with Contracts and get back to you." He looked at Carl. "I do know a lot of people have invested with him on this project, and I suspect if he fails to close there will be a lot of very upset folks. He's got a lot of irons in the fire, so I'll have finance recheck on how extended he is and whether he can stay fluid. It could be a lot of trouble for him if he misses the end of the month."

"Well," Carl said as he half turned in the doorway, "he's not the only one with a lot riding on this project. We haven't had a decent project in nearly a year and we need this one as much as the next guy."

"I understand," Robert said. "Does Mike have anything more?"

Carl leaned out into the aisle and checked Mike Hammersmith's office door. "He's not in yet. I'll ask him what he knows when he gets in. Let me know what you find out."

"Will do," Robert said as Carl stepped back into the aisle and started to his office.

☐-☐-☐-☐-☐

Billie went in early to finish the detail checks she needed for the Duckard Project, and with the last comparison completed and the folder closed, she sat back in her high-backed chair and closed her eyes. Everything checked except for a couple of items that she noted and sent back to the projects group. The ownership issue bothered her, but she knew the buyer still had twelve bank days to close his purchase. She also knew that she had no information on how that was progressing, and had no reason to think it would not happen.

She stretched her shoulders and relaxed her achy muscles, absently thinking about the previous night with her friends. It was supposed to be a normal Wednesday girls' night at Lori's suggestion, but Stacy had shown up with a man in tow, her new significant other, and that had shifted the dynamics more than Billie thought it would. After two cocktails, she was done; too much "look at me," "look at us" from Stacy's side of the table.

As Billie brought her mind back to business, she heard Mr. Boster talking across the cluster of cubicles in the center of the main office. At first, she was not listening, but as he continued, she realized he was talking to Mr. Lange about the Duckard Project. Slowly, she heard Mr. Boster's concern that the property buyer might miss the closing date, that the loss of this project was something the company did not want to experience.

Well, she admitted to herself, *no one wants to lose a multimillion-dollar contract.*

Back to her computer, she continued the search she had started, querying for the title information on the old department store and the five other buildings in the same block. Using the search engines she had access to and the appropriate pass codes assigned by the design firm, she finally connected with a database that identified a Pastoric Group as the title holder on four of the six properties in that block. Billie sighed. There was nothing on the department store building and the next one, immediately to its east. Four searches later she found a clue for the last two properties and it led her back to the tax rolls; wire transfers with no source names mentioned paid all the taxes quarterly.

Billie turned her efforts to the city and the county records departments and uncovered a couple of references to a Tri-Funds and a CR Associates, both listed as joint title holders for the two Duckard properties. *And I'll bet...* she said to herself as she returned to the tax roles for the first four properties. *Yup, more noname wire transfers for those payments. No surprise there.*

She stared at the screen and leaned back in her chair. Something was certainly unusual. Not wrong, but unusual, and she could not tell what. Yet.

Billie keyed a straight internet search for a Pastoric Group, and as she expected, there were no active websites for that specific company name. She tried a number of variations, but still came up empty-handed. Searching for Tri-Funds and CR Associates gave the same results.

Dejected, she cleared the screen and logged off, got up, and grabbed her coat. She needed to get out and walk a little to clear her mind and sort through what she thought she knew. It was not making sense; not yet.

◻-◻-◻-◻-◻

Holding her short jacket tight against the dreary cold and blustery wind, Billie quickly mounted the steps and pushed the Streetcar's outer entry door open. Pushing through the second, she absently shuddered and stomped her feet as the hostess greeted her and asked if she was alone or joining someone.

"No," Billie said. "Just me. I also need to talk to someone about the guy that cleaned up the spill Tuesday."

"Oh, that was just Billy," the hostess answered nonchalantly as she led Billie to a table for two a short distance left of the front doors.

The waitress seated Billie, placed a menu in front of her, and asked if she wanted anything to drink.

"Tea, please," Billie said, still clinging to her jacket. "Very hot."

The hostess nodded and went to the drugstore-style counter, spoke to the girl there, and then went through the archway into the back rooms. Billie watched for a moment and thought about how odd it was that his name would be Billy also. She absently shook her head and turned her attention to the menu.

The waitress returned with a cup, two tea bags, and an insulated pot of hot water, and asked if she had decided on anything.

"I think the tortilla soup," Billie replied. "And could you see if the manager or the owner is available for me to talk to?"

"I'll see if he's available," the waitress said as she entered Billie's order in her digital pad.

"Thanks," Billie said, and then picked up the squeeze bottle of honey from beside the napkin holder and stirred a dribble into her tea cup.

The waitress turned and greeted a couple that had entered

38

while they had been talking.

Billie was pouring hot water over her second tea bag when the waitress brought her soup, a basket of chips, tortilla ribbons, and a small bowl of salsa on the side.

"Can I get you anything else?" the waitress asked, and quickly added "besides the owner" when Billie started to ask.

"Okay. Do you know anything about this Billy?" Billie asked before the waitress could leave.

"Like what?"

"Like, does he do that sort of thing to everyone? Often?" Billie said, trying to figure out what exactly to ask. "I think he must have a screw loose. Does he?"

"Look," the waitress said. "I can't talk about people that work here. He washes dishes and cleans up our messes. More than that, I can't say."

Billie watched as the waitress turned and went to check on another table. Billie's frustration was quickly growing.

-¤-

"She's cocked and loaded, Billy," Angie said when she came back into the dishwashing area. "She still seems upset about Tuesday, and Carole says she wants to talk to Sid."

"Rightly so," he said. "I think I really embarrassed her, and now she definitely has a reason to be pissed at me. Shouldn't have done that in front of her friends."

"Is this someone you actually know?" Angie asked.

"From a long time ago, but probably not anymore," Billy said cryptically without looking up.

"Wow, and she's really cute. I didn't think you knew anyone cute or that actually knows how to dress. And a girl too." Angie shook her head and turned to go back into the dining room. "Too bad you pissed her off."

¤-¤-¤-¤-¤

"Well, I don't know if she's the same redhead," Sid said when he caught Billy before he left for the day. "But I think I got her calmed down. And I did promise that you would not make any more bizarre appearances in the dining room, nor would you embarrass our customers again—her or any others."

"Thanks, Sid," Billy said as he put his apron on the hook by the bathroom door. "I'm going to get cleaned up and then I need to run. Thursday nights are always busy, as you know."

"You should sleep in on Fridays, Billy," Sid said. "You need more than four hours' sleep."

"That's what weekends are for," Billy said, and slipped into the bathroom for a shower.

Sid shook his head as he went into the dry storage area and collected the day-old bread and pastries, a few canned goods, and a bag of oranges from the cool room. He set the items out on the counter until he had enough to fill the canvas bag hung by the back door.

Dressed in his worn clothes, Billy stepped out of the bath and slipped on his stained coat. Ned handed him the canvas bag that Sid had filled and Billy swung the strap over his head and shoulder.

"Sid had to take a phone call," said Ned.

"Thanks, Ned," Billy said, and turned to the door. "See you in the morning."

"Sid said he'd have another bag on Monday, after the weekend. Where do you take this stuff?" Ned asked.

"Sid gives it to a few of the needy folk." Billy smiled. "He likes for me to drop it off when he can spare a little."

Ned nodded and Billy slipped out the back door and turned north.

Six

Billie parked her SUV in the lot across the street from the Streetcar Diner. The diner shared the lot with the strip mall around the corner on Duberry.

She slipped into the back seat and put on a heavy pair of slacks over her leggings, slipping out of her skirt in the process. With her stylish leather coat pulled tight around her and a leather and fake fur cap that reached down over her ears, she crossed the street near the alley behind the diner and waited. She remembered that Sid had mentioned Billy usually got off about six, and she hoped she figured right—that he would use a back door instead of leaving through the customer-filled dining room.

After about twenty minutes, Billie heard the back door onto the alley open. She peeked around the corner, stunned to see the same disheveled man she had seen at the kiosk by the bank step out under the security lamp and turn north.

Damn! What are you, ten? This is so wrong.

When I was ten, this wouldn't have scared me this much.

When you were ten, nothing scared you.

She took a deep breath and hurried into the dark alley, nervously following his silhouette as he walked toward the lights on St. Charles. At the street, he went east a block to Eighth Street West and then turned north.

Billie glanced each way at the crossing streets, watching the man's dark form between the splashes of light at the corners. Her nerves tense and her heart nearly in a panic, she quickly ducked into a storefront alcove each time the man she thought was Billy paused under a streetlight and looked around. Eight blocks north, he turned west two blocks to Tenth Street West.

She tried to make herself relax, wondering where in the world he was going. Absently, she checked the time on her phone and abruptly looked around, realizing its glow made her stand out in a neighborhood that was getting darker by the block.

She thought about when she had seen someone walking along the sidewalks: two guys, three blocks back. And now, as she followed Billy around the corner onto Tenth, she noted they were getting close to the homeless village two blocks ahead, north of Hadley. The village was a full city block filled with a strange concoction of cardboard and canvas hovels, and homeless people. She had never been there but she had heard about it a lot. What she had heard was nothing good.

Billie faltered and looked down at her jacket, her boots, and the sharply pressed slacks. She thought about the style of her hat and knew she could not go any farther. *God, Willum. What am I doing? This is wrong in so many ways.*

Remembering the many newspaper accounts of what usually happened to women alone after dark in unsavory places, places like this, she knew she did not belong there. She was not nervous anymore; suddenly, she was afraid.

Billie quickly turned around and hurried back down Tenth, hoping she could get to where it intersected with Duberry at Baker before anyone noticed her. At each street, her heart pounding in her chest, she paused and listened for anyone following her, coming toward her, any sounds that were not normal, but all she could hear was the blood surging in her ears.

Between streets, the sound of her hard bootheels clacking on the sidewalk shouted to everyone, *Look at me!* Clack. *I'm here!* Clack. *Come and get me!* Clack. Her heart raced; she had to get to Duberry, where she knew she would feel safer.

Billie got back to her SUV, jumped in, and locked the doors. After a few very long minutes, scrunched down in the seat, her breathing slowed and her heart stopped threatening to burst. She thought about how crazy and irresponsible she had been to blindly follow someone she only thought she knew. And to follow him into a disreputable section of town, making herself the easiest of all targets.

She shook her head and wondered what could possibly be possessing her; why she was following someone that obviously had intimate ties with the lowest life in the city. And worse, she had voluntarily followed him. She, Billie Mattis, the one that could not defend herself if her life depended on it, was wandering around in the worst part of town, alone. And she admitted, there, in that part of town, her life probably did depend on being able to defend herself.

You stupid, stupid girl! You're nuts. This is not like you at all. You can't do this alone.

Alone? Hell, what am I saying? I shouldn't be doing this at all!

Gripping the steering wheel, forcing herself to relax, she admitted she was completely nuts! But deep inside, she knew she would follow him again, to find out what he was, what he did, where he went. No one she knew would go with her, especially for the unimportant reasons she had. Might be different if she were following a known criminal, but she knew that would not matter. She was going to have to do this alone, and that scared her all over again.

She needed to find another way—some way that she could follow him and maybe blend in. Maybe. *Damn, Willum. This is going to be tough. Tougher than I thought. And what am I going to do if someone chases me, or...*

Sitting in her SUV, she tapped her phone and connected with the internet. She searched for a used clothing store and found three. The nearest was just eight blocks east of her apartment on the next street south, Comanche and Seventh Street East.

Billie drove to the simply named Recycled Clothing Store. It was open, but her fears won out: the parking lot was empty and dark and she was nervous and afraid again. *I'll come back tomorrow or Saturday in the daylight,* she placated, and turned back to her apartment.

Friday, April 15

Work on the new city park renovation project was not keeping Billie's interest like the Duckard Project had, and she found her afternoon filled with numerous pauses and false starts. Returning to her office from her third visit to the break room, she knew the day was going to be a total bust. She stopped by Mr. Boster's office and told him she was going to run some errands and would see him in the morning.

For the first time in her life, she felt uncomfortable and out of place in broad daylight as she parked her large British SUV, her graduation present from her parents, in front of the Recycled Clothing Store. It too was situated in a less-fortunate city district and was patronized by people of similar repute.

Billie got out, crossed the numerous handicapped spaces in the nearly empty parking lot, and wished she had something more nondescript to drive. Inside, she forced herself to take her time and objectively survey the contents of the store beginning with the casual, more stylish selections that hung near the front of the main room. The quality of some of the contributed clothing surprised her and made her accept that the less fortunate also had an eye for nicer things. As she continued looking, she tried to ignore the questioning glances from the store staff and other customers, but the feeling that she herself was being judged for simply being there would not leave her. Dressed in nice clothes, a stylish jacket, and her hair nicely curled, she felt strongly that they saw her as looking down on them by what she wore.

Turning to the racks at the back of the store, she realized her parents had raised her in a very biased manner, and she wondered why. Was it on purpose? Or was it just something that happened when you grew up in a seemingly controlled environment and never had to associate with anyone of different lifestyles or go anyplace outside your routine circles of likeminded friends? Even in college, she realized she had avoided the "average" people on campus and kept to friends she knew from home and others of similar status and interests.

Billie searched a rack of clean but worn jeans and was surprised when she found a size and cut that would fit without being too flattering. She smiled, looking at herself in a tall mirror. It was the first time she had ever shopped and not looked for the nicest or the sharpest styles in anything she considered. Searching a bit more, she laughed when she found a perfect bulky sweater in a color that did not look totally garish; she figured her plain camisoles would protect her from its roughness.

Finally, Billie made her way to the cashier and paid for the sweater, jeans, a knitted cap, a quilt-stitched "puffy coat," and a pair of not-too-badly-worn, low-topped, low-heeled boots. As she set the bags in the back seat of her SUV, she felt excited, uncertain, anxious, and a little afraid.

◻-◻-◻-◻-◻

"You're late," Lori said as the elevator door opened and Billie saw her and Becky standing beside her apartment door. "Did you forget about Friday Happy Hour?"

"I...guess I did," Billie stammered, and unlocked her door.

Billie pushed the door open and quickly went up the spiral stairs to her loft bedroom and shoved the sacks into her closet. She was thankful they had not pressed her to show them what she had bought. Besides not wanting them to see the uncharacteristic purchases, she did not want to announce what she was planning.

I may be stupid, stupid for doing this, but I'm certainly not dumb—not dumb enough to tell them about it.

She hurried through her dressing room off the bath, ran a brush through her curls, and straightened her blouse. Quickly, she descended the stairs with her coat in her hand and stopped between the girls and the door.

"Ready? Do I look okay?" she asked absently, and turned to the door.

"Let's," Becky said, and followed with Lori close behind.

-☐-

Becky seemed on a mission, following the short-skirted hostess through the throng at The Marquee Cocktail Lounge. Lori and Billie followed as closely as the crowd allowed. The hostess gestured pleasantly to a corner table and Becky quickly took the seat at the back side so she could watch for suitable "opportunities" among the patrons—male opportunities, of course. Billie took one side and Lori sat across from her, hemming Becky in.

"All of our beers, normal cocktails, and wines are half priced until eight," the hostess said as she laid a drink and food menu pad on the table. "Make your selections and a waiter will bring them." Then she turned and left.

"Do you think she would be so curt if we were men?" Lori asked with a smirk at Billie.

"Where's Stacy?" Billie asked with a shake of her head as she selected her preferred cocktail from the pad, inserted and withdrew her card, then slid the pad to Becky.

"She's running late at the bookstore," Becky said as she entered her selection. "Something about end-of-the-month inventory and stock ordering. She said she'd check and see if we're still here when she gets through, but if you ask me, I think she plans on seeing that fellow Tom again tonight."

"How long has she known him?" Lori asked, and took the pad. "He didn't say much Wednesday."

"Yeah, Stacy did all the talking," Billie said. "I think she was trying to impress him."

"A year or so actually," Becky continued. "But they hadn't gone out together until last week."

"Her last beau lasted how long? Six weeks?" Billie asked, and smiled at Lori.

"How about you?" Lori asked Billie. "Are you missing your ex yet?"

Billie shook her head and glared at Lori. "No! I don't think about him until someone brings him up. Damn, Lori, I'm trying to forget him." Billie inhaled and held her breath, forcing herself to calm down. She did not need this twice in one week.

"Okay, okay. Sorry," Lori said, and entered a choice on the menu pad.

"What about that guy in the diner?" Becky asked. "Wasn't that the strangest thing?"

Billie smirked and looked at Lori. "Yes, it was the strangest," Billie said.

Becky caught Billie's tone and looked at her. Lori snickered.

"Is he the same guy?" Lori asked.

"Who? What same guy?" Becky looked from one of them to the other.

"I really don't know," Billie said. "Maybe. I'm still trying to find that out."

"Have you talked to him?" Lori persisted.

"Billie! What are you talking about?" Becky glared at both of them.

With a laugh, Billie explained the day long ago when Lori and she had come into the city with her mother and sister, and how the almost exact same events occurred.

Becky was very quiet when Billie finished, and Becky slowly looked at Lori. "You were there and remember all of that?"

Lori nodded. "I heard the bowl fall and break this time, but I couldn't see it like I did before. I didn't know what to say when Stacy said he had cleaned Billie's boots. I was shocked to see it all repeating."

"And you think it might be the same guy? And he did the same thing?" Becky asked, suddenly full of curiosity.

"Lori does," Billie admitted. "I did talk to the owner and he apologized for causing me any discomfort or embarrassment. He said he'd already talked to the guy that cleaned my boot."

47

A toned and muscular waiter in a sleeveless black T-shirt sporting the Marquee logo interrupted, stopping beside the table. He set their drink orders in front of them and took the time to smile and nod at each before he turned back to the bar.

They laughed as he walked away.

"Does this guy have a name?" Becky asked, and glanced at Lori.

"Sure," Billie said offhandedly. "The owner, Sid, said his name is Billy Carson. He has worked at the diner for about seventeen years."

"A 'Billy'?" Becky stared at her.

"Was that the name of the guy we saw with your mom?" Lori asked, still pushing.

"I don't know, Lori," Billie said, and shrugged. "I don't know if he told us that day."

Billie smiled and turned to Becky, leaned close, and asked, "Say? Can you do some checking for me in the museum's local archives?"

Becky nodded and Lori scooted her stool closer so she could hear.

"I've searched the internet for him, and everything I found was for someone much older, younger, or on the wrong side of the country. I can't find anything on him or his parents in the public records."

"It may take a few days, but I'll start checking tomorrow," Becky said, and smiled as she sipped her drink. "Why? Why are you suddenly interested in this guy?"

"I don't know for sure," Billie said. It was not quite a lie because she really could not explain why, but she did not look Becky in the eye. "Maybe it's a bad case of curiosity."

Are you going to tell them you can't get him out of your mind?

No.

"Seems strange, Billie," Becky said softly. "You've never been this curious about a guy. Never since I first met you."

"Please don't say anything about this to Stacy," Billie said, looking at them over the rim of her glass.

Lori looked at her, confused, and Becky smiled.

"I don't want to hear any of Stacy's snide remarks. Okay?"

Seven

Saturday, April 16

Billie, in her usual bright skirt and leggings, colorful coordinated blouse, and leather coat, slipped into the Streetcar and joined the lunch crowd.

"Hi," Carole greeted. "One, or are your friends meeting you?"

"Just me again," Billie said, and followed Carole to another table for two near the front door. As she sat down Billie asked, "Is Billy Carson here?"

"No," Carole said, and shook her head. "He's off on weekends. Could someone else help you? Sid's here."

"Sure, if he has a minute," Billie said.

"I'll get him," Carole said. "Take a look at the menu and I'll be back to get your order. Anything to drink?"

"Hot tea, please."

Billie watched a moment as the girl walked back to the kitchen and disappeared through the archway. She turned to the window, and absently looked at the traffic passing on Duberry and wondered where Billy spent his time off.

She had just settled on a food choice when Carole led Sid up to her table.

"Afternoon," Sid greeted. "May I?" he asked, gesturing to the second chair.

"Sure. Please," Billie replied, and Carole asked if she was ready to order as she set the tea service and two tea bags in front of Billie. "Yes. The Famous Onion Burger, fries, and a black and white shake with a little coconut and crushed pecans."

Carole entered the request into her handheld digital pad and hurried to the back counter to make the shake.

"What can I do for you?" Sid asked, and folded his hands on the table in front of him.

"I don't remember introducing myself the last time, but I'm Billie Mattis." She extended her hand in greeting. "Thanks for letting me blow off steam, but I have more questions about Billy, I'm afraid," Billie started, and took a long sip of her tea.

"And what might those be?"

"I've finally convinced myself to talk to him," Billie admitted. "So I came by but the waitress said he was off on weekends."

Sid nodded and Billie knew by his look that she needed to get to the point.

"Do you know how I can get in touch with him? I need to understand why he did what he did."

Sid cocked his head and then absently shook it.

"Can you tell me where he lives?" Billie asked before Sid could answer. "The waitress told me he wasn't here and I would like to talk to him."

"No," Sid said softly. "I don't know where he lives. You can leave a message for him if you'd like. I will put it in his mail slot."

"Mail slot? You have a mail slot for him?" Billie asked. *A mail slot? How odd.* She just stared at him.

"Yes." Sid smiled. "I have a slot for Billy and slots for a number of his friends that don't want mail delivered to their homes."

"That's a surprise," Billie said, and stared at Sid. "Why wouldn't they want mail delivered?"

"He will surprise you. Anyway, there are a lot of reasons, Billie," Sid said. "Many folks don't have a secure mailbox, and some may have a snooping neighbor, and others may not have a permanent address. There are lots of reasons, and I help out a few that I can. No big deal. It works for them and it works for me."

Billie smiled. "That's very nice of you to help. I'm almost dizzy, suddenly starting to see life and parts of this city differently. Better, maybe."

Sid nodded and smiled. "Well, as we get older we either see things better, or sometimes worse, but definitely differently."

Carole returned and set the shake on the table, smiled, and told Billie her burger would be out in a minute or two.

"Sid," Billie said. "Where does Billy go? Hang out? I'll leave a note, but I'd like to find him and talk to him."

Sid shook his head. "You might be able to find him, but he could be anywhere in town. I don't know his routines or where he goes. He could be anywhere."

"I know this is personal, but does he see anyone? Anyone regularly that might know?"

"Billy's not that kind of guy."

"What?" Billie asked, but it really was not a question. "I knew it. He doesn't like girls."

"No. Nothing like that," Sid chuckled. "I think he likes a redhead he knows, but he doesn't have a standing relationship with her or anyone else that I know of. Billy's a very private type of guy. I think he stopped talking about himself and what he does when his folks died."

"Okay," Billie said, reluctantly forced to accept that she was going to have to wait. She sighed, dejected, realizing that Sid was not going to tell her anything more. "I'll stop pestering you. Will you tell him I'll come by next week and see if he'll talk to me?"

Sid shook his head and pushed a small pad of paper to her. "I'll just forget."

"Aah yes. A note." Billie smiled and dug for a pen in her handbag. She took the pad and wrote her simple request in a neat, legible hand, and signed it. She folded the small sheet in half and wrote Billy's name on the front. "Will you please leave this for Billy to read at his convenience?"

"Certainly." Sid smiled. "It will be my pleasure. Now, if you don't have anything more, I do need to get back to the kitchen and be sure that burger isn't getting too done."

"Thanks, Sid," Billie said as he got up.

Halfway across the dining room, Sid passed Carole bringing Billie's burger and fries.

◻-◻-◻-◻-◻

Even on weekends, his days off, Billy was a creature of habit. He stretched quietly when he woke, rolled over on his thin mat, and pulled the tattered blanket up around his neck. He slowly opened his eyes, knowing it was late even though the only light was from the few overheads in the next room. He listened, but did not hear the children, nor murmurs or any conversations, a reminder of which day of the week it was and that he had slept in later than he normally did. Everyone was gone, doing their Saturday things.

He rolled over and sat up on his knees, folded his blanket, and rolled it up inside the mat. He tied it and stacked it in the corner as usual before he headed to the bathrooms. Refreshed, his face and hands washed, he returned to his small plot of floor space and retrieved his boots and a clean change of not-so-abnormally-worn clothes from his backpack.

He stopped at the last of the three refrigerators by the bathrooms and took his cup from his plastic bin on the bottom shelf. He picked out one of the small chunks of white cheese that he had sliced and individually wrapped and a packet of coffee. In the bathroom, he filled the coffee maker, set the cup on the hot pad, and went to change.

He stretched as he settled in front of the washbasin, then he shaved and combed his mussed hair, straightened his shirt, and wrapped his dirty clothes in his damp towel, knowing Mary would wash them at the Streetcar with his work clothes when he took them in on Monday.

Ready for the day, he cleaned the coffee maker, unwrapped the cheese, and picked up his cup. He walked across the large and unusually empty basement room to the stairs, but instead of going outside at the door, he wandered around the main floor, absently checking the large covered windows and the few remaining display counters.

His mind wandered back to Thursday night as he climbed the stairs to the second floor. He remembered how surprised he was when he had realized the redhead, Billie, was following him, alone. Somehow, he decided, he was going to have to arrange to talk to her and set things right between them. What she was trying to do was entirely too dangerous. Then he wondered if she even knew how to defend herself; surely she did.

After he wandered around the top floor, Billy made his way back to the basement, rinsed his coffee cup, and put it back into his bin in the refrigerator. He took his better, less-soiled jacket out of his backpack, along with the folded note he had picked up on Friday before he had left the diner for the weekend.

He started out checking his mail slot each day after Sid had set the slots up for him and a few of the people in the village and the basement, but over the years and with little personal correspondence, Billy had settled on twice a week. Now, he only checked his slot on Fridays and Tuesdays—sometimes on Mondays. Anything that came in over the weekend he saw on Monday or Tuesday, and anything after that he saw on Friday.

Billy quickly reread it, folded it, and put it in his shirt pocket. Then he slipped his jacket on and stepped out into the alley through the door at the top of the first flight of stairs.

-¤-

It had been a couple of months since she had asked him to meet her, Billy thought as he crossed St. Mark, walking south with the taller city center buildings just a block back to the west. He paid them little attention, lost in thought, wondering what was wrong as he arrived in front of the museum; she only asked him to meet her when she needed a shoulder to lean on or sometimes to cry on. He took a deep breath and smiled, knowing she needed his help and he was glad to give it; his shoulder was always available.

He turned, stepping up on the first of the short flight of wide stone steps in front of the stone edifice. The petite, dark-haired woman in jeans and a leather jacket stepped through the double glass doors to greet him.

"Afternoon, Monica," Billy said as he took her hands. "I hope I'm not too late."

Monica smiled and glanced at her watch. She shook her head. "I still can't figure out how you do it, Billy. No watch and you're three minutes early."

He chuckled, took her arm, and led her down the steps. "You remember that little coffee shop a block down on St. Anne, diagonally across from campus? Amber's?" he asked as they started south along Second.

"Yeah," Monica said. "Quaint place, if there's such a thing as quaint in Chesterfield."

"I thought we could talk there," Billy suggested. "Out of the weather and with something warm to drink, if you like."

"That sounds great, Billy," she said as they crossed St. Charles.

-¤-

"How's your son doing?" Billy asked as he pulled a chair out for her at a table in the corner of the small shop's nearly empty seating area.

"He's wonderful. Doing great and smart as a whip," Monica said, beaming as she talked about him. "He follows Dad and Nikki everywhere around the restaurant and tries to mimic whatever they're doing."

"Tell your dad and sisters 'hey' for me," Billy said. "And I'm very glad to hear he's healthy, happy, and into everything. Sounds like an inquisitive mind in the making."

"Very inquisitive," Monica said, still smiling at her memories. Then her expression turned somber. "I still can't thank you enough—"

"Stop. You already have, Monica. Many times over," Billy

said, and looked at the serving counter. "Can I get you a coffee, espresso, tea? Anything?"

She dropped her eyes a moment and then looked back up. "You know what I'd really like? A Brazilian roast with a shot of brandy and a sweet roll of some kind."

"Sure," Billy said, and went to order the coffee.

He returned with a tray and set her coffee, a shot on the side, and a cinnamon roll in front of her, and his herbal tea and a cherry pastry at the chair beside her.

He sat down and smiled at her as she poured part of the shot into her cup. "Okay. Tell me what's wrong. Is this just because or is there something wrong?"

"It's the nightmares. I know it's been four and a half, almost five years," she said softly, and sipped the coffee. "But I still have nightmares. I'm twenty-four years old and there's nothing threatening in my life now. I'm a mom and the little one is doing great. Dad, the restaurant, and my work there are good, satisfying, and then there are nights like Thursday! And again last night! I think I woke the whole house." Then softly, she added, "Both nights."

"I didn't realize it's still affecting you so much," Billy said, his voice full of concern. "I know you can't forget with the little one around all the time, but I hoped your professional help had made things better."

"It did for a while," Monica said. "But it comes back every spring about this time. Gets worse in early May. I can't seem to shake it."

"I understand," Billy said, remembering the night in early May when he had found her five years before, beaten, raped, clothes shredded and exposing her to the unusually cold elements of that dark night's late freeze, left to die.

She chuckled involuntarily. "I'm embarrassed every time I think about it—half naked, bruised, and bloody. I'm still surprised you found me."

"I'm so very glad I did," Billy said. "There was no way I could leave you there like that. I've known you and your family most of your life, and...well, you know."

"Thank you, Billy," she said, and patted his hands. "I know you can't do anything to help my nightmares, but I think I wanted to see you again today because you've always been such a positive, stabilizing force for our family and for me. You were the first person I thought of when I calmed down Friday morning: always with the right attitude and response, always optimistic and full of hope, always a comforting friend."

"Don't let the façade fool you," Billy said, and smiled. "Not everything in my life is a bowl of fruit and cream."

"I know," Monica said, and took another sip of her coffee. "But it's how you deal with it and handle it that impresses me, Dad, and my sisters. Thank you."

"Again, Monica," Billy said, and smiled, "you're welcome. You can ask to talk to me anytime. About anything."

"Thanks," she said, and smiled. "And thanks for the coffee," she said, and took a bite of her roll. "I can't do anything like this around the restaurant or the house. Not with the little one trying to taste everything he can."

Billy nodded. "There's no judgment, Monica."

"You never do." She smiled. "Oh, by the way, I wanted to tell you that we paid off the loan we got to fix up the restaurant. It's ours again, free and clear. One more thing to thank you for."

"Not me. You and your sisters did the work. I just pointed you in the right direction. I think it's absolutely wonderful you've been able to pay it off," Billy said. "It's a good reason to celebrate."

"Yes. We're going to have a mortgage burning next weekend," she said with a conspiratorial smile. "Will you come?"

"Oh, Monica. You know I'm not good at those kinds of gatherings," he said, suddenly bashful. "Besides, you and your sisters did all of the work. I don't really belong there. I'll just congratulate you and see your dad sometime next week and let you enjoy your celebration."

"Billy!" Monica said. "You know Dad would like you to be

there."

"I know." Billy shrugged and smiled sheepishly, playing the part to the hilt. "We'll see, but don't count on it."

Monica smiled, shook her head, and sighed. "Okay Billy. We know how you are."

Billy glanced around and then asked, "Is there someplace else you needed to go? This is a long ways from your home."

"No. Before you mentioned coming here, I was going to suggest going to the Library," she said, and smiled.

"The Library? The pub and student hangout?" he asked with a sly look. "Or the real one on campus?"

"The first one." She smiled. "I parked in the garage behind the police station and walked over to the museum to wait for you."

She slipped some bills across the table to him. "For the special coffee."

He pushed the money back. "You can buy another time. Call me if you need to talk again."

"Okay," she said, and put the bills away. "Walk me back to my car?"

Eight

In reasonable spirits, Billie left the Streetcar, got into her SUV, and turned east on St. Charles, following the old interurban trolley line, which she suspected was the inspiration for the Streetcar Diner. She continued east when the old trolley line turned north on a sweeping curve only to turn back east two blocks north on Archer. The tracks were long gone, but Billie liked that the city kept the curved streets and added the walking and sitting gardens in the quadrant of each curve. It seemed special, especially when you walked the route, following the footpaths and the historical signage placed along it.

Billie was lost in thought, thinking about how little she actually found out talking to Sid. She felt he had to know more than he was telling, and then quickly chided herself. She was a virtual stranger to both of them, so why would he tell her anything specific? There was no telling what he might think she would do with personal information about Billy—the private man named Billy.

She slowed for pedestrians as she passed the police station on the north and then again when she had to stop at Second Street East. She glanced each way and waited as a couple crossed in front of her, walking slowly to the south.

Suddenly she recognized Billy, wearing cleaner clothes, walking with the petite, black-haired woman with shapely legs in tight-fitting jeans and a tailored hip-length jacket! Billie's mouth fell open as she remembered Sid's words in the diner. She stared after them as they went down the sidewalk along Second. Transfixed, frozen in place, she watched them casually walking away, her hand holding the crook of his arm.

The blare of a car horn brought her back to the moment and she slowly crossed Second and turned south at the next corner. She tried to shake the image from her mind as she hurried through the college to Cheyenne and back west to her apartment.

What are you doing? Why are you acting this way?

He was with a girl! Sid said he didn't have a girlfriend.

So what if he does? It's none of your business who he sees or likes.

Well...Well...I was just surprised.

Really?

⊡-⊡-⊡-⊡-⊡

Billie sat on her three-section sofa for a long time, staring out through the full-height glass wall of her twelfth-floor loft apartment. She absently refilled her tea from the small pot she had placed on the end table as she stared at the view of the city center north of her building.

She knew she had no claim on him, and she could not understand why she had felt so surprised and deflated when she saw him walking with the dark-haired woman. After all, having lived there for the last seventeen years he had to have friends—even women friends.

So stop getting yourself so worked up. So what if he has a girlfriend and Sid doesn't know about it. He said Billy was a private person, so why would you think he would tell Sid everything?

She sighed and sipped her tea. She looked at the large pendulum clock on the far wall of her dining area; two more hours and she could relax with the girls. But no matter what she told herself, she still felt discouraged. Then she wondered, remembering another part of Sid's conversation.

You said you thought he liked a redhead he'd met. I'm a redhead... She smiled to herself. *I wonder how many redheads there are in Chesterfield. Can't be that many.*

She picked up her digital pad, flipped the cover open, and

quickly connected with the internet.

Stop! You dummy, get a grip, she chided herself, feeling flushed at her idiocy. *There's no database on people by the color of their hair, stupid.*

So all I know about you is that you dress horribly, except for today. You visit unsavory parts of town. You get your mail at the diner. You have at least one dark-haired female friend and Sid thinks you like a local redhead. I wonder...You did clean my boots, and you seemed...Well, it certainly felt like you were being more than just friendly, Mr. Carson.

Monday, April 18

The breakfast customers had begun to diminish and Billy cleared the table after an elderly couple left. He quickly reset the napkin box, shakers, and condiments, and pushed the chairs back in place. At the sink, he rinsed the dishware and silver and stacked them in the dishwasher tray. Sid stopped beside the deep sink as Billy finished, closed the dishwasher's door panels, and wiped his hands on the towel he carried over his shoulder.

"She's the same girl, isn't she?" Sid asked, remembering he had given Billy her name.

Billy nodded and smiled.

"You know she really doesn't know anything about you, Billy."

"She did finally ask to meet so we can talk," Billy said with a smile. "Maybe she isn't so angry anymore."

"Yeah, I know she wrote you a note. She seems nice, Billy," Sid continued. "Maybe you'll still think so too."

"Yeah. It's been so very long," Billy said, and turned to look him. "How can I explain who I am to her? No one except you, Aunt Mary, Mr. Filton, and Mr. Gibson know the truth—the whole truth. And now, I'm certain Mike Hammersmith's going to try something again. I have to stay alert and try to catch him in the act this time. But I can't endanger anyone else—especially not Billie."

"Does she know about any of the help she's gotten?" Sid asked, and patiently waited for Billy to answer.

"Of course not," Billy said after thinking for a long moment.

"You know, you don't have to tell her everything," Sid said. "You can still be private and keep most of your secrets secret."

"I know that too," Billy said, and knew his expression was showing his sadness as he fought his internal desire to blurt everything out to her. "I just worry. Time suddenly seems to be against me. Again."

"Yeah," Sid admitted, but then his face brightened. "Did I tell you that Mom got you another set of pants and some shirts for work?"

"No, you didn't," Billy admitted. "Why'd Aunt Mary do that?"

"I'm sure she'll tell you. She'll be down and talk to you shortly, but she wants you to keep one change of your daily clothes here and enough changes of work clothes so you don't have to worry about them being wrinkled or dirty."

"I don't understand, Sid," Billy said. "Our arrangement has been working out fine."

"She also put a change of better clothes," Sid continued, ignoring Billy's questions, "in the closet in the bath so you'll have something nice if you go somewhere with Billie."

"You know I won't be going out anywhere. And why would she think I would be taking Billie anywhere?"

"She just thinks you might," Sid said with a smile. "And Mom doesn't want you to look as homeless as you seem to be all of the time. Let her dote on you a little, Billy. Even if you don't think you'll wear them."

"Sure," Billy said as he caught Sid's shoulder and forced a tight smile. "I'll let her."

"And when you see Billie," Sid added, "talk to her. She seems to want to know you, so help her remember you or just give her a reason to understand you're special too. But you do owe her some courtesy, especially after all these years."

"Thanks, I'll try," Billy said.

"Good," Sid said firmly. "When does she want to get together with you?"

"Whenever I say," Billy said. "Tonight and tomorrow I have to be at the village and the department store, and tomorrow I also have the soup kitchen. Maybe Wednesday will—No, she's out with her girlfriends on Wednesdays after work."

"Can you get a sub and meet on Thursday?" Sid asked. "Have her come here and I'll set up the end booths for you so you won't be disturbed."

"Yeah," Billy said, and smiled.

"You can get ahold of her?"

"I can. She gave me her phone number in her note."

"Good. I'll set things up here. Are the others helping you watch?" Sid asked, and opened the dishwasher when the chime sounded.

"Yeah. We're split between both places," Billy said as Sid slid the dishwasher trays out to drip dry. "Falcon has recruited a few of the younger fellas from the village to help. The drug dealers suddenly seem to be on every street corner, trying to get in from all angles. We could lose everything if they get in and start selling."

"Good luck," Sid said. "Here, I'll put these away."

"Thanks. I need to use your computer for an hour or so."

Sid nodded. "I figured. Take as long as you need."

-¤-

Billy finished and logged off the computer, leaving it in the same state as he had found it so Sid would not be upset with his use of it. He got up and opened the office door, startling the older woman coming down the hallway toward the diner.

"Sorry, Aunt Mary. I didn't hear you coming."

"Hello, Billy," she said, one hand on her chest and the other gripping the handrail along the wall. "I thought it might be Sid in the office."

"Nah. Just me playing around on the computer." Billy turned and gave her a gentle hug. "Thanks for the clothes. Sid told me about them."

"You're welcome," Mary said. "I know you don't want to look fancy and put your friends to shame, but every man ought to have at least one nice change of clothes."

"Yes, Aunt Mary," Billy placated. "But my friends and I can't go around in good clothes." He took Mary's hand and led her to the door to the kitchen. "Come on. I'll bet we have a table just inside the dining room for you, and Julie will bring you your tea. I'm sure Angie has one of Melony's special rolls for you."

"I appreciate all of you," Mary said, "but come sit with me for a few minutes. I think you have some new decisions to make."

-¤-

"Thank you, girls," Mary said to Angie, Julie, and Melony as they started back to their stations. "And you too, Carole," she added, waving to the girl standing behind the long soda counter.

"So you think I've reached a decision time?" Billy asked with a knowing smile. Little actually got past Mary, even if she wasn't in the diner every minute of every day.

"You have," Mary said firmly, and stirred her tea. "For a while I thought you might have forgotten, and you puzzled me. You never went after anyone, never had that special look—not until that spilled soup and you remembered." She sipped her tea and Billy felt she was waiting for her words to soak in.

"I always remember, especially at night when things are quiet, when I'm watching and waiting, when I try to sleep. Those memories have been the hardest for me to deal with, knowing how the situation affected her and her family. I'll admit, though, I was very surprised when I realized Billie had been coming in and I didn't recognize her. I lost track of her for a while after she graduated."

"I think the memory of a twelve-year-old with red ringlets

and freckles that came into the diner one day for lunch may have blinded you," Mary said. "When they came in that day, two years after the accident, I was sure you would have said something to her. Something to let her know."

"You know I couldn't, Aunt Mary. No more than I can now," Billy said with more force than he intended. "Sorry, but there's too much happening and I think it's going to get rough again. I just told Sid that I can't risk getting involved with her and possibly getting her hurt."

"So you think Mike's up to something?"

Billy nodded and slowly smiled. "After I lost my one chance to pin my folks' death on him, I became more and more disillusioned. I just can't figure out what would drive him to kill someone." Billy sighed and then smiled at Mary. "But in December, I baited a trap for him and now I just have to get the timing right. I'm worried that if I get distracted—"

"Well," Mary said, "you be careful playing with matches. You need to think about yourself and not get hurt either."

"I'll do my best, Aunt Mary."

"And now that you know she's here?" Mary continued.

"Yeah, I do, Aunt Mary," he said. "She still has a few gorgeous freckles, incredible hair, and bright green eyes. And the rest of her grew up very nice as well. I'm going to try to see her Thursday night."

Keeper and His Tiger: An Unexpected Complication

Nine

His forehead wrinkled with displeasure, Frederick Westman stared at the computer monitor and reached for the button on the intercom.

"Mitchell, come in here," he said coldly, and released the button before he got an answer.

"Yes, sir," Mitchell said as he hurried through Frederick's open office door.

"Have you looked at the Duckard's purchase?" Frederick asked, turning his head and looking at Mitchell over the rims of his glasses.

"Not since Friday," Mitchell admitted.

Frederick tapped the monitor screen. "Our offers to pay the back taxes on that property and the rest of that block have been rejected."

"What? Rejected?" Mitchell questioned. "I was told by our source at the City Treasurer's office they were all in arrears."

"You better get down there and recheck," Frederick said, his icy stare holding Mitchell's disbelief at bay. "If someone's paid the taxes, I want to know who it is! If not, I want to know the story! The whole story!"

"I'll get on it immediately," Mitchell said.

"Also find out who has the title to those properties!" Frederick shouted after Mitchell as he scurried down the corridor. To himself and the otherwise empty office he said, "I know Hawke's Enterprises never got the chance to complete the purchases, so who? Who has them now?"

Interrupting his thoughts, the phone console beeped.

"Yes?" he said as he touched the hook key, his temper still coloring his voice.

"Mr. Lange on one," the secretary's voice announced, and he grabbed the hand unit and inhaled deeply.

"Hello, Robert," he said in a calmer tone when he had keyed the line. "What can I do for you this morning?"

"A question has been raised concerning the Duckard Project," Robert's voice said pleasantly. "I was asked to confirm your progress on the purchase. That everything is on track to close on the twenty-ninth."

"We're working the details, Robert," Frederick said.

"Good. I'll pass that along to Mr. Hammersmith. Mike has a lot riding on the renovation of that block."

"I'll keep you informed," Frederick said, keeping his emotions out of his tone. "Anything else?"

"No," Robert said. "This has a very high priority here and Mike will not be happy if you miss your date."

"No need to remind me, Robert. I know Mike. If there is nothing more, I should get back to work. Have a nice day."

"You too."

The connection broke and Frederick reflected on Robert's implications. He knew that Mike would be upset if he missed his date, but he also knew that missing the date would mean he would have to pay back a number of investors, and he would have to pay back a lot.

"Donna," he said as he tapped the intercom again. "Get me the financials on all of our open development projects."

"Yes, Mr. Westman."

¤-¤-¤-¤-¤

"What's the story, Mace?" Billy asked when he met Mace and his wife Pigeon at the south end of the dim alley in the block just east of the Duckard's buildings. "Hey, Pidge."

"He's been there about two hours, Keeper, and I've talked with him," Mace said. "He isn't inclined to leave."

70

"Is he argumentative? Does he have any of the signs?" Billy asked.

"Signs, yes," Mace said. "Argumentative, not so much."

"Okay, Mace," Billy said, and stepped away from the wall. "You go and squat on one side of the mouth so he can see you. And Pidge, you take a position here just above the cross alleys. Stop anyone that comes this way."

"Okay, Keeper," Pigeon said, and settled down beside the dark dumpster.

Billy and Mace started walking up the alley, and when Billy stopped in front of the man, Mace went on the short distance to the end of the alley and settled down in a crouch beside the wall across from him.

Billy squatted down and watched the man in the shadows. "I believe Mace explained the situation," Billy said.

"You the Keeper?" the man asked, his voice low and slightly slurred.

"Yes. I'm Keeper," Billy said, "and I cannot let you stay here."

"Why not?" the man said. "It's public prop'ty."

"Aah, but it isn't," Billy explained. "And the owners expect me to keep it clean and safe."

"Clean and safe? Whaz'at s'posed to mean?" The man's voice pitched a little.

"You've brought drugs and booze with you," Billy said simply. "No drugs here. No buying. No selling. No sharing. No using."

"That's perznal bidness."

"Not here it isn't," Billy said. "There are eight blocks here that are off-limits to drug users and boozers. If you try to stay here, either I will evict you or the police will evict you. Only those with permission can be here."

"Who sez?"

"The owner says. And I am the keeper of his property." Billy offered his hand. "I can help you up and point you to a place over by the bus station if you would like."

"Don' need no help." The man jerked his hand back.

"If you can shake the drugs and stay sober for a year, I can talk to the owner on your behalf," Billy said. "But to be allowed to be here, you have to earn it. Get a job, help at the kitchens, or—"

"Yur shittin' me," the man said in disbelief.

"Not in the least," Billy said. "Mace, give me a hand."

Billy and Mace caught the man's arms, stood him up, and turned him toward the street. A bottle slipped out of his torn pocket and broke on the pavement. Mace reached down and picked up a small plastic packet that fell when the man jerked, trying to catch the bottle.

"Looks like enough for a pretty good high," Mace said, and Billy nodded as they half carried the man onto the sidewalk. "Your rehabilitation has just begun," Mace said, and dropped the packet through the grille over the storm drain.

"Nooo," the man said, staring at the black grille. "Now what'm I gonna do?"

"Hopefully dry out," Mace said as he moved the man in the direction of the bus station. "Remember. Don't come around these eight blocks. If you do, Keeper will know and we'll go through this all over again."

¤-¤-¤-¤-¤

About dark, Billie parked her SUV on Hadley, just west of the homeless village. She followed Billy at a distance, hoping he wouldn't notice the repeating appearance of her vehicle as she tried to keep tabs on his whereabouts. She picked out an old jacket and the same leather and fake fur hat, just in case, but she planned on staying in her SUV and watching where he went after he left the village. Sid said he did not know and she found nothing from the internet, so she sat impatiently, hoping maybe she might find out where he lived, or at least where else he went at night.

Dusk turned to full dark and she waited, hoping she was close enough to Duberry that no one would bother her. She checked her watch frequently, bored, wondering what he did in the village that took so long. Finally, about eight fifteen she saw him cross Hadley a block east, going south.

She made sure her automatic lights were off, then started her SUV and drove slowly east with only the streetlights on the corners to guide her. At the corner of Tenth, she stopped and looked south. He passed under a streetlight a block down and then turn east on the next street.

She knew she was being childish, stalking him instead of just pulling up beside him and asking him where he was going. Everything about her said just go and ask, but she realized she did not want to admit that she was actually afraid to.

Instead, she drove south one block and turned to follow one of the streets north of him. She stopped at each north-south street corner, looking for him and waiting until he appeared and crossed into the next block east. The neighborhoods got darker, some streetlights not lit, less and less people about and fewer houses with lights on as she passed. The number of empty lots increased and the darkness fed her nervousness.

After two miles of depressing houses and dark lots, she stopped just above what was once the eastside, Mansions Bluff trolley station and maintenance depot. She waited, watching the street to her south, but Billy did not arrive as she expected. When he was still absent after another few minutes, she turned south and drove slowly, hoping to see where he might have turned or stopped.

Circling the block twice with no sign of him, she felt completely deflated and knew she deserved the disappointment. Billie took a deep breath and slowly drove back to Seventh East and then turned south. He was nowhere to be seen.

In deep contrition, she followed the old trolley route south. She was at an unfamiliar loss to understand her intense sense of depression and her inexplicable inability to answer Becky's question of why this was so important. At Cheyenne, she reluctantly turned west and drove back to her apartment.

Ten

Tuesday, April 19

"Matches is up to something," Falcon said when Billy met him on the corner of Duberry and Tenth. "Mouse said she heard he's out to enlarge his market area."

"That means the village or the city center," Billy admitted, and glanced at the sun, gauging how much daylight was left. "If he shows up before I get there, can you keep a lid on it?"

"Sure," Falcon said, and cocked his head. "You have somewhere else to be?"

"Just for a few minutes," Billy said, and smiled. "You remember Danny Willis, the owner of Danny's Steakhouse?"

"Yeah. The one you helped out a while back."

Billy nodded. "His daughter told me they paid off the renovation and reorganization loans and are having a mortgage burning party this weekend, so I need ten minutes to offer my congratulations and tell him I won't be at his party. I won't take long."

"Okay, Keeper." Falcon smiled. "We'll keep things under control until you can get there. Tell him hello and congrats from me and Sparrow also."

◻-◻-◻-◻-◻

Billie stared at her computer monitor and shook her head. She had lost count of the number of times the contracts and the client's project description words had blurred and run together into a meaningless jumble, smearing together and making them

unreadable. She shook her head and looked at the clock icon—
three-thirty.

Damn!

Time was slogging past like a river of molasses, and Billie
logged off the company system. She shut her computer down,
pushed her chair up to her desk, and took her coat off the rack
behind the door.

*What's wrong with me? I can't get him out of my mind. He's
like a bad dream...in a way.*

You know what's wrong. You just won't admit it.

I vowed I wouldn't let anyone get close again—

Then you saw Billy.

Damn! Yeah.

Billie closed her office and left. She absently nodded to
the receptionist as she waited for the elevator. Then, barely
remembering the five-block drive, Billie closed her apartment
door, thumbed the deadbolt by rote, and hung her coat on the
pegs on the wall.

She stood in front of her three-piece sofa, staring out
through the glass wall. It did not take her long before she
focused on the area northwest of the city center—the break in
the budding trees where the homeless village sat.

Am I doing the right thing? she asked herself without
realizing she had.

No! You're going to see him Thursday. Talk to him then.

*I have too much time invested to let this opportunity slip
away. I need—*

No! This is stupid! her mind shouted. *It's too dangerous and
you know it.*

But I want *to see what he does when he goes there. It'll be
okay.*

No! It won't and you know it! Willum would not approve.

Billie shook her head, forcing herself to stop listening to
her rational sense. She knew she knew better, but she *wanted*
to know. Sid would not tell her anything and it had her tied up

in knots all night and most of the day. Why did Billy spend his time with the homeless people, look so much like the homeless people, and Sid not seem worried about it?

Billie hurried up her spiral stairs, grabbed an old school backpack she had stuffed in her closet, and shoved the dress-down clothes she had bought in it. She pushed a pair of heavy socks in the side pocket and the worn pair of boots in the front pouch. Then, with a quick look around her bedroom, she zipped the pouches closed, threw one of the straps over her shoulder, and hurried down to her SUV in the parking garage.

Forcing herself to act and not think, she tossed the backpack in the back seat, got in behind the wheel, and started the SUV. She drove as casually as she could to Duberry and north as the sun finally set. Stopping just north of Danny's Steakhouse and moving to the back seat, she slipped the worn pants over her slacks, then put the heavy socks and boots on, pulled her old jacket tight, and zipped it so it would hide her brightly colored blouse.

She hesitated, then inhaled deeply.

You're really going to do this?

Yes. I said I was going to. I want to see what he does, what goes on while he's here.

With renewed determination, she grabbed the knitted cap and moved back to the driver's seat. As she closed her door, she glanced west and saw Billy leave the side door of Danny's Steakhouse and head north on Tenth West. Wondering why he would be at Danny's, she drove north, toward Hadley and the village.

It isn't safe here.

I'll...just stay for a minute or two. Not long.

A minute might be too long. Why are you doing this? Honestly.

You know why. His coming here is so different than what he seems in the restaurant.

You don't know how he is in the restaurant or what he's normally like.

Sure I do. Well...maybe a little.

Billie glanced at her hands where she was gripping the steering wheel. Her knuckles were white and she was trembling.

Now see what you've done.

Billie stopped a block south and a block east of the village. She checked the time and then took her watch off and slipped it into her left jacket pocket. She felt for her phone in the right pocket as she got out and pulled the knitted cap down on her head to cover her ears. She absently brushed her hair back over her shoulders with both hands as she turned to lock her SUV.

Okay. Just a little ways and you'll be there. One step at a time. And then another. You can do this.

She glanced around her as she started up the block to the village; her rational side remained silent.

At the southeast corner of the city block full of cardboard and canvas lean-tos and tents, she stopped beside a tree and waited for Billy. Knowing when he had started up Tenth Street, she knew he should get there soon. She glanced around again, noticing some of the people huddled beside a cardboard hovel not too far away.

At twenty after six, Billie saw Billy cross Hadley on an angle from the far corner of the block. She watched his confident swagger as he walked to the middle of the block and then calmly into the throng of makeshift shelters. Billie tried to keep her eyes on where he was, taking a path that looked like it would take her to the middle of the village. Carefully watching her steps, trying to avoid the people's belongings, she worked her way through the clutter. Then as she neared the center of the block, she heard confrontational voices.

The people near her were so intent on listening to the voices, they did not acknowledge her presence as she hurried to get closer.

This is not good.

Hush!

Billie stopped in a narrow gap between two shelters,

looking over the shoulders of a small group of men and women. She could not believe her eyes, seeing Billy and two other men—one tall and lanky and the other about Billy's height and a little heavier—to one side of a large steel barrel with a flickering fire inside. Looking to her left, they were face to face with two men wearing slightly better jeans, boots, and jackets; the air felt taut, crisp with tension.

Billie stepped around the group in front of her and eased closer. She focused on the five men and moved toward the barrel until she could make out their words.

"I've told you before," Billy was saying calmly. "You cannot come in here and try to sell your wares. You have to leave or I will see to it you are carried out. No drugs in the village." Billy's tone was sharp and firm.

"Yeah, yeah, Keeper," said the man wearing a brown jacket and standing in front of Billy. "But who sez?" He did not sound like he expected an answer. "This is a free country, man. These folks have a right to choose."

Billie wet her suddenly dry lips as she watched Billy lean forward, toward Brown Jacket. "I say." The air nearly sizzled as Billy hesitated for just a second before he continued in a tone that made the hair on her neck stand up. "And the owner of this block says. If anyone wants to live here, they *do not* have the right to choose. But you do. You can choose how you want to leave."

Billie cringed, disbelieving what she was seeing. Billy's stance was confident, authoritative, and unyielding—so very different from the eager-to-please, compassionate Billy she saw in the diner. She watched the shadow of his hard-set jaw, his facial muscles dominant and stark in the firelight. She could not see his stare, but felt his concentration as he confronted the brown-jacketed man before him.

"You think you can win in a fair fight?" Brown Jacket asked, and Billie felt, more than she heard, a tremor in his voice. The man beside Brown Jacket took a small step toward the tall lanky man beside Billy.

"Nothing's going to be fair about it, Matches," Billy said,

in the same soft, firm voice he had used before. He nodded slightly toward the lanky man, keeping his eyes on Matches. "Stretch and Hammer will see to that."

"Step aside, Keeper," the man in a heavy sweater standing beside Matches said. His voice raised above Billy's. Sweater took a step forward and everything seemed to happen at once.

Billie inhaled sharply as Sweater lunged at the lanky one she thought was Stretch. She did not see where the knives came from, but was relieved when Stretch stopped Sweater's swipe at his middle, wrenching his arm around, spinning and tossing him on the ground with his arm twisted up behind him. Stretch took Sweater's knife and tossed it into the fire barrel.

Barely seeing Billy behind Stretch, she realized she heard knives clash, metal against metal like miniature swords, and when she focused on him, he was holding Brown Jacket, his arm twisted up behind his back, between them, and Billy's knife pulled tight against Matches' throat.

It was over in a heartbeat and Matches slowly raised his knife hand and let the knife fall to the ground. The man Billie assumed was Hammer quickly kicked it away.

"Now, Matches," Billy said, his voice still soft and dangerous. "One flinch and your head will be roiling around in the dirt beside your friend. You can either go away and tell all of your friends the village is off-limits, or I can deliver you in pieces and let the newspapers spread the word. The choice really is yours."

"Okay. Okay," Matches said slowly, and opened his raised, empty knife hand.

"I ought to confiscate your wares," Billy added, "and put them in the barrel, but I don't want the smoke or the smell ruining our air. If I see or hear of you hanging around here again, I will personally make sure you visit the fine folks at St. Charles and Main. I hear they have wonderful, all-expense paid accommodations."

Billie inhaled and absently smirked as she realized the address Billy was talking about was the police department downtown.

She watched as Stretch and Hammer escorted Matches and Sweater down the path and out of the village. When she looked back to the area around the fire barrel, she clutched her arms across her chest, suddenly feeling a chill; she could not see Billy anywhere.

Billie sighed and began to tremble, the images of what she had just seen replaying in her mind. She watched the small crowd of people that had gathered a short distance from the fire barrel slowly disperse and heard fragments of their mixed comments on what they had just seen. Then as she decided she needed to get out of there, something tugged on her hair from behind. She looked over her shoulder and saw a husky man, taller than herself, letting a long strand of curls slide through his fingers.

Shit! Shit! Shit!

I told you.

Shit! This can't be happening.

She started to back away, but the man tightened his grip. "My, my. What d'we have here?" he said in a voice that matched his appearance.

"Let go. Don't touch," she said, her voice louder than she expected as she snatched the curl from his hand.

"Now missy," the man insisted, and Billie stepped back again, stumbling over something.

She quickly looked down and repositioned her foot, trying to put space between her and the man.

"Tha's no way ta be. I sure do like red. Reminds me of some'un spunky."

"Let go," she repeated, with more heat in her tone.

His hand suddenly clamped her upper arm and he began pulling her. His grip reminded her of Blake and how he would grab and jerk her around, forcing her do what he wanted. The remembered fear paralyzed her, keeping her from moving, speaking.

"The lady is not interested, Lenny," a firm yet familiar voice said as Billy stepped between her and the man. "I've already had enough trouble for one night. Go back to the bus station and leave her alone."

"I don' see yur mark on 'er," Lenny said, and jerked her arm again.

"She has," Billy said in a steely voice. "And she does not want to go with you. Now go back to your place before you upset me."

"I don' wanna go. I have a righ' ta see my friends," Lenny said.

"Not in your condition. Not when you've been drinking and you don't listen when a lady says no." Billy's voice went soft again and Billie knew she did not want to see the look in his eyes.

Slowly, Lenny dropped his grip on her arm and turned, stumbling back through the mass of tents, and disappeared into the darkness.

Billie inhaled and rubbed her arm as Billy slowly turned to face her.

"And just what are you doing here?" he asked, his face neutral. "This is the worst possible place you can be and the worst time for you to be here."

"I...I just—"

"Come on," Billy interrupted, his voice softer as he turned her toward the fire barrel and the main path through the village. His hand settled gently on her back just above her waist and he pushed her toward Hadley. At the street, he stopped. "What on earth possessed you to come here? Tonight of all nights?"

Billie inhaled and straightened her shoulders. "I wanted to know where you go and why you come to the homeless village. Why you dress the way you do. And now—"

"I said we could talk on Thursday."

"I know, but I—"

"Stop! Thursday! And stop following me around. It isn't safe."

"You know?" She could not believe he did.

"Of course I know you've been following me. And you have to stop it." He sighed and let his shoulders fall. Then in a softer voice, he asked, "For your own good, stop. Where's your car?"

"One block over and one down," she said, and pointed to the appropriate street corner. She tried to see his eyes, but the shadows were too deep. "Are you mad at me?"

"Hell yes!" he said sharply. "Of all of the things you could do, this is the stupidest thing I can think of." He inhaled and sighed again. "And no. I figured you'd try to follow me, but I just wish you hadn't tried to come tonight. Things are very tense right now and I can't look out for you." He gently caught her shoulder and turned her toward the corner. "Come on, I'll walk you."

"Billy? What's going on? Why do you care if a couple of drug dealers try—"

"Thursday! Thursday, Billie," he said, letting his voice soften again. "Save your questions for then."

They walked in silence and she slipped her hand in the crook of his arm, trying to get a sense of what he was thinking as they passed under the streetlights.

You know what he's thinking. He's upset with you.

I know.

I'm surprised he's still willing to talk to you on Thursday.

Me too. I almost blew it, didn't I?

Yes! Yes, you sure did.

Billy stopped beside her SUV and opened the driver's door for her when she unlocked it.

She looked up at him. "I was so surprised at—"

"Go," he said firmly, but without the heat she felt earlier. "Please. It's very dangerous here. Bring your questions Thursday. And don't try following me around anymore."

"Okay," she said as he helped her up into the SUV. "I'll go home and I'll talk with you on Thursday. I won't follow you again unless you don't tell me what's going on."

"Thanks," he said, looking at her for a long moment before he closed her door.

He was still standing in the middle of the street, watching her, as she pulled away and turned south on Tenth West.

Eleven

Wednesday, April 20

"What have you found out?" Frederick asked as Mitchell came through his office door.

"I went like you asked, and the clerks there looked up the properties for me," Mitchell said, standing uncomfortably in the open door.

"Sit down, for God's sake," Frederick interrupted. "You're making me nervous. Now go on."

Mitchell settled into the straight-backed chair at the end of Frederick's desk. "The city records show those properties haven't been in arrears anytime in the last twenty years. Not once since they were built, actually." He wet his lips, expecting Frederick to say something. "They were not in arrears even when Mike Hammersmith thought W. C. Hawke was trying to buy them."

"What?"

"They were not for sale or in jeopardy of tax action then either," Mitchell said firmly.

"But Contracts has been watching those properties for years and they said they saw a posting about Christmastime." Frederick stared at Mitchell and then reached for the intercom.

"Jeffers?" he said when the connection made. "Bring the files on the Duckard Property and come to my office."

In a matter of minutes, a white-haired man entered the office door with a thick file folder in his hand.

"Show me the posting you said you saw in December on the tax sale," Frederick said flatly.

Jeffers opened the folder, thumbed through the sheets for

a minute. He flattened his hand on one and laid the folder in front of Frederick.

"December twenty-first," Jeffers said, "a Tuesday. We alerted you at nine-thirteen a.m. on your phone and made an 'Offer to Pay' at ten-oh-six a.m. as you requested. You were in a meeting and we had to wait until you came out at ten o'clock."

"How long was the posting up?" Frederick asked.

"We looked again…" Jeffers flipped to the next page. "…at nine a.m. the next day, the twenty-second, and the posting was gone. After an 'Offer to Pay,' they usually remove the postings. The notation here indicates that we notified you of the removal, and I believe you commented the removal indicated the offer was accepted."

"Yes, yes," Frederick agreed. "But Mitchell talked with the city clerk and our source in the clerk's office yesterday. They say those properties were never posted as in arrears, not once in more than twenty years! How is that?"

"I do not know sir," Jeffers said, closing the folder and standing up with it tightly under his arm. "We responded to the public postings and saw no reason to second-guess them or the need to call and verify the posting. That is not part of your company policy or normal procedures."

Frederick studied the man for a long moment.

"Thank you, Jeffers," he finally said. "That will be all. You as well, Mitchell. I need some time to think."

-¤-

It was late and most of the Westman Associates' employees had gone for the day when Frederick finally tapped the intercom.

"Mitchell, have someone look around the Duckard building and the one to the east. See if anything's going on that we should know about."

"Yes, sir," Mitchell answered. "Are you looking for anything in particular?"

"Yes, but I'm not sure what. I want to know why someone

has kept those properties paid up and has not done anything with them. Why would someone spend that kind of money and not try to recoup any of it?"

"Yes, sir. I'll get someone to nose around a little."

Twelve

Thursday, April 21

Angie looked up from serving desserts to one of her dinner tables in time to see Billie hurry across the street from where she had parked on the south side of St. Anne. She caught the inner door and pulled it open as Billie reached the top of the steps.

"Billie?" she asked as she closed the door behind her and Billie nodded. "Hi. I'm Angie. Nice to meet you again. Please come this way."

Angie led her to the three "reserved" booths at the far end of the dining room and gestured for Billie to take a place in the middle booth.

"I'll let Billy know you're here," Angie added. "Is there anything I can get you while you wait?"

"I don't think so," Billie said as she laid her jacket on the bench beside her.

When Angie disappeared through the swinging doors in the archway, Billie looked around the dining room. She wrung her hands and tried to concentrate on the streetcar motif details of the room.

He said he wasn't mad at you.

I know. But he seemed concerned.

You can do this.

But what if he thinks about what I did and decides he should be mad at me? Actually, he probably should be anyway.

Stop fidgeting! You made it into the homeless village and back home again. You're still in one piece—no small thanks to Billy, though.

I know. I know. A big *thanks to him for saving me from that man, and for getting me out of there without anything else happening.*

"Hi. I'm Julie," the waitress said, startling Billie out of her thoughts. "Sorry to interrupt your thinking, but do you like red or white?"

Billie stared at her for a second.

"Wine?"

"Sorry. White, I guess. A chardonnay."

"Sure." Julie smiled and walked back to the long counter at the back of the dining room.

-¤-

Billy was leaning back against the end of the grill, looking through the corner of the serving window at Billie.

"Don't keep her waiting," Sid said, and glanced toward the window without looking through it.

"I was pretty tough on her Tuesday," Billy said, and looked at him. "I'm actually surprised she came."

"You had to be, from what you said. She shouldn't have been there, and I think you did the right thing. So now, visit with her and be your normal, likeable self." Sid smiled. "Or at least be pleasant. We talked about this the other day. Remember?" Sid snapped his damp towel at Billy and turned back to the orders on the grill.

"Yeah. We did." Billy smiled. "And I will." He straightened and stood up, smiled at Sid, and walked to the archway.

-¤-

Billie was watching Julie until Billy pushed the swinging doors open and stepped into the dining room. He was wearing his normal white pants and shirt. She saw Billy's smile and the tension in her shoulders and her apprehension eased.

"Hey," he greeted as he stopped at the end of the other

bench. "No red boots?" he asked as he sat down across from her.

Billie folded her hands and pushed them down in her lap, not wanting him to see her nervousness. "No. No red boots. I think you said they didn't look good with my hair."

"Well." He smiled. "They were certainly a distraction. Your hair is far more stunning than red boots. And I must say the rest of you grew up very stunning as well."

Billie stared at him. Suddenly she could not remember what she wanted to say.

It's a compliment, dummy. Just a compliment.

I know. I wasn't expecting—

Just thank him!

"Uh, thanks," she answered softly. "Lori said you were the same boy...sorry, man now"—Billie stumbled over her choice of words as her thoughts and questions tumbled and collided in her head—"that cleaned my boots years ago."

What's wrong with you? You act like you've never talked to a man before.

"I am," Billy said.

Billie took a deep breath and looked at him as he folded his hands and leaned against the table.

You're not ten! Get over it!

"I'm sorry, but I don't remember you or the first time you cleaned my boots very well," she said. "And I didn't hear everything you said the second time, um, last week."

"That's okay." He smiled, and unexpectedly she could not take her eyes off him. "I'm around but not very memorable."

I disagree with that.

"I've been in here many times," she said, forcing herself to relax, "since I moved back to town, after college, and I don't remember seeing you before the spilled soup. Have you been here all along, or have you been away?"

"I've been here," he said. "I've seen you and your friends a few times when you've come in, but I'm always in the back unless there is an emergency like—"

"—like spilled soup."

He nodded and chuckled and she smiled.

"Yeah. I have to admit I didn't realize I knew you until last week. I think it might have been the boots."

She nodded absently, slowly wringing her hands in her lap with less fervor. "But you don't really *know* me. The whole 'cleaning my boot' scene is vaguely familiar, but Lori had to remind me what happened and what you said. When was it? Nine, ten years ago?"

Surprised she could not recall how long it had been since that meeting, even after she and Lori had talked, Billie caught his eyes, startled by the warmth she saw in them. She unexpectedly felt like she was interrupting some private thought and forced her gaze to move away. But she lingered on the cleft in his chin and his powerful, squared jawline that exuded confidence and control. His shoulders were wide, supporting muscular arms with well-developed biceps and forearms. She suspected there was not any excess fat on him anywhere. But when she looked back at his face, it was his slightly crooked smile and his soft, light brown eyes that—

Snap out of it, stupid! Get a grip. You don't know him either.

"Fifteen," he confirmed, and she was afraid she physically jerked when he spoke, jarring her from her thoughts.

"Fifteen? Really?"

"Yeah. When I heard the bowl hit the floor, I came out and was only concerned with the spill until I saw your red boots with soup spatters on them. Something clicked and the words seemed to come out on their own. I'm sorry that I embarrassed you."

"Thank you. Stacy was put off some, but Lori and Becky were okay." She smiled and looked at the wall for a second. "Because I let Stacy's unpleasant comments and opinions influence me, I came and complained to Sid about how inappropriate and invasive your actions were. I may have yelled some."

"Believe me, Sid already knew what had happened. He

doesn't miss anything that happens here in the diner."

"Are you in trouble?"

"Only with you."

"You were, but now...only a little...maybe." She took a deep breath. "But I think I'm the one that's in trouble now."

Before Billy could say anything, Julie stepped up and placed a chiller beside the table and a carafe of iced water between them. "Can I get you anything else?" she asked as she sat two wine glasses beside the carafe.

"Thanks, Julie," Billy said, and shook his head.

Billie saw Julie smile at him and wondered what was being said between them. Then Julie left and Billy picked up the bottle and poured the wine into her glass.

"Have you eaten?" he asked. "I know the owner and can get us a killer of a deal if you're hungry."

Billie shook her head. "Thanks, but I ate at home. I didn't expect this...this...V.I.P. treatment, and you didn't mention dinner."

"No, I guess I didn't. Sorry. I should have said something when I called you, but when we saw each other on Tuesday night, my mind was on other things."

"Yeah, I know," she said, and took a sip of her wine. "I am sorry about Tuesday night. I saw your confrontation with the other men—the drug dealers, I think they were. And that brings me back to my questions."

Billy nodded and poured the iced water into his wine glass. "But I have one first. Why have you been following me around? And going into the worst parts of town, at night, alone with no one to protect you? Are you completely—"

"Stupid?"

"I was going to say 'daft,' but 'stupid' works."

Billie stared at him, her irritation growing until his concerned expression slowly melted into a wide smile. She could not help but smile in return.

"Yeah, 'stupid' fits," she said. "I guess it started when I came back here to talk to you, to apologize for reporting you to Sid." She sipped her wine again, wishing it would stop the trembling she was feeling. "Sid wouldn't tell me where you lived or where you went at night, so I thought I'd follow you home and then we could talk and I could apologize in person. I figured I needed to do that." She hesitated and took another deep breath. "But you went to the homeless village instead and I lost my courage." *God, I seem to have so little courage left. It all went away when Willum—*

She stopped her thought and took another, longer sip of wine before she looked back at him. "Sorry. A bad memory." She took another breath and saw that he was patiently waiting for her to continue.

"Then on Saturday I came by the diner again but you were off and I saw you later over by the college. But you were busy, walking with a woman on Second Street East. I didn't want to interrupt. Was that a girlfriend or someone special?"

Billy nodded and smiled. "A good friend. I've known her, her folks, and her sisters for many years."

Billie absently nodded, somehow relieved she was just 'a good friend.' "Well, anyway, not being able to catch you and talk led to Tuesday night's stupid escapade."

Billy raised his glass and took a long sip of his water. His eyes were soft—maybe understanding, she thought. Hoped.

"I was scared. Part of my brain was telling me it was dangerous and all of that, but I didn't listen. The other half kept telling me it couldn't be that bad. Then I saw you and the drug dealers and the fight, and knew better. But I couldn't move or run away. I was mesmerized watching you and the men, seeing how determined and confident you were. When it was over, I watched the other two men take the dealers away, and when I looked for you, you were gone and I got scared all over again."

She put her hand on the table to stop her trembling before she picked up her glass again and took another sip.

"When the big guy pulled my hair and grabbed my arm, I about lost it. I just knew I was going to die...or worse." Her heart was suddenly racing and she took a couple of breaths to calm herself. She looked up and held his eyes. "I was suddenly terrified, frozen with fear, and then you stepped in between us and everything was better again."

"I know you know, but in that moment, in that place, your red hair was a flag in front of a bull. You really should not have been there," Billy said softly, then took a sip of his water as she studied her wine glass.

"I know." Billie looked up and held his eyes again. "Thank you."

"You're welcome, Billie." He was still smiling at her. "But don't make a habit of going into places like that and expecting someone to help you out."

Billie smiled sheepishly and nodded. "Obviously you know a lot of those people."

"Certainly. I've lived here in Chesterfield for seventeen years and have made a number of wonderful friends at all levels in the city."

"I've been back since college and only have three friends to speak of. And one of those is from my childhood."

"Three in a couple of years is not bad, Billie."

"So tell me," she said, setting her glass down in front of her and leaning forward. Forearms on the table, she smiled and looked him in the eye. "I know I'm pressing my luck, but where do you live, Mr. Billy Carson? Just in case I want to come and visit sometime."

Billy slowly shook his head.

"What? You're not going to tell me? You don't want me dropping in to visit?"

He shook his head again without breaking eye contact. "No," he finally said in a loud whisper.

"Why not?" Billie asked in a raised voice, unexpectedly feeling like he had slapped her and she suddenly wanted to scream at him.

"I'm sure this is making you angry," Billy said. "But you don't need to know where I live."

"Need to know?" Billy stared at him in disbelief. "Are you kidding me? You think people have to have a 'need' to know where you live?"

"That's right." Billy said, and sipped his water. "I can't tell you where."

"Can't or won't?" Billie challenged, trying hard to keep her voice from reflecting the hurt she felt. "You make it sound like 'knowing could be dangerous.' Like a spy drama or something."

"Or something," Billy said cryptically. "The men you saw Tuesday night and many of their cronies have been trying to find out where I live for more than ten years. If they knew, they wouldn't come visiting to talk, so I won't give anyone the chance of finding me while I'm sleeping."

"You're kidding. Right?"

He shook his head. "Not for a second, Billie."

A whispered "wow" slipped past her lips.

"I simply need to stay alive to help the people that trust me to help them."

"Alive?" She blinked and sat up straight, uncertain she had heard him correctly. "I thought you meant they might beat you up or something. Not...My God, Billy. What do you do besides pick fights in dark places and save red-haired damsels from their idiocy and foolishness?"

"That's about it." He smiled with a shrug. "That's what I do—especially saving red-haired damsels."

Billie studied his face, his unreadable expression, completely missing his implication. She knew that was all he was going to tell her, but she had to try once more.

"You said you'd tell me what's going on with you and the homeless village, the long walks in the dark each evening, and things like that."

"I just did, Billie," he said, and leaned forward, resting his arms on the table. He smiled pleasantly, but she did not feel the warmth she had felt before. "I just told you: I help people that can't help themselves. Those people trust me to help them, and that help causes me to have a few enemies. It's just that simple."

Damn! I need to know more than—

No. You just want to get what you want. Listen to him. He's trying to tell you.

Billie sighed. "Okay. How do you help them, besides defending them against the drug dealers?"

Billie suddenly felt there was another layer peeking out from behind the Billy that he had been showing her—something genuine, something driven from deep within him. She could not tell if it was his subtle change in posture, the way he said the words, or something in his eyes, but when he mentioned helping the people he spoke of, she saw a spark, something she had not seen before.

He shook his head very slightly. "That's about it, Billie."

Billie sighed, feeling defeat. "Okay, I give up. I don't know how to explain why I would like to know more about you and the years that I missed between our first meeting and now. I pestered Sid to find out anything I could about you, but Sid wouldn't tell me much." Billie hesitated, uncertain if she should tell him. "But last Saturday when I left you the note asking you to meet with me, he did tell me that you lost your parents, and I want you to know how terribly sorry I am that that happened. I know loss, but I can't begin to imagine what it would be like to lose my parents."

"Thanks. I was fourteen when they died and I came here. Mary made sure I had proper schooling and helped me get a little college education as I grew up. In the beginning, she let me work here so I could have some pocket money, letting me do the menial tasks, you know—take out the trash, wash the dishes, mop the floors. Anything that was not associated with food preparation." He chuckled. "I'm certainly not a restaurant-quality cook."

And you're still doing the menial tasks... "I don't mean to sound rude, but why are you still doing—"

"The same things?" He raised his eyebrows at her, then smiled. "I guess because it suits me and it suits my needs at this time. Sid and Mary have been very good to me and let me work at things I'm comfortable doing. I don't need much and this works for me. Sid and Mary have been the very best a person could only hope to know."

"Thanks," Billie said, smiling as he refilled her wine glass. "After Lori and I talked about that visit, I began to remember some things that were happening about that time. I know I don't know you other than you were the boy that told me so many years ago that I had to focus on what I had, what I could do, and not on the past and what I had lost. I think I told you about the trouble I was having in school and that I was close to failing a number of classes." She sipped her wine and studied the table, thinking. "I also think you bet me I'd never be able to get my grades up enough to pass. It was spring and I only had a couple of months left that year."

She glanced up and realized he had been studying her; she caught his gaze as it drifted down from her hair to her colorful blouse. She thought he would have looked at the rest of her if the table hadn't blocked his view.

He smiled and looked back to her face, and she relaxed. At least he seemed to like what he saw.

"I understand you did," he said softly. "I lost my bet but you never came back to collect."

"What was the prize? I forget."

"A black and white shake with coconut and crushed pecans," he said softly, still holding her eyes.

She knew she was staring with her mouth open; it was still her favorite shake.

"And, I also understand you did well through the rest of your grade school, graduated fifth in your high school class, and went on to a bachelor's and then a master's in business up at state. You must be doing pretty good after all of that."

"Wait. What do you mean you 'understand'?" She leaned forward again, his words suddenly causing her to feel threatened. "What have you been doing? Checking up on me?"

Billy chuckled and put his hands up between them. "It isn't like that. Think about it. When we made our bet, Miss Wilhelmina Mattis—who by the way told me in no uncertain terms she did not like her given name very much—told me 'to just wait and see' how well she would do. I told you I would."

"You remember that?" Her tensions slowly began to ebb as she accepted his explanation.

"I had to, Billie. You and your red hair, freckles, red boots, pointed hat, effervescent manner, and incessant questions about the diner gave me no choice but to see how well you did. That meant I had to keep tabs on you every now and then."

Is he really telling me the truth?

Think about those two guys you dated in college and how they treated you and what they really wanted. Then think about Blake and I think you can see a difference.

Yeah, I think about them more than I should and I can see a big difference. Billy's far from pushy—maybe too far the other way.

Are you going to trust him?

Yeah, I think I am. Mostly.

"I guess I ought to be flattered," she said, considering that he did not act like he was gathering information for his personal gain. After her previous experiences, especially after Blake, she felt like she would know if he was.

"Thanks," he said, then smiled and sipped his water.

"As for how my life's going, I'm doing okay," she said, pondering his question. "My sister went off to college while I was still in high school. To keep from dealing with my parents' expectations, I just followed your advice and stayed focused on school."

Billy cocked his head in silent question.

"My sister was my anchor after so many things went wrong in my life," she said, and took another sip of her wine. Billy refilled her glass as she continued. "Then I met this boy in a diner and he gave a twelve-year-old girl some great advice. I took it and his challenge and stayed out of my parents' way." She smiled at him and her words. "Like someone else I know, 'just staying out of the way.'"

Billy smiled. "You were okay when your sister left for

college?"

"Only because I had something to focus on," Billie said, and smiled at him. "I lost someone that I felt very close to when I was ten, and I drifted in a deep depression for years. Maybe I still am. Your kind advice helped me more than you can possibly know. It gave me purpose when my sister left, and even through college and seeking work after. Thank you."

"You're welcome again," Billy said, and smiled hesitantly. "I didn't know, but I'm glad it helped. What keeps you busy now?"

Billie smiled, straightened in her seat, and squared her shoulders. She sipped her wine again and then turned her glass by its stem as she began to explain her work.

"I review design proposals and confirm that proposal details match with the customer requirements. When they do, I compare the final contract details with the confirmed files." She chuckled. "I'm a glorified fact-checker, but it's wonderful to see how a construction project goes from a customer's wishes to a tangible entity."

"Very good. It sounds important."

"I think it is," she admitted, a little pride in her voice. "If I happen to find a discrepancy and we can get it corrected before the contracts are written or signed, I can save Mr. Boster a lot of money."

"Mr. Carl Boster?" Billy's tone was suddenly mirthless and as dusty as a dirt road in late summer.

"Yes," she said softly, concerned by the change she saw. "What is it? What's wrong?"

Billy did not answer and she could see that he was lost in deep thought.

"Mr. Boster is my boss. He's a junior partner in the company we work for," she said, trying to explain and ease the sudden tension between them. "Is that a problem?"

"No. No, of...course not, Billie."

She could see that he was forcing himself to remain civil. Something about Mr. Boster bothered him. It bothered him a lot.

"Carl Boster is...a reasonable and reputable man," Billy continued after a moment, "and I'm sure he sees you as a very valuable assistant. It must be very rewarding for you."

She absently nodded. "It's different work than I expect to be doing when I graduated, but it has its rewards. I didn't know you knew Mr. Boster."

Billy nodded but the warmth in his eyes was gone. "I met Carl and Robert Lange when they first came to Chesterfield, before they partnered. They had had their own separate offices then."

"Billy? What's wrong?" She knew something had drastically changed between them, and it was beginning to bother her as much as it seemed to bother him. Suddenly Billy felt very distant, and she realized she did not like it. He was shutting her out. "What did I say? Is there something I can do?"

He shook his head. "No, Billie. It isn't anything like that. I'm just surprised that you work for them and I didn't realize it. It caught me unaware. I guess the best way to put it is that I don't trust Mike Hammersmith, and knowing you work there, for him, doesn't make me happy." He inhaled deeply and held her eyes. "But I know it isn't really any of my business where you work or who you work for."

"Why do you distrust Mr. Hammersmith?" she asked, watching his posture for any more changes in his body language.

"I suspect Sid probably mentioned," Billy said, "that my dad and Mike did not like each other. Not even a little would be an understatement."

"No," she answered. "Sid won't tell me much of anything about you. He says if I am to learn something about you it will have to come from you." She watched his steady hand as he picked up his glass and sipped the water before he continued. His internal emotional control amazed her.

"My dad tried to help a few people and businesses to keep Mike from taking over their properties when they fell on hard times. He helped them pay their mortgages on time, pay their taxes when they couldn't, and sometimes to make their payroll when they were short. Things like that."

"How could he do that?" Billie asked. "Wouldn't that take a lot of money?"

"He just helped where he could," Billy said, and Billie was certain there was more he was not telling. "Carl Boster and Robert Lange are good men, and they'll look after your interests as much as they can."

"Well, thank you. I guess I'll have to rely on Mr. Boster and Mr. Lange to stay between me and Mr. Hammersmith." She smiled at him. "I'll try to stay out of his way."

Billy smiled at her repeating the phrase.

Billie looked up, acutely feeling Julie as an intrusion when she interrupted, stopping beside the table.

"Billy," Julie said softly. "Sorry to interrupt, but there's someone here that says she needs to speak to you. She says it's urgent." Julie gestured to the swinging doors and the kitchen beyond.

Billy glanced back to Billie. "Will you excuse me for just a minute? I need to see who's here."

"Sure, Billy," she said, and watched him as he followed Julie through the swinging doors. As the doors closed, Billie saw a petite brunette smile at Billy's arrival.

-¤-

"Hey, Lynx," Billy greeted softly as he led her away from the others in the kitchen.

"Stretch sent me," Lynx said in a loud whisper. "We have snoopers down at the store. Stretch said to get you if I could find you."

"How many?" Billy asked as he grabbed his backpack from his bathroom.

"Just two, I think."

"Okay. Give me a minute," Billy said as he set the backpack beside the back door. He turned to the swinging doors. "I'll be right back."

-☖-

Billie was surprised at how quickly Billy returned, but instantly saw the concern and stress on his face. He slipped onto the bench where he had been sitting and leaned close.

"Billie, I have to leave. Sorry, but some friends of mine are having some trouble."

Billie absently nodded, surprised when he covered her hand with his and held her eyes.

"It's okay, Billy," she heard herself say.

"I'm sorry. I'll call you and we'll get together again to continue our talk."

Again she nodded absently. "I'll be waiting."

"Thanks, Billie," he said as he got up. His hand lingered on hers a moment before he turned and disappeared through the swinging doors.

Thirteen

Billie stared at the archway doors as they slowed and stopped swinging. She felt depressed by Billy's leaving, but forced herself to accept that something important had come up.

She took another long sip of her wine and admitted that his leaving did not feel like it was planned. She was wondering what kind of trouble his friends were having when Sid stepped through the archway and gestured to Billy's empty seat.

"May I?"

"Sure," Billie said, and forced herself to smile.

"I was surprised when I saw Billy leave," Sid said as he settled in the seat and leaned against the bench back. "Is everything all right?"

Billie nodded. "A brunette came to talk to him and then he said he had to leave. Something about some of his friends are having some kind of trouble."

"Hmm."

"He didn't say what kind of trouble." Billie did not look directly at Sid, but wondered if he would know what kind of trouble Billy's friends were having.

"That does happen every now and then," Sid said, and smiled at her.

"He said he'd call me so we can continue our talk."

"That's good," Sid said. "I'm sure you haven't had enough time to get answers to all of your questions."

Billie had to chuckle. "No. You're right about that."

"I'm glad he's willing to talk again," Sid said, and turned to slip back out of the booth.

"Do you know where he went?" she asked quickly.

Sid shook his head. "Like I told you before, he could be anywhere. And he doesn't confer with me when he has things he needs to do."

"Sorry. I was just wondering."

"I can see that you are curious, but be patient, Billie. It looks like he wants to talk to you and he'll answer your questions when he's ready." Sid hesitated and then added, "I think you may have given Billy a problem that he hasn't had to face before—at least something to think about. "

"Thanks, Sid," she said as he got up and then went back into the kitchen, leaving her to think and finish her wine.

◻-◻-◻-◻-◻

Billie sat curled up on her three-section sofa, silently debating with herself.

Was she a friend or was she a 'friend'?

I don't know. I only saw her for a second or two.

But they left together?

Yeah. I guess. He said there was trouble and that they needed him.

Another fight?

I don't know. But I think that if there was, Billy would be involved, helping his friends.

The reading light illuminated her lap and the digital pad she was studying. Searching for details was something she knew she was good at.

He said he helped people who need his help. She thought a moment and the homeless village quickly came to mind. *If I were to help those people in need, other than defending them in the village or on the streets, where in town would I go?*

She entered a search for organizations that offered appropriate assistance. A number of organizations and their websites popped up on her screen and she quickly glanced

106

through them, shaking her head.

I don't think Billy would go to one of these. He would be involved in something more personal, more hands-on. Someplace where he could control things if a bad situation developed.

She remembered him at the village, face to face with the drug dealers, and how he had maintained control, making certain the dealers could not influence the people there. She changed her search filter and looked at volunteer organizations. In minutes, she had narrowed the responses to three categories: one providing work opportunities for unskilled or less-skilled persons, the second providing inexpensive or free clothing and nonperishable food items, and the last providing hot and cold meals.

She smiled and selected the last item on the list, "charity kitchens."

A new list of a number of small church kitchens and three nonprofit "soup" kitchens rewarded her.

Billie quickly read the half-page list and settled on the three soup kitchens.

I'm betting you help by serving at one of these. They feel like something you would support. All are hands-on, face-to-face services where you can see the people you seem to know and would help.

Billie leaned back and took a long sip from her glass, feeling good about her "find," but studying the addresses closer, Billie realized they were all in less-desirable parts of town.

Where would you expect them to be? They are where the people are that need them.

I know that.

And Billy would be comfortable there.

Yeah. I know that too. Even if he went to the east one. It's probably in the worst part of town.

Billie closed the pad's cover and set it aside on the sofa, wondering what Billy was doing. How he felt after their talk and his rushed departure.

She took another sip of her water and watched the soft,

sometimes-twinkling lights of the city through the apartment's glass wall. She thought about the *unseen* things she was beginning to see when she paused and looked out at the city. Then she remembered the change she saw in Billy when he talked about the homeless people and his helping them. As she relaxed, her thoughts returned to their meeting that night.

At least, she thought as her mind settled on a pleasant memory, *I think Billy cares about me, some, maybe. Otherwise he wouldn't have stopped that man from dragging me off.*

He might have done that for any woman in distress.

She pondered that possibility for another minute.

But if he didn't, he wouldn't have walked me to my car and told me to go home.

Maybe he just wanted you to go away. He did say he didn't have time to watch out for you. Maybe you were in his way.

She sighed and took another sip of her water.

But Sid did say, she argued with herself again, *I've given him a problem he hasn't had before. And I saw how he looked at me when he said the rest of me had grown up and looked stunning. No one's ever said that to me before.*

Maybe he hasn't seen very many women and thinks—

Maybe he likes what he sees. Maybe I have *given him a problem he doesn't need to solve. One that he just needs to let solve itself.*

Maybe.

Wait! The man in the village said I didn't have Billy's mark on me.

Billy said you did.

What mark was Billy talking about? I don't have any marks on me.

She sighed. *Put that on the list of things to ask about, along with all of the others.*

Thinking about the confrontation Tuesday night, she remembered the moment Billy stepped between her and the man that had grabbed her. Her fears had instantly evaporated when Billy interceded. She wasn't afraid when he walked her to her car and she wasn't afraid when he watched her drive away. He stood in the middle of the street to be sure she turned away from the danger.

Billie realized she was not afraid for him either. She knew he could take care of himself, recalling how quickly he and Stretch had stopped the dealers. Calm and assured, they made the situation look rehearsed. Then Billie wondered again, what his *mark* on her was.

Billie relaxed, warmly toying with the possibilities.

Sometime, long after midnight, she fell asleep, curled up on her three-section sofa.

Fourteen

Billy followed Lynx out through the diner's back door. They hurried up to St. Charles and then straight across to the city center. A block south of the department store block, Lynx told Billy she was going back to her spot, watching the perimeter with the others. Billy nodded and followed the dark alley north.

-¤-

"That you, Keeper?" a tall and lanky shadow asked as it rose up in the alley in front of Billy.

"Yeah," he whispered back. "Where are they, Stretch?"

"Next block," Stretch said. "One's been trying to get an alley door open on the south side of the east building, and the other is in the main alley trying to get into the department store. They haven't gotten in."

"Who's with you to help?"

"Mace is here. Hammer's still up watchin' the village. Mace and I can go after the man at the east building, and you, the one at the west."

"Got it. I'll go around and come in from the north."

Crossing the Duckard's block along Baker, Billy stopped at the mouth of the north-south alley. In the dim half-light he could just see the man at the door near the far end of the west building.

He followed the wall on his left so the light from the street would not make him a silhouette. Billy slipped around the piled trash and stopped directly across from the shadowy figure working at the people-sized door accessing the alley. Billy stepped across the alley and touched the man's shoulder from behind.

"You need to stop that," Billy said firmly. "That's called breaking and entering."

The man jumped in surprise and yelled, spun away from Billy, and darted around the corner of the building. Billy chuckled as the man disappeared into the cross alley.

He turned back to the darkness and heard Stretch confront the second man. Someone yelled, something went *thud,* and silence followed. Billy waited. Finally Stretch walked into the half-light, smiling.

"I think we'll tie this one to the police call box two blocks down with a note pinned on him," Stretch said with a chuckle.

"Good idea, Stretch," Billy said.

"You let yours go?"

"Yeah. I figure he needs to tell whoever sent him that they did not succeed. Do you need me anymore?" Billy asked, and Stretch shook his head. "If not, I'll make a quick check to see if there are any more."

"Wonder what they were looking for," Stretch said as he turned and walked back into the darkness.

Billy wondered if his bait might have something to do with why they were there.

He listened and heard Stretch talking with Mace. One of them hefted the unconscious man, remarked that he was heavy, and then he heard them walk down the main alley to the next street south.

Fifteen

Friday, April 22

Mike Hammersmith stormed into the design offices, shattering Billie's concentration. He stomped down the long aisle to his office, yelling, "Robert!" She cringed, but the slam of his door did not come.

Now what? Billie listened, bewildered, swinging her chair from side to side, but did not get up. She stopped and saw the designers standing in their cubicles; their curious gazes followed Robert Lange as he left his office and hurried into Hammersmith's. He closed Mike's door more calmly than she expected.

Billie tried to go back to her contract comparison, but her curiosity won out over her common sense. She rapped her fingers beside her keyboard and listened to the bits and pieces of conversation among the murmurs that drifted out of Mike's office. She heard Mike mention "a default" and "a setup" and then "being toyed with." But all she could really tell was that Mike Hammersmith was angry.

¤-¤-¤-¤-¤

Robert closed the door and took the chair near the end of Mike's desk.

"So? What has you all stirred up this morning?" Robert asked as he opened his digital notepad.

Robert had worked with Mike long enough to know him and his fits of rage, but today was worse than he had seen before. At least, Robert was glad Mike's rage did not seem to encompass him or Carl.

"Our source at the title office confirmed that Duckard property was never in arrears." Mike slapped the desk and then absently thumbed the corner of the desk pad. "When our finance office saw the public notice, I knew I had that property, but now it looks like there is something unusual going on."

"Unusual?"

"Finance showed me a copy of the public notice last night, and when I stopped by the records office, they claimed it isn't their form!" Mike got up and started pacing. "They said it wasn't an official notice and showed me the differences between the one Finance copied and one the tax office had published in the past. The logos, shadow marks, even the font used for the records office address are slightly different." He turned and stared at Robert. "Someone set this up, possibly knowing I would see it and jump on it."

"Hmm," Robert muttered, and rubbed his chin. "But you didn't jump on it."

"Yes, I did. Well, no, I didn't. Not me personally," Mike admitted as he rounded the end of his desk, dragging his finger along the edge as he thought a moment. Then he started back. "I had Westman front the inquiry and payment, but the crux of the matter is that someone is toying with us. Did they expect me to jump or were they fishing, waiting to see who did?"

"If it is someone fishing," Robert said, tapping a note in his pad, "I think they know by now."

"Yes! And that is my point exactly," Mike said sharply, stopping to stare at Robert. "They know."

"Well, Mike," Robert said without rising to Mike's tone, "you couldn't have purchased the land for taxes or as a purchase without everyone knowing it was you doing the purchasing."

"Don't you toy with me, too, Robert. Of course I could." Mike stopped and put his hands on his hips, daring Robert to contradict him. "The current owner has."

"Not exactly, Mike," Robert said. "Contracts say the property is owned by Tri-Funds and CR Associates."

"But Contracts cannot find out who Tri-Funds and CR Associates are!" Mike shouted. "There is no public information on them! No websites! No principals listed anywhere. There are no stock listings. No profit or loss records, no tracks. They could be ghosts, for all we know."

Robert nodded. "Okay. I'll call the corporation commission and see if we can get a lead through the state." Robert made another entry in his notepad.

"Well, I think we've been lured into jousting windmills," Mike said with a little worry still in his voice as he sat down. "But why, Robert? Who would care? W.C. Hawke has been dead for years. There's no one else that could be doing this."

"I'll see what I can find out," Robert said, then stood up and left the office.

-¤-

As Robert walked back to his office, he stopped at an open door and knocked on Carl's doorjamb. He gestured for Carl to follow him.

In the quiet of his office, Robert sat down and Carl entered and closed the door.

Robert explained his conversation with Mike and the conclusions Mike had come to.

"How would someone post an unofficial public notice for delinquent taxes?" Carl asked when Robert had finished. "I would think it would have to be done by someone in the records office or in the tax office."

"I don't know who has access to the files that are ready to be published," Robert said. "But what I'm more concerned about is why someone would do it."

"But you just said—"

"No, I don't mean to see who responded," Robert said, thinking. "I mean, what would be accomplished? All that has happened is that two companies have spent a lot of money they

115

wouldn't have spent otherwise. What's the gain in that?"

"To get us to spend money we don't have?" Carl asked. "Maybe this person thinks he can run one of us into bankruptcy."

"Maybe, or revenge for some misdeed in the past," Robert said. "But I wonder if it isn't something more." He rubbed his chin a moment longer and then looked at the clock. "I've got to call the corporation commission. We'll talk about this later."

◻-◻-◻-◻-◻

"You missed all of the detailed small talk," Lori said as Billie sat down at the tall table and looked around the Library's crowded room.

This definitely feels like a Friday night.

"What small talk?" Billie asked as she pulled the menu pad to her and started swiping through the choices.

Man, after this week, I think I could start drinking this stuff by the gallon.

"Becky talking about her cleaning," Lori said, and nudged Becky.

"Not just," Becky defended, and sipped her Manhattan. "And to top it all off, Wednesday the first of three shipments for our Spring and Summer Exhibitions arrived. So now I'm helping unload the new stuff and clean it along with the old stuff."

Billie made a selection, inserted her card, and noticed Becky's glance at a table behind her. "How big are the shipments?"

"Mostly small stuff—artifacts and a few antiquities," Becky said, and ate the cherry out of her drink. "But three statues will need a crane. I don't know about the other shipments."

"Should be an interesting exhibit," Billie said as she turned to look toward the bar and the table that had caught Becky's interest. One of the men at the table seemed to be watching them. "Are we going to get an early invite when it's set up, or do we have to wait for the public opening?"

"I can probably get some backstage passes," Becky said, and laughed.

"That'll be nice," Billie said, and smiled. "You always do such nice work finding interesting exhibits and arranging the displays."

"We missed you Monday and Wednesday," Lori said. "You weren't ill or anything, were you?"

Oh damn, Billie thought, knowing she could not tell them what she had been up to. *Damn, I need to ask him what I can say.* "No. Wasn't ill or anything," she said instead. "Just bushed. Worn out. There's too much going on and too little time." *At least that's not a complete lie.*

"Yeah, we're busy at work too," Lori continued, and pulled the menu pad to her as the waiter brought Billie her drink.

"Anything else for you?" he asked, and Lori hesitated.

"Yes," Lori said, and raised her empty glass.

"Bring another, all around, on my card," Becky said, and the waiter nodded and turned back to the bar. Becky glanced at the table with the two men.

"Oh," Becky added, and pulled the menu pad back to her. "My dad got me started last weekend on shots of this stuff." Becky keyed her selection, swiped her card, and pushed the pad aside. "You'll love it. Smoothest spiced rum I've ever tasted. Sailor Jack's; it's addictive."

Lori giggled and Billie took a long sip of her brandy martini, savoring the stimulating flavor.

"So how bad is your work?" Becky asked.

Billie shook her head and began telling about the drama surrounding the department store project.

"And today, old Mr. Hammersmith stormed into the office, very upset, before the morning had even begun," Billie said. Then in a more sober voice, she continued. "Now he thinks the project will default and be put away in the vault. We'll know next Friday, but he thinks someone intentionally put up a false public notice to see if he would bite on it, or maybe *knowing* he would bite on it."

"A prank?" Lori asked.

"I don't know," Billie said, shaking her head. "Mr. Lange thinks there's probably something deeper, but he hasn't voiced any of his reasons."

Billie finished her drink as the waiter brought the second round and the three shots.

"Very nice choice," he said as he set the shots in front of them.

"Okay," Becky said softly. "I'm not suggesting we do shooters, but just take a sip of these and we'll see how long they last."

As she picked up the shot glass, Billie wondered about Becky's new "friends" at the other table, but was happy that Becky had not extended an invitation to them.

Sixteen

Sunday, April 24

Billie's depression got deeper each day since Thursday, and today had not helped. She could not enjoy the small barbeque sandwich she ordered, nibbling as she wondered why she had not heard from Billy. She sipped her soft drink and watched shoppers drift by the Finch Meadow Mall's food court. It was a pleasant afternoon, weather-wise, but the pessimism she remembered in the Boster, Lange and Hammersmith office on Friday did not help and she felt like everything around her was closing in, making it hard for her to breathe. Fate seemed to be against her, especially after she went by the Streetcar on her way home Friday and found out that Billy had taken the day off and would not be back until Monday. Today, she just went shopping to have something to occupy her "depressed mind" and "idle hands."

You've only known him for two weeks.

Well, this time, she admitted. She toyed with her chips as she thought about Billy. *Why does his silence bother me so much?*

It shouldn't. You've only been with him twice.

But I like how I felt when I've been with him.

Yeah. He saved your hide and didn't bawl you out for your stupidity. That's why you like being around him.

Probably right. He treated me nice and liked how I looked.

Billie bantered with herself, but knew she had never felt like this before—especially not as a grown woman, and certainly not over anyone she had met in college or since. Sometimes her feelings scared her, and this was one of them.

She sighed and resigned herself, looking forward to another

119

night alone, watching streaming reruns on her digital pad.

At least sunsets are getting later, she told herself in an effort to cheer herself up, *and that means the weather will be getting warmer soon. I can get into that.*

It was not much of a consolation, but it did raise her spirits some as she drove north from the mall and turned off Second Street West to her apartment and parking garage off Cheyenne.

Swinging into the drive, her heart jumped; Billy, wearing his less-worn pants and a clean shirt, his jacket unfastened, was sitting on the brick planter to the right of the turnstile. Desperately trying to keep her giddiness in check, she stopped and lowered the car window.

"Hey, what're you doing here?" she asked, forcing herself to stay calm as he stood up and walked over to the car door.

"Hoping I would find you before you went off again," he said with a bright smile.

"Follow me in and we can go up to my place," she said, gesturing for him to follow her.

She parked in her assigned space, got out, and led him to the elevators.

"I didn't know you were looking for me," she said as the elevator doors closed and they started up. She stood to one side with her hands clasped behind her. "But I was hoping you would want to finish our conversation. I stopped by the Streetcar on my way home Friday and Angie told me you had taken some time off. I hope it wasn't because of something I did."

"Sid said you came," he said, and shook his head. "I'm sorry I wasn't there."

"I was too," she admitted as the elevator stopped and the door slid open. "I'm in twelve-oh-seven." She unlocked the door, led him in, and tumbled the deadbolt behind him. "Can I take your jacket?" she asked as she hung hers on a hook behind the door.

He handed his to her and she hung it beside hers.

"Can I get you anything? Wine, a soda, water?" she asked as

she stepped into the kitchen.

"Water would be fine," he said, and walked over to the large front window. She saw him look at and around the window and guessed he was looking for some signs of the curtains.

"It has hidden curtains in alcoves on either side of the window," she said as she came back into the living room and handed him a glass of iced water. "When they're drawn back, it gives the illusion of a missing wall instead of just a window. It was one reason I liked these apartments."

"You're not having anything?" he asked as he took the glass.

She shook her head. "I was window-shopping at the mall and ate there before I came home." She smiled and sat down on one end of the three-section sofa. "Have a sit," she added, and patted a space.

"You have a nice place here," he said, and she thought he was trying to find a good way to start whatever it was he wanted to say. "Secured entry to the garage, into the building, locked apartment doors. Must feel good to be so secure."

"Thanks. And yes, I like the security and I like privacy. I usually don't have anyone visit."

"What? No late-night poker games or girl talk sessions with your friends?" He smiled.

"No. Not here," she admitted. "If we socialize, it's usually out, or occasionally at Becky's or Lori's."

"Surprising, but I guess girls live differently than guys," he said, still smiling at her.

"I'm sure we do," she chuckled. "So? Why were you looking for me?"

"I wanted to apologize for having to leave so suddenly the other night," he said, and set his glass on the coaster on the coffee table in front of the sofa.

"You did say it was urgent. I hope everything went okay."

"Thanks, it did. It was important that I go. I really wasn't trying to brush you off."

"Was the woman just a messenger?" she asked, turning to

face him with her legs curled between them as he sat down. She did her best to put on a positive air of confidence and control.

"Yeah. Her husband sent her to find me."

She saw him smile as he picked up his glass and took another sip, and wondered if it was her asking about the woman that was humorous to him. Billie was certain he was not telling her everything.

"How was the rest of your work week?"

"Tense, especially Friday." Billie glanced at the window. "Hammersmith was in a state I'd never seen before. Irate, angry, a complete terror. I know the project is a big one, but I've never seen anyone go off so much on a supposition. He doesn't know if the project is doomed yet or not. He just thinks so."

"Do I understand all of that?" Billy asked.

"No, I guess not," Billie admitted. "This last week was just a hectic one, and now I will definitely rely on Mr. Boster to stay between me and Mr. Hammersmith." She smiled at him. "I'll try to stay out of his way."

Billy smiled at her repeating the phrase. "I'd like to get past that part," he said, "if you don't mind. I'm not mad."

"That's good." Billie said softly. "If I heard you right, Thursday night you said you help people that can't help themselves."

Billy nodded.

"Does that mean you volunteer someplace?"

Billy smiled. "Yes, I do. Most nights of the week, when I'm not busy with something else."

"I thought so. Which one?"

"Why do you want to know that, Billie? I certainly don't recommend you follow me to one of the soup kitchens. None of them are in very nice neighborhoods."

"I think I may make you mad at me again. But I have a favor to ask," she said, "and I don't mean for it to anger you."

You're an idiot! Are you really going to ask him?

Yes, I am.

"Okay," he said, and she could see his concern in his eyes. "What can I do?"

"Take me with you. The next time you volunteer at the soup kitchen."

His eyes went wide and his expression hardened as his body straightened. "No! No! And no!"

"Why not? I want you to show me part of your life. I want to get to know you, to help too. At least at a kitchen there won't be any fighting."

"No," he said firmly.

"Billy," she said in a soft, pleading voice. "This week I realized my parents raised me in a very sheltered, biased vacuum. I never thought about the average people—much less the less-fortunate people—until this week, and I'm ashamed of how I've felt about them."

"I'm glad you realize your biases are wrong," he said, "but you're not going into that part of town as long as I'm alive and can prevent it."

"What do you mean I can't go into those parts of town? You'll prevent it?" she asked sharply, her voice rising in defiance.

"Sorry, Billie. I know I can't force you" —he held his hands up between them—"but it isn't safe there. It can be very dangerous."

"Aren't there women volunteers at the kitchen?"

He looked at her a long moment. "Yes, some," he finally admitted.

"So why can't I go and help? You'd be there too."

She watched him and saw him look at her length, seeing all of her at once, yet stopping his gaze everywhere he thought was interesting. He inhaled and she forced herself to wait and endure his sudden, open, and unapologetic appraisal of her appearance.

"Billie." He closed his eyes and she saw him shudder. "Bluntly, there are some there that would see you and would drag you off, strip and rape you before you could scream for help. I...can't even consider—"

123

"Hold it," she said, and jumped over the back of the sofa. "Thank you for liking how I look, and for worrying about my safety. I understand and sincerely appreciate your fears and concerns," she said as she darted up the spiral stairs. "I worry about what could happen too, but wait there and let me show you something."

"You don't know what you're asking me to do," he said. "I don't know if I could protect you there."

He ran out of arguments as they bantered, him from the living room and her from the open loft bedroom above the dining room and kitchen. Finally he stopped, listening to the rustling of clothes and sacks that drifted down into the living room. The sounds fell quiet and he turned at her footsteps on the stairs.

He stared in disbelief, seeing a frumpy girl in baggy jeans and a bulky sweater with her hair stuffed out of sight under a bulging knitted hat.

"After you made me leave the village, I went shopping a second time to get something even more dressed down, less conspicuous. If I take my makeup off and you show me how to act and how to talk..." She stopped when he did not move or say anything.

He slowly got up and walked to her. He took her hand and slowly inspected the sweater, plucked her sleeves, turned her around in front of him, tweaked her jeans, and looked at her from hat to boots.

"I...I won't need a jacket with this sweater, and the cap hides my hair better..."

When he turned her back to face him, he was smiling. "You'd actually dress down and go out in public again, looking like this?"

"Is it all right?" she asked, looking down at herself, suddenly concerned that she had forgotten something. "Like you said, I think having my hair out last week was a really big mistake."

"Yes. It certainly was," he agreed, and turned her around again. "When I saw you, all I could see was your beautiful hair

124

and the tense situation. I knew the combination was explosive."

"I'm sorry, Billy," she said softly. "I thought I knew what I was doing, but I obviously didn't know what to expect."

"I was surprised to see you there, and I'm surprised now, but for a different reason," he finally admitted. "You know you'll be forever banned from all high society if any of your friends ever saw you looking like this."

"I don't think they would recognize me if they did," she said, still frowning.

"You might be right," he said, and led her back to the sofa. "But tell me why? Why do you want me to do this?"

"Will it work? And keep me from being dragged off, stripped, and raped?"

"With a couple of minor additions, I think you might be safe enough," he said, seeing her smile brighten, "if you stay close to me, but that smile will have to go until we are back in a safe part of town. No one in the kitchen is very happy, much less ecstatic."

"Then you'll take me with you?" she asked, suddenly feeling like that little girl following that special boy around a diner's kitchen.

"God, give me strength. I must be completely out of my mind," he said as he stood up, and she watched him glance up at the tall ceiling and then around the room before he looked back at her.

She squealed and jumped up, threw her arms tight around his neck, and hung against him in a very enthusiastic embrace. With his arms holding her in reflex, she kissed his cheek and slowly, very slowly, lowered herself back to the floor. Seeing his surprised smile, knowing he felt her body against him, she happily knew he did not see her as a twelve-year-old girl anymore.

She slipped her arms around his waist, looked up at him, and waited. "Show me the minor improvements and how I should act and talk. Please. I want to learn."

Seventeen

Tuesday, April 26

"It doesn't look like anyone has been listening to your offers on that city block or on those two buildings," the pert woman from Contracts said as Frederick stared out of his wide office window.

"So it seems, June," he said absently. "Have you looked at our default status on this one?"

"Unfortunately, you did not have us review the last revision of the contract you signed," she said, catching his attention. "There is a rather unusual penalty clause."

"Unusual?" he asked before he meant to say anything.

"Yes, sir," June answered. "You obligated the company to a ninety percent default payment." She waited as he looked back at the window. "You will owe Boster, Lange and Hammersmith ninety percent of the design and development contracted total if the project fails for any reason."

He did not say anything.

"You also leveraged the investments in this project to pay for the overages on three of our other projects," June continued, and he listened in silence. "Three out of your current five projects will have to be completed and the customers will have to satisfy their obligations before funds are available to pay Boster, Lange and Hammersmith."

"How long?" was all Frederick asked without turning away from the view through his window.

"Thirty days from Saturday if the contract defaults," she said softly. "Normally, project payments would be paid in project quarters, but—"

"Thank you, June," he said firmly. "That will be all for now."

She folded her binder closed and stood up. "Sir, if there is anything I can do to help..." She slowly turned and left the office, fully aware that there was nothing she could do and little that he could, either.

Wednesday, April 27

Trying to remember everything Billy had told her, Billie folded her frumpy clothes, as he called them, into the worn backpack he gave her. She dressed in a regular pair of fitted slacks and a modest top, hoping that when she left the building she would look normal enough the security people would not ask questions and still look common enough for the walk Billy said they would have to take before she could change. He was cryptic in his explanations, but she trusted he had his reasons and tried to do everything he asked as she got ready.

This is probably the second dumbest thing you've done yet.

No, it isn't. I have to face this. I have to face my fears.

By jumping off a cliff? In front of a speeding truck? Into a volcano?

It isn't that bad.

We'll see.

Billie glanced at her touch screen phone and realized it was after six and she had to meet him at six thirty west of the bus station. That was seven blocks north and two blocks east; she knew she had to hurry.

She threw on an older yet nice-looking jacket, grabbed her backpack, and hurried to the elevator. At the bottom, she slipped out through the carded turnstile and at the corner, started north on First Street West. Billie turned east and glanced behind her.

Damn. Is someone following me? That's all I need.

She looked again.

Double damn, someone is following me!

Her heart began to pound again as she hurried her steps.

Stay calm, slow down! Billy said don't run, just keep a steady walking pace. Always act assertive but never act afraid. That's easier said than done.

One block from the intersection where she was to meet Billy, she stepped around the corner of the building on her right and waited. Billie knew she had a few minutes and if someone was following her, they would reach the corner before she had to move on.

The minutes passed slowly, and she turned to face the corner. Clenching her fists and inhaling deeply, she slouched against the stone façade beside a store's large window. Suddenly a disheveled-looking man stepped around the corner, stopped, and looked straight at her.

"Very good, Billie," Billy said, and smiled. "You did that perfectly."

"What? Billy? You scared the crap out of me. You were testing me?" Instantly mad and relieved at the same time, she drew her hand back to slap him, but he caught it and gently pulled it to him, holding it against his chest.

"I had to prove to myself and to you that you had listened and could make this first step work," he said.

"Really? By scaring me half to death?" She did not smile at him.

"Come on," he said, and pulled her behind him. "There's a public bathroom in the next block and you need to change before we go any farther."

At the marked doorways in the side of the stone building, Billy told her to see if it was empty. Billie checked and, seeing it was empty, went in and got dressed while Billy stood guard.

Changed, she put her good clothes in the backpack, and in a matter of minutes came out as the person of meager means he had seen in her apartment.

She was shivering and he slipped an arm around her shoulders as he led her to the dirt strip beside the parking garage north of the bus station.

"Damn, it was cold in there," she said, her teeth still chattering as they crossed the street. She leaned against him, savoring the warm feeling of his arm around her, but she held hers folded in front of her.

I don't know why, Billy, but you give me confidence. It's like when Willum would walk with me and put his arm around my shoulders.

She looked up at him and saw his steady, assured expression watching the street as they walked.

Teach me how to be strong. I don't want to be scared anymore. Mold me into something new—better. Tonight, I'm your clay and you're my sculptor.

Then her mind took an erotic turn and she thought about what else his sculptor's hands could mold.

-ۃ-

"Sit down," he said, interrupting her thoughts as he stood on her left. He leaned back against the parking garage wall and lowered himself into a cross-legged sitting position. She followed his example and her mobile phone chimed as she reached the ground.

"Damn! Forgot about that," she said as she retrieved the phone and touched the face. "Hey." She spoke softly, not quite in her usual voice. "No, not tonight." She listened to the caller. "I'm not feeling up to it tonight. Maybe Friday night." She listened again. "Okay. Call me."

She touched the face and silenced the phone. "I'm sorry Billy. I forgot all about my phone and that Lori would call to see where I am."

She saw his stern look as he slowly nodded. "Turn it off. No chime, no vibrations, nothing. Hide it deep in your backpack."

"Okay," she said sheepishly, and opened the flap on the pack. "I really am sorry, Billy."

"I know." He smiled thinly. "I forgot to mention it too."

"Thanks for not being mad at me."

130

"You're welcome. Now," he said as she finished hiding the phone and set the pack down beside her, "let me see your hand."

She extended her left and he took it, pulled a pen from his pants pocket, and pushed her sweater sleeve up to her elbow. "What are you doing?" she asked as he began drawing an intricate, stylized chain around her wrist.

"Don't worry. Most of the women have tats," he said when she twitched and started to pull back. "It's water soluble. Use soap and your makeup remover and it'll come off with some scrubbing. I'll see that you're serving with me tonight and you won't be in water very much."

She slowly relaxed and he continued to draw. When he was finished, she studied the design, twisting her wrist one way and then the other. She almost did not hear him ask for her foot.

"Boots again?" she teased as he took her leg and pushed her pant leg up.

He patted her leggings and smiled at her. "Good girl, those'll help keep you warm." He looked at the worn boots and asked, "Are these your favorites?"

"Why yes, the best ones I have," she replied with a smile.

"I'm afraid they should be a little more scuffed up," he said, and picked up a coarse rock and began scrubbing the toes and sides of the heels. Then he leaned over and took her other foot.

"You really do have a thing about boots, don't you?"

"Only when your feet are in them," he answered without looking at her.

She stared at his unexpected answer.

He set her foot down, pushed himself up, and turned, catching her hands and pulling her up. He took a long flip-blade knife out of his pocket and opened it. He wiped it on his coat. "Before you use this, wipe it like this as if you're cleaning it. It's clean, but wiping it makes it look like it doesn't matter."

She looked at him, puzzled.

"When we're walking—like when we leave to come home— take an apple, and if you get nervous or something happens that starts bothering you, slowly peel the apple. Like you're looking

131

forward to having dessert. I don't know who we might run into, but you need to seem comfortable and not act very alert or on guard, even though you will be."

"Okay," she said, and took the knife.

He showed her how to open it and reclose it.

"Do that a few times so you don't have to think about it when you use it."

When he was satisfied she was ready, he led them up to Crescent Street and started east.

"The serving line is a series of tables beside each other along one side of the main dining room," Billy explained as they walked. "Normal arrangement with the line starting on the servers' left; trays, plasticware, napkins, then sandwiches or soup, followed by breads, spreads, and fruit next, and finishing with drinks, water, tea or coffee, and a dessert."

Billie's hand kept returning to her pocket and feeling the unfamiliar knife as she matched Billy's long strides with her shorter legs, listening to his description of what she should expect.

"Remember, most of the people you will see are just like you and me, just less fortunate than the average folks," he said. "But there are some, and you'll know them when you see them, that think everything they see is theirs for the taking. If any fellas like that make a pass at you, just smile and blow it off and stay close to me. I'll also be watching you, but let me know if anything happens that you don't like."

Eighteen

"Hey, Keeper," the kitchen manager asked as he and Billie stepped in through the side door. "Gotta trainee in tow?"

"Sure do, Randy," Billy said. "This is Billie, and I'd like her to help me on the serving line so she can see how things are done."

"I think we can manage that, Keeper," Randy admitted, nodding as he walked back to the prep area. "Get your things settled and give her a quick overview. I'll open the line in about five minutes."

Randy walked to another group of people and Billy led Billie into a back room where everyone stashed their things while they were there. Billy set his backpack on top of Billie's and then took her into the serving and dining area, giving her an explanation of what they saw as he went.

"Looks like you'll have breads and fruits." Billy smiled and pointed as he led her up to the back of the serving table. "I'll be right beside you with the soup."

Billie nodded as he explained things, and eagerly followed him wherever he led her. She did not dare think too much, afraid she would fall apart if she did. If she held onto something—maybe tongs, or the table, or his hand—maybe her shaking would not be too obvious.

It took a few people going through the serving line before Billie felt like she had the hang of the system and, mostly, the people. She appreciated how Billy told her often that she was doing very well, and when she started running low on fruits he shouted back to the kitchen and a runner brought a new tray and exchanged it with the old one. When his pot of soup ran low, Billy shouted for another and a runner exchanged it with a full one.

By the time the first hour passed, Billy could see her confidence. He noted that she followed his advice and was careful to not show her pleasure, though she did occasionally say hello or something encouraging as people filed through. He kept a close watch on her, and about halfway through the second hour, she got her first real test.

A tall, lanky man with a cultivated swagger and full of arrogance saw Billie and stopped in front of her. Billy turned to say something, but Billie glanced at him and smiled sweetly up at the man.

"Please move along," she said.

"Or what?" he demanded, and started to reach across the counter.

Billy started to intervene when Billie slipped her hand into her pocket, leaned over the table toward the man, and continued. "Or I'll jump this table, cut your balls off, and leave the rest for my squeeze to take out with the trash."

The man stopped, stared at her, and then slowly withdrew his hand with a soft, forced chuckle, collected his tray, and quietly moved along. Billy stared at her for a long moment, then slowly turned back to his soup ladling. He looked sideways at Billie and caught her eye, hoping his guarded smile and wink showed her he approved.

Sometime in the third hour, one of the runners caught Billy's arm and nodded to the door into the kitchen where a medium-height, slender woman stood with her coat still tightly wrapped around her.

"Charley, can you handle this a minute?" Billy asked a helper, and patted Billie on the shoulder as he followed the runner to speak with the woman.

"Cat, what's up?" he said softly, knowing Billie was listening, trying to hear what they said.

"We got druggies—Pink and one of his cronies snooping around our block," she said. "They seem to be interested in getting into our building and the one to the east. I sent Stretch

134

and a few of the other men out to keep an eye on them."

"Good for you," he said, and caught her hand between both of his. "Go back and tell them I'm on my way." He watched her turn and slip out through the side door, and then he went and told Randy that they had to leave.

He stopped beside Billie and waved to another man standing near the kitchen doorway behind the serving tables.

"Mickey, can you take over the breads and fruits? We have to leave," Billy said, and glanced at the man at the soup pot. "Thanks, Charley. Sorry it's sudden again."

Both men smiled and nodded.

"That's okay, Keeper," Charley said. "They'll be shutting down in a half an hour so anyway. Go do what you need to do."

Billy turned to Billie. "We have to go."

He led her into the back room and grabbed their backpacks and coats. As they started toward town, leaving the dimly lit area in front of the kitchen behind, he explained.

"That was Cat—real name's Mindy. She and her husband are good friends of mine, and they're having some trouble down town. We need to hurry. Can you run in those boots?'

"Sure. They're a little loose, but I can manage," she answered as she pulled her backpack on, settled it on her back, and pulled the straps tight.

Billy started a steady jog and made sure she was able to stay beside him. He smiled, pleased that she could.

"Faster?"

"A little," she admitted.

With her company, the ten-block jog passed quickly. He slowed them a block east of the department store and stopped at a corner of the building, then he turned and looked at her. "If a fight starts, stay behind me and be ready to push that knife into someone."

"You're kidding?"

"No, I'm not," he said in a very soft voice and looked at her, quickly glancing down the length of her five foot one figure, unexpectedly taking note of their difference in height. Then, holding her beautiful eyes with his, he thought for a moment about all of the years he had watched her grow up and how he felt, his feelings for her safety suddenly conflicted, knowing he was about to lead her into something she could not possibly be prepared for. How could he tell her he was sorry for what might happen? Then he decided what he needed to do, and without explaining or saying anything, he cupped her face between his palms and kissed her, slow and tenderly, holding her lips until they needed to breathe.

-¤-

Her stomach knotted at his admission that the knives were not stage props and things could get very serious. She straightened her shoulders and forced herself to accept the reality that went with her decision to go with him that night.

I told you.

Hush!

She was with *him* and she knew he would do all he could to protect her, but he kept looking at her as if there was something more he wanted to say. She looked up at him, focused on his eyes, partially obscured by the shadows from the streetlight at the distant street corner.

Before she could acknowledge his comment or ask what more he was thinking about, he cupped her face in the palms of his large, gentle hands. Softer than she expected them to be, the question was quickly pushed out of her mind when he drew her face close to his and kissed her, softly, tenderly.

Her eyes instinctively closed and she savored the feeling as their lips touched, hers eagerly surrendering, conforming to his without resistance. She knew she was melting, her legs weak. She felt supported only by his strong hands and arms holding her face against his. She wanted to wrap her arms around him, but in the moment of surprise, she could not feel them and make them respond; she hung limp in his grasp, floating on the sensations he sent down her spine, tingling every part of her. Even her toes had disappeared.

Nineteen

When their lips parted, he looked deep into her surprised eyes as they opened, heard her soft inhale to catch her breath, and then demanded in a whisper, "Just do *not* get hurt. Come on."

She stared at him, wide-eyed, and stumbled forward as he took her hand and pulled her around the corner into the alley.

"Watch behind us," he said, and quickly led her into the shadows at the east end of the cross-passage between the two buildings. "We'll go up and down these alleys and see who's out and about."

Still holding her hand, Billy led the way.

Halfway up the alley in the second block, Billy heard men talking softly. He stopped Billie and put his hand over her mouth as he leaned close to her.

"This one's for real," he said, and turned toward the voices at the end of the alley. "I'm sorry I can't avoid this one. Stay here by the dumpster and wait for me."

"Not on your life. You're not going to leave me standing alone in the dark, freaking myself out at every tiny sound, worrying about what you're doing. I'm going to be right beside you," Billie said, her eyes flashing and her voice tight and controlled. "If it gets too serious, I can still scream."

Billy stared at her dark, nearly invisible silhouette. "You know you're going to drive me to drink, don't you?" He sighed, feeling the heat of her determination. "All right, all right, remember the apple? When we confront someone, stay just behind me and slowly, nonchalantly peel your apple. If I gesture for you to come closer, or stand up or anything, hold your knife in one hand as if you're ready for battle, and the apple in the other. Remember which edge of your blade is sharp. Then follow my lead and my actions. Be assertive, but not cocky. Don't talk."

She dropped her backpack beside Billy's, flipped the knife open, and pulled the apple from her pocket. "Let's go, before I lose my nerve."

As they walked, she stayed as close behind Billy as she could. He noticed her hands were shaking.

"You'll do fine," he whispered, and squeezed her shoulders to reassure her.

As they stepped around the last dumpster, Billy saw there were three men and moved to the middle of the alley. He stepped forward with his long-bladed knife in his right hand, and Billie positioned to his right and slightly behind him.

"Hello, Pink," Billy said softly when they stopped near the edge of the building's shadow. "What brings you into my 'hood?"

The three men stopped, and the tall one doing all of the talking turned slowly to face Billy's voice.

"That you, Keeper?" the man asked softly.

"You know it is," Billy said, and slowly moved forward.

He glanced sideways and saw Billie was where she was supposed to be and was slowly peeling the apple. Her ten-inch blade flashed in the dim light.

"I asked you a question, Pink. You got no reason to be here."

"Now, Keeper, my man. We all know there's a lot of opportunity here in the center," Pink said, slowly spreading his arms out in an encompassing gesture. "I know you chased Matches out of the village, but this 'hood's crampin' my space."

Billy did not see any knives, but knew they each had one, and maybe something more.

"This is not your 'hood, 'my man,'" Billy said, emphasizing Pink's words. "No sales in the center. Now you need to leave while you can."

Pink chuckled and the two men followed his lead and also

laughed.

"I think it's time for you ta step aside, Keeper," Pink said, the challenge clear. "The center is ripe an' you're gettin' old, been here too long. You need ta make space for the future."

Billy motioned for Billie to move forward and saw her move to his side as he spread his stance and leaned forward on the balls of his feet. Pink noticed her as she mimicked Billy's stance. Pink and his men settled into a similar but less-poised crouch.

"Come on, Pink. Show your lackeys how good you are. Three against two ought to be easy," Billy said as he slowly led Billie to his left, toward Pink's weaker side. He was about to say something more when he heard a low, soft, guttural growl coming from beside him. He glanced at Billie, barely turning his head, and saw her snapping her blade from side to side, drooling long strings of saliva, teeth bared and growling so low he felt it more than he heard it.

He saw Pink stare at her, suddenly reconsidering what he did not know. Pink chose to test the situation and took a quick step forward, but was startled and jerked upright as both simultaneously lunged at him in return. Billy's swipe caught the front of his shirt, narrowly missing his chest. The shirt gaped open from the slice of Billy's blade.

Pink's two men had not moved.

"I'll take a piece with the next swipe," Billy warned.

Billie continued to growl, and Billy could see that Pink slowly realized he was facing something seriously unknown, alone.

"Okay, Keeper," Pink said softly. "I'll let you have this one, but we'll be back."

"This is not your 'hood, Pink. I don't dislike you, man, but if you want to stay in one piece you better think again about tryin' ta do bidness in my 'hood."

"Later, man," Pink said, and slowly stepped back onto the sidewalk, fingering the wide rent in his shirt. He motioned to the two men with him and they quietly walked to the east and past the corner of the building.

"Turn around and watch our backs," Billy said without rising from his crouch.

He saw Billie turn and felt her back up against him, still in her crouched position, and suddenly he was having a tough time staying focused on Pink and his two men, his body betraying him. They waited, and after what Billy thought was a suitable time, hoping he had himself under control, he forced himself to ask softly, "Anything in the shadows?"

"I don't see any movement," Billie answered, and he slowly straightened up, feeling Billie again mimic him, still tight against his backside.

He inhaled deeply, then turned and looked at her for a long moment, stirred by her closeness but forcing himself to keep his hands to himself. He smiled hugely and started back down the alley. They picked up their backpacks and Billie walked quietly beside him.

"Cat? Are you watching?" he said softly into the darkness.

"Yeah, Keeper," the female voice answered. "Are they gone?"

"For tonight," he said. "Let Stretch and Mace know it's clear."

Only the silence of the alley answered as Billy turned them into the narrow cross-passage.

"Your squeeze, huh?" Billy asked absently as they listened to the sounds of the city and walked down Second Street.

Billie did not answer, and Billy turned them to the west on St. Charles.

After a couple of blocks she asked, "Why'd you kiss me?"

"So you'd know I was serious. So you'd know I don't want you to get hurt."

"Oh," she said, and looked at him.

"Sorry if you think I was out of line," Billy said, "but I wanted you to know how I felt. I couldn't think of a better way to tell you."

"You could have just told me."

"I did."

"Hmm," she said, and stepped closer and slipped her arm around his waist.

Slowly, he laid his hand on her shoulder and asked her about the growl.

"I was so scared and I didn't know what else to do. I had that piece of apple in my mouth and was about to spit it out when I started to drool. That's when I figured any special effects were better than none, so I used it, hoping it would make them wonder. And I thought twitching the knife might make them think I was a little deranged."

He laughed. "Well, I think you just might be, and Pink sure did wonder."

"I did all right then?" she asked.

"Like I said before, I am surprised," Billy admitted. "You are full of surprises—especially with that guy at the kitchen. How in hell did you ever think of that retort?"

"Too many late-night movies and long nights alone." She smiled. "It just came out."

"And how did you follow my movements so quickly? I didn't even know what I was going to do next."

"Dance classes," she said, tightening her hold around his waist with one hand and pulling his other arm around her shoulders with her other hand. "And drama classes. I couldn't always remember the steps, so I learned to anticipate and follow the person next to me. I got very good at mimicking."

"I'll say," he chuckled. "Poor Pink didn't know what he was up against. He must've thought we choreographed the whole routine." Then he turned serious. "I'm glad it didn't deteriorate into a real fight. That was too close."

They walked in silence for a moment.

"I would've stuck one of them if I had to," she said softly. "I don't want you to get hurt either."

He saw her look up at him, her face deeply concerned.

"I'm glad," he said, and squeezed her shoulders. She responded by squeezing his waist again.

"Why does everyone call you 'Keeper'? At the kitchen? Pink?"

"On the streets, that's who I am. I take care of that area and the northwest village, keeping Cat and the others as safe as I can. So I'm known as Keeper."

"You keep them safe? Like I saw in the village?"

"Any way and as much as I can," he repeated, and smiled down at her.

"So if you're Keeper, what does that make me?"

"We'll have to think about that some," he said, and saw her smile at the thought of a continued association.

"Where are we going?" she asked, looking around at the unfamiliar street.

"To the diner. You can shower and change there before I walk you home."

-¤-

Billy let them in, relocked the door, reset the alarm, and was showing Billie the bath, the soaps, and towels when he heard Sid coming down the hallway.

"Go on," he said, and pushed Billie into the bathroom with her backpack and closed the door. "It's just us, Sid," he continued, and turned in greeting as Sid reached the doorway.

"Us?" Sid asked, looking around the kitchen.

"Yeah. Billie needed to get cleaned up so her security people will let her into her building," Billy said with a chuckle.

"She needs to get cleaned up?"

"Yeah. She dressed down and I took her to help at the kitchen," Billy explained.

"To the kitchen? On Crescent? Really?" Sid asked, wide-eyed.

"Yeah. She was amazing." Billy looked back at the bathroom door and smiled. He explained the bones of what had happened and how Billie had handled each challenge. "All I can say is there are three mean street thugs, drug dealers, that have a new respect for the lady that calls me her squeeze. I actually think she would have engaged if Pink pushed hard enough to make it a fight."

Sid smiled and glanced at the bathroom door. "Well, I'm glad for you she didn't fall apart. But you know, she actually could be an asset, helping you gather info on Hammersmith and Westman. If she's half of what you say she is and you consider that, with respect to the business world, she could really help you."

"Yeah, I guess she could." He smiled.

"But, for her to help, you'll have to let her in on some of your secrets."

"Yeah," Billy said, his expression sobering. "I'll have to think about that some."

"I'm sure you will," Sid said, and patted Billy on the shoulder. "See you in the morning, cousin. Goodnight."

Billy watched Sid as he disappeared up the hallway, then he turned to look at the closed bathroom door. Listening to the sound of the shower, he sighed, letting his thoughts of a beautiful Billie fill his mind.

-¤-

"Well, you asked to see part of my life," Billy said as they stopped across the street from Billie's apartment building.

"I did," she sighed. "Last week and tonight were real eye-openers. I had no idea that you face so much danger. And so often."

"I know," he agreed, and squeezed her shoulders. "Are you all right? With everything?"

She quickly turned, put her arms around his waist, and held him tight, her cheek resting against his chest. "Yes, I think so. I have to admit I was very scared at times. But then I'm always scared, and I don't know if I would have been okay if you weren't there. I've got a lot to think about, Billy." She hesitated. "I wish you would come up."

"Not tonight. Wrong dress, and even though I've been up

143

once, this is too soon," he said without relaxing his hold. "I have a lot to think about too." He pushed her back a little and looked down at her smiling face. "You've only known me a little over two weeks, and I've exposed you to the darker dangers of our society, and your life's been threatened once, possibly twice. And even though you were wonderful tonight, taking my world and its dangers in stride, trusting me to keep you safe, I don't feel good about placing you in that danger."

"I know you don't, but I'm glad you did," she said, "and very glad I was a little help for you and not trouble this time."

"You're not trouble, Billie." He smiled. "But I must caution you to not tell your friends about tonight, about where you went or what happened. Not a word. Probably shouldn't mention your following me into the village either." He put his finger against her lips. "Not a word, please," he repeated softly, feeling his finger tingle at the touch of her lips.

She studied his face for a long moment before she said, "Okay."

"I know it will be hard. They will ask where you went and what you did, but I must stress that it is very important to keep this a secret—for your safety as well as others."

"I won't tell," she said with a quick shake of her head, and pushed herself up on her toes and kissed him slowly. "That's for taking me and protecting me." She kissed him again, as tenderly as she dared. "And that's for caring for me enough to worry." She let herself back down and turned to the street. "Will I see you tomorrow?"

"I have to serve again," he said. "Game?"

"If you don't have to be the marshal and me your deputy again," she said, and smiled. "Yeah, I'm game."

"The Forest, at six-thirty?" he asked. "I'll bring some sandwiches from the diner."

"The park on St. Charles?" she asked, and he nodded. "See you then."

He waited and watched from the shadows as she hurried across the street and slipped through the front lobby door, waving back before she disappeared inside.

Twenty

Friday, April 29

Clearing tables, Billy and Ned were getting the dining room ready for the lunch crowd when Sid came into the dining room and tapped Billy on the shoulder.

"Mr. Filton is on the phone for you," he said softly. "In the office. I'll finish this one for you."

"Thanks," Billy said, and wiped his hands on the towel he had over his shoulder. He stood up and turned to the archway into the back rooms. Billy stepped into the office, closed the door, and picked up the handset.

"Hello," he said.

"Billy? It's Grier. I got your message," the voice on the other end said. "What can I do for you?"

"Thanks for calling me back," Billy said as he settled into Sid's chair. "Are you where you can talk, or should we meet?"

"I can talk for a few minutes."

"Okay. Can you tell me the status on the River Crest Apartment property?"

"They're ready for occupancy," Grier said. "They've been ready for about two months. City inspections are complete and all permits are closed."

That is wonderful. "Good, good," he said. He anxiously leaned forward, arms resting on Sid's desk, and explained what he wanted to do.

-¤-

Billy saw Sid pumicing the griddle when he came out of

the office and back into the kitchen. Sid looked up with a questioning cock of his head and a smile.

"Good news, Sid," Billy said, and stepped closer, seeing Niles at the stove, just past the grill. He lowered his voice. "The apartments are ready, and this is the day Westman and Hammersmith know for sure they can't get their hands on the Duckard block. Still."

"So?" Sid asked. "What now?"

"I've been thinking about what Mike will do next," Billy said. "He obviously knows by now the public notice was a fake, but what I can't figure out is why he continued the contract with Westman when he figured it out. I'm also not sure why Westman made the Offer to Pay instead of Mike."

"Maybe there's some muddy water between the two of them," Sid said, and set the water bottle, pumice block, and scraper aside, satisfied the griddle was clean enough for lunch.

"Yeah," Billy admitted. "Ever since I started watching those two, they've had a strange love-hate relationship. Well, maybe it's been more hate-hate from Westman's side."

"Bears a little closer look?" Sid asked, and checked the ovens.

Billy nodded and noted that Niles had gone into the cold room.

"You might also want to watch for changes around your neighborhoods," Sid continued. "Mike never was one to come right out and say what he means."

"Yeah, I know." Billy smiled. "I figure that's why we're seeing a sudden increase in drug dealers trying to move into the village and city center."

"If they get in," Sid said, and stopped to look at him, "you know it'll only take an anonymous phone call to turn their world upside down."

"I know." Billy nodded. "That's the part that scares me the most."

"Have you talked to Nolan?" Sid asked, and closed the oven door. "Or Gibson?"

"Not yet," Billy said as Niles came back with a number of items stacked in his arms. "Hey, Niles. Let me help you there."

Billy helped unload the stack and placed the items on the preparation counter in the middle of the kitchen.

"Thanks," Niles said, and wiped his forehead with a paper towel. "Sid? Have you ever thought about a separate cooling unit for the kitchen? I have to go into the cool room to stop sweating. It shouldn't be this way."

Sid nodded and went to the back door. He pushed it open and set the heavy iron doorstop in front of it. "There. Separate cooling."

Billy chuckled at Niles' expression. "I'd say no, Niles."

Niles shook his head and started opening the containers, and Billy gestured for Sid to follow him to the dishwashing station.

"I told you I took Billie to the kitchen," Billy confided.

Sid nodded and smiled.

"We went again last night," Billy said, then leaned back against the counter and explained the incidents that happened Wednesday night, and that Thursday was much quieter, without confrontations.

"Yeah, you said she can mimic you,"

"Yup." Billy nodded. "Almost as fast as a mirror." Billy chuckled and shook his head at the memory. "Sure startled Pink. I've never seen anything like it."

"You didn't see any of that when you checked on her in school?"

"No," he said, as if that would be obvious. "No one records that level of detail. Beside, that wasn't why I was checking."

"If you say so," Sid said softly, looked at him with a raised eyebrow, and then turned back to his kitchen duties.

⊡-⊡-⊡-⊡-⊡

Sid saw Billy repeatedly step to the archway and glance into the dining room and then return to his dishes. After Billy made the round trip a few times, Sid wandered to the archway and satisfied his suspicions. He smiled and walked over to Billy.

"Take a minute, take your apron off, and go talk to her," Sid said in a low voice so only Billy could hear. "You're going to end up breaking my dishes if you keep walking back and forth with the soapy ones in your hand."

"That bad?"

"Yeah," Sid said. "And mop this up before someone slips." He gestured to the trail of sudsy water dripped between them and the archway.

Billy finished loading the dishwasher tray and quickly mopped the floor. He hung up his apron and stopped in front of the archway as he looked for Billie at her table. He was about to push the swinging doors open when Billie pushed them in and smiled at him.

"Sorry," she said with a wide smile. "Were you coming through?"

"I was," Billy said, and returned her smile. "But I don't have to now."

He saw Billie's cheeks redden.

"I was going to ask you," he started, "if you'd meet me tomorrow after lunch. In the Forest?"

"Sure," she said. "I was wondering if I'd see you this weekend. I have our girls' night out thing tonight, so I can't go to the kitchen."

"That's okay. I've got business in the village in the morning, so after lunch is best for me," he said softly, slightly louder than a whisper. "How about one tomorrow?"

"One. In the Forest," she repeated, her green eyes shining brightly. "See you there."

Twenty-One

Saturday, April 30

"Morning, Helen," Billy said as he folded his legs and sat down in front of her makeshift tent. The woman in her late fifties with unruly, salt-and-pepper hair sat up with a blanket wrapped around her, and he glanced around as he slipped her a small pastry box and a still-steaming coffee in doubled foam cups. "Brought you something."

He tried to not openly show preferences, but he was aware that everyone knew he had his "favorites." Some were special to him because their personalities just clicked, and some because they showed an interest in improving.

"Thanks, Keeper," she said, and wrapped her hands around the warm, foam plastic cup. "You're such a blessing."

"Not me, Helen," he said. "I'm just the delivery boy."

"Well, then please thank Sid and his mom for me," Helen said, and sipped the warm brew.

"I will." He smiled and saw four familiar faces coming up the path.

He waved and one smiled and led the others to him.

"Do you mind if we sit here a bit and talk a little business?" he asked as the four stopped and crouched down in front of them. "You remember Mace, Hammer, and Ferret and Mouse."

"Certainly," Helen said, and quickly finished eating her cinnamon roll. "Morning to all of you, but if you'll excuse me, I need to go wash and freshen up. Stay here and talk as long as you want."

Ferret was closest and helped her stand up. She thanked him as she tightened the blanket around her and slowly trundled off toward the portable toilets. Ferret watched her for a minute, then folded his legs and settled down between Billy and Mouse.

"Why didn't Helen ever get a street name?" Mouse asked as Ferret sat down.

"Just didn't," Hammer said, and looked at Mace.

"When her husband died and left her with virtually nothing," Mace said, and stirred the dirt in front of him with his finger, "Helen had nowhere to go. A couple up on the north side of the village took her in, and after a year or so Keeper was able to find someone that would give her a job." Mace turned his head and looked at Mouse. "She wasn't able to help with the watching or defending the village, so no one ever gave her a name."

"So she didn't have any family to help her?"

Billy shook his head. "No, Mouse, she didn't. They never had any kids, and both of them were only kids themselves and survived both of their folks. "

"She's still working? Right?" Mouse asked. "At that pet store on David and Sixth Street West?"

Billy nodded. "She still is."

"Do you remember when the portables came, Keeper?" Ferret asked, jerking his thumb up, pointing back over his shoulder. "I remember how happy we all were when they did, but I can't remember the time."

"Let's see," Billy said, and scratched his head. "I'd been here two, maybe three years. So fourteen or fifteen years ago."

"Sure was a great improvement," Mouse said as she snuggled against Ferret.

He slipped his arm around her and watched the others as they sat down.

"Those and the water. Did we ever thank the people that own this block?"

Billy shrugged. "I'm sure someone did, or those wouldn't still be here."

Mouse smiled.

"Okay. You asked us to meet you. What's up?" Mace asked as he sipped the coffee he had brought.

"You made that last all the way up here?" Hammer asked, and gently punched Mace on the shoulder.

"Yeah," he said emphatically. "Pigeon will only make me one each morning, so I hafta make it last."

They chuckled and then turned to Billy.

"I know you all have noticed the sudden rise in dealers trying to push the doors open," Billy said when he saw they were ready. "I think that's by plan."

"By plan?" Mouse asked.

"Yeah," Billy said, and nodded. He had spent half the night trying to think of how to tell them what he needed without telling them too much. "You've heard the rumors that someone was trying to buy the Duckard's block in the city center." They nodded. "Well, I know it was more than a rumor. And yesterday it fell through."

The four smiled hugely and patted each other's backs.

"But…" Billy held up his hand and looked at each of them in turn. "…I think *if* the city feels those mid-city blocks, or the block the village sets on, is a haven for druggies, peddlers or users, they will come in and clean house."

"Does that mean what I think you mean?" Mouse asked.

Billy nodded. "Yes, Mouse," he said, and looked at her youthful, almost naïve expression. He knew she wasn't naïve and was only a few years younger than he was, but she had that look and he knew she could use it to her advantage. "They will have reason to evict everyone, and we can't let that happen if we can help it."

Billy looked at each one of them and then continued. "I need for you four, and any of the others that you feel can help, to listen for anything that will help us head off the dealers. There are changes coming and we need to know all we can about the dealers—who's pushing them, feeding them, supplying them. Anything that might give us a clue to what we can do to stop them, or that we can use against them. Proof would be better, but I'll take whatever I can get."

"Where do you want us to start?" Ferret asked.

"You know better than I do," Billy said, and chuckled at a thought.

"What?" Hammer asked.

"Just remembering." Billy smiled and looked at Ferret. "It was Ferret and Mouse that found my Mary at the Streetcar out of all the Marys in town when I first came here. I don't need to tell you where to start any more than I need to tell you how to breathe. Thank you. All of you."

They all stared at Billy until Mouse finally stood up and wiped her suddenly moist eyes with her sleeve. "Oh shit, Keeper, someone had to find her," Mouse said, and turned to the path they had come up earlier. "You sure weren't gonna get it done."

Mouse stuffed her hands in her pocket and started walking. The men quickly stood up and slapped Billy's shoulder, agreeing they would see what they could find out. Ferret caught up to Mouse and slipped his arm around her shoulders as Hammer and Mace hurriedly followed them.

Twenty-Two

Considering the weather was still brisk, Billie pulled her casual slacks over her leggings, slipped into a warm blouse with a medium-weight V-necked sweater over it, heavy socks, and her older pair of walking boots. She threw a wool scarf around her neck and put on her older, worn leather jacket. Then she confirmed she had her knife in her handbag and thought about Wednesday night.

Smiling at her memories and Billy's encouraging comments, she took the elevator down to the parking garage.

Driving? Or walking?

She reluctantly stared at her SUV and decided.

Walking. The Rover is too...overbearing, I think. One of these days, I really need to get something more...normal.

She exited through the turnstile and stepped out onto the chilly but sunny street. Six blocks north and four west, she stopped on the south side of the city block commonly referred to as "the Forest."

I guess it's still a little cold for most folks, she thought, surprised to see the park was nearly deserted. She slowly walked along the south sidewalk and pondered the few people she saw: an older man sat on a bench at the near corner of the park with a small dog on a short leash, a woman and a small child played in a sandbox in the southwest corner, and there was a man lying on a sunny bench halfway up the paved walking path that wandered north through the park.

She watched the man on the bench as she walked up the path. As she entered the sunny clearing, he sat up and turned to face her. Billy was wearing his pale blue plaid shirt, lightly worn denim jeans, and an old but clean brown jacket; his appearance surprised her.

"What happened to you?" she asked when she was close enough for him to hear her.

"Mary said I had to look decent if I was going to see you in public," he said with a smile, "especially if I see you in the daylight in public."

Billie chuckled and grabbed his hands.

"So? What's your day looking like?" he asked.

"Well," she said as he led her back to the bench, "I guess I'm on the hook to go out with the girls again tonight."

He nodded and she continued.

"Then tomorrow I have to drive out to Mom and Dad's place for Sunday lunch. I'll get back about seven, or a little after."

"Aaah, a full schedule with little time to spare," he teased. "I certainly hope you have a good time with them."

"Thanks," she said with a smile as she sat down on the bench beside him. "Come with me?"

"Can't," he said. "Wish I could, but not yet."

"You know, I didn't sleep a wink the last two nights," she continued, reluctantly accepting his answer.

He turned and faced her, his left arm bent between them, resting on the back of the bench, and his right across his lap. "And why is that? After that little bit of exercise and fresh air Wednesday and Thursday nights, and a relaxing night partying with your friends last night, I would've thought you'd have slept like a baby."

"Riiight," she said with a wide smile. "I kept thinking about the things that could've gone wrong, the things that could—"

"Me too." He smiled and took her hand with his right. "I was awake all night trying to justify getting you into such a serious situation. You could've been—"

"But I wasn't," she said, and squeezed his hand. "But, you *did* put me into that situation unprepared." She held up her other hand when he started to argue. "You need to teach me how to defend myself, how to act in a fight, what I should do. I can't very well help if I don't know what to do or if I'm too scared because I might do something wrong. And I'm scared of that almost more than I'm scared of not knowing what to do. We need to work on preparing me for the next times."

"Next times?"

"You heard me, Billy. I want to help as much as I can, go with you to the kitchen as often as I can, help you watch when I can, and you need to teach me what I need to know. Wednesday night without knowing what I should be doing was haunting. I was just too dumb to know how much I don't know. I just followed your lead, but Thursday night, as we got closer and closer to the alleys, my mind started listing all the 'what-ifs.' By the time we got there, I was terrified."

She watched him digest what she was saying, waiting for him to decide one way or the other. After a significantly long silence, she pushed, "I know you said I did everything like I should've, but I have to know what to do. I was just following what you did, and I sure couldn't do what we did if you hadn't been showing me what to do." She looked up, searching his eyes. "Are you going to teach me, or do I learn by myself, on my own? If I learn on my own and I do it wrong, then my getting hurt will be completely on your head."

Slowly, he shook his head. "I'll teach you, if only to show you how dangerous it really is."

"Thanks," she said, but restrained herself from hugging him and thanking him like she wanted to. "I already know it's dangerous. Just tell me where and when."

"Are you really all right?" he asked. She knew he saw the cloud of seriousness cross her face.

"Yes. Well, not really," she admitted. "I suddenly feel like I've been dropped into an alternate reality and nothing makes sense anymore."

"Like what?"

"I think I need to grow up, Billy," she said softly. "When I met you a couple of weeks ago, my life was almost carefree. I have friends that I party with three nights a week, sometimes more, and we gossip about the guys in the bars, or at the comedy center, or in different movies, or...My only problem was an abusive boyfriend, and he's thankfully a forever ex. And now, I find all those carefree things shallow and meaningless. I've met Lori and Becky for drinks twice this week, and both times I've felt like an outsider, uninterested in things that I used to eagerly look forward to.

"When I went and got clothes for my spy trips, I realized how many people there were, struggling to have a small piece of what I take for granted. The recycle shop had many racks of pretty clothes, but the bulk of the clothes were just functional, necessary apparel. A lot of women looked at the nice stuff, but they bought the everyday stuff—only what they needed or could afford.

"Then I followed you and went with you and saw what so many are facing each day—things I thought were just in movies or books. And Wednesday night, facing Pink, I surprised myself when I realized I was ready to fight beside you and possibly harm another human being to protect the safety of people I had not even met. I suddenly don't fit in my world anymore."

"But you do still fit in your world, Billie," he said, and pulled her hand to him. "That world and this one are still the same world. You've just gotten to see a different part of it."

"I see what you mean." She studied his face, his calm yet confident expression, the commitment behind his eyes, a peek at that other "layer" of Billy she was just starting to see. "Will you teach me and let me help?"

"I will have to trust you with part of a secret before I can tell you how," he said, and slowly turned to look around the park. "Can I trust you, Billie? I have asked myself that question for a number of years, ever since you graduated from high school."

"From high school?" She knew she was staring.

"I told you I was asked to watch and see."

"I want you to know you can trust me, Billy," she said, and squeezed his hand. "If there's something you want to share with me and it needs to be kept secret, I'll do my very best to keep it."

She saw him smile at a memory as he looked across the sunny park, and then he stood up and she glanced down at her hand firmly held in his, pulling her to follow.

"Come with me," he said as he picked up a folded blanket he had on the bench. He led her to a large conifer in the northeast corner of the park, crouched under the boughs, and set the blanket on the ground near the trunk. He turned and sat down on it.

"Maybe your friends won't see you here conversing with a degenerate stranger," he added as he leaned back against the tree, pulled her down crosswise on his outstretched legs.

Hesitant, she finally settled on his lap but did not let herself curl her left arm across his shoulders or around his neck. He slipped his right arm gently around her waist and let his left rest across her knees.

"Now, there are a few things I need to tell you about, and I need you to keep the secrets. There are other secrets that I may share later, but we'll start with these."

"Sid said you were very cautious about who you trust," she said, and studied her hands clasped in her lap. "I hope I can be worthy of your trust. I'll try, Billy."

"When I was young," he started, "my dad used to wrestle and play very competitive games with me. I enjoyed those times with him, away from his work, away from Mom, away from everything else. In those times it was just the two of us." Billy gently took her right hand with his left and began rubbing her palm with his thumb. "As I got older, he taught me various martial arts moves, wrestling moves, how to shoot many of his guns, and later, after they had died, I realized he had been teaching me how to street fight, how to defend myself. Like you, growing up with decent means was great—carefree. Then when I was nine or ten, I realized that my dad was very concerned about people and small businesses when they faced hard times."

She forced herself to sit still and listen quietly.

"I went with him many times to the soup kitchens around town, and when he stopped to talk to different people that were having problems. It was a year or so later when I overheard him one night on a phone call with Mike Hammersmith, arguing over someone I didn't know. Dad accused him of dealing underhandedly to take the property out from under whoever it was. That's when I realized life wasn't like I thought it was, and after that I paid attention to who Dad championed and fought and thwarted. Eight out of ten times it was Hammersmith he fought with."

She waited when he stopped, watching his hand caressing hers. Finally, she glanced up at his silence, seeing his serious face staring out into the park, seeing nothing—yet, she thought, maybe everything.

"Early in the summer before they died," Billy started again, "Dad went against Hammersmith once more, and when I asked him about the people that might be hurt, he smiled and told me that even if Mike won, the people would be safe. It was again after he and Mother died and I came here that I understood what he had done to protect them."

"What did he do?" she asked, almost afraid to break his train of thought.

"I need to wait and explain those details in another discussion, Billie. Can you wait until then?" he asked, and looked back, watching her eyes gently.

She nodded, resigned, and changed the subject. "How did they die?"

"It was a car wreck," he said softly. "We were coming home from a weekend visiting with some friends of theirs. Mom and his friend's wife were good friends, and they had a great time cooking and retelling stories from their college days. I think they might've gone to school together. Dad and his friend played cards and talked about construction projects."

Billie gently squeezed his hand, and remembered how Willum used to come to the ranch sometimes and ride with her and Sandy.

"Anyway, on our way home, the car went off the road, flipped, and ended up in a ditch. I was sleeping in the back when it happened, and I woke up—or regained consciousness, whichever it was—in the trees off to one side of the road. The car was fully engulfed in fire, and I saw a man walking away with a gas can in his hand."

"Murdered?" She stiffened in disbelief, squeezing his hand tightly as her surprise quickly pushed her thoughts of Willum out of her mind. "They were...killed?"

Billy nodded. "Slowly, I realized what had happened, and I knew I couldn't be found; something told me that if I was alive, I had to hide to buy myself some time to figure things out. Dad always said to be patient and not charge into a confrontation too soon. Figure things out before you act. So I made it into the city, to the one place I knew I would be safe, and I found Mary and told her what had happened."

"Mary? The Mary of Mary and Sid at the Streetcar Diner?"

"Yes," he admitted. "We've known Mary and her son Sid for nearly forever. They let me work for pocket money, but I stayed where I was safe and where it would keep them safe and they wouldn't be implicated in anything I did."

"Can you tell me where that is?" she asked, trembling with the thought that he might still not want her to know. "Where you go to hide and be safe?"

"I'll have to check with the others first, but maybe I can show you," he said, and squeezed her shoulders. Then she felt him tense up. "Billie, I have to tell you. My secret is that I am a homeless person."

"What?" she said as she stiffened and turned to look at him.

"Please wait," he said, holding her waist and hand tightly, keeping her from jumping up. "You know me, and yes, I am one of those looked down on by everyone in *normal* society. I have reasonably high values, but I simply choose to not live in a house alone, like everyone else. At least not yet."

"Do you like being homeless?" she asked when he relaxed his hold.

"Of course not." He smiled at her. "But right now, I have people that I protect and I can't do that if I live away from them."

"But you have a job. You're respected there, you're..."

"Yes I do, but I also care about the others. They have jobs too. I have been able to get jobs for many under my protection," he said, and again squeezed her and then made himself relax. "Those have some means and they share with others, just like I do. They get food legitimately, they don't panhandle, and I have been able to give some of them hot and cold running water and electricity."

"Then why do you go to the soup kitchens? Sorry. I know why."

"Obviously to help feed those that don't have jobs or means," he said, seeing her questioning look. "It takes volunteers to make it work."

"But you go to a kitchen in the worst part of town. I hear the other two are in much nicer areas."

"I go there so those that come there see Keeper face to face. So they know I'm here, doing what I do, helping those that need it. I try to give them hope. If I went to one of the other kitchens, people like Pink, Knife, and those behind them would overrun the city center and the village, and soon no one would be safe. I've trained some of the others to help watch and to be available to fight for the rest, but it takes a leader. I'm it, just me, sort of by default."

"Not so," she said, slipping her arm around him and snuggling against his shoulder. "Well, maybe not for much longer."

You really are nuts.

"Once you teach me, there'll be two of us."

He thought without speaking for a long time—long enough that Billie was concerned and looked up to see what he was doing or looking at.

"Sorry. I'm just thinking," he said softly, and she leaned her shoulder against him. "About three or four months after I moved into the city center, a man came and squatted in the alley two blocks south of where we met Pink. He was a shabby man and he drank, and one night Russell—we call him Mace—

heard him telling someone about a hired job he had done, to cause a car wreck and then set it on fire to be sure the occupants died. Russell said he was obviously tormented by having done such a deed, and had taken to the bottle.

"Russell befriended the man and was there the night he admitted that a man named Hammersmith had paid him a thousand dollars cash to make it happen."

"What? Mr. Hammersmith?" She stared at him.

I know Hammersmith has a temper and is unpredictable, but...murder...?

"Yeah, Hammersmith. Then he gave him another thousand when he finished. He also named Westman as an accomplice, but we never heard how he was implicated."

"You're sure? Could there be another—"

"No, Billie. There's no other. I'm sure."

Billie forced herself to sit still and slowly get her breathing under control.

Things like this just don't happen. I've never known anyone—

"When Russell told me about it, I went into a rage, but when we got to the alley, it was full of police and reporters. Either the man killed himself or someone killed him for talking. I never found out which, but he had most of the money in his pockets."

"You lost your proof," she said, forcing her incense down, making herself think about what he was telling her. She would think about the rest of this later. "And now you're waiting?

"Yes," he said, "but things are starting to happen." He sat her up to face him. "Will you help me, let me know what Westman and Hammersmith are doing with their new, big development project?"

Startled, she looked at him.

"Certain things have already happened to confuse their efforts…" He smiled. "…but it would help if I knew or had a clue as to what they are thinking, planning next. The top is probably going to blow off pretty soon, and I want to be sure the right parties get their long-awaited dues. I don't mean to be asking you to snoop or do anything illegal or that will get you into trouble, just to let me know if you hear anything odd or curious."

"Sure. You know I will, Billy," she said, and leaned her left shoulder against him again. "I know you won't tell me everything, but I will help however I can, however you need me to."

"Thanks, Billie," he said smiling at her, slipping his arm up and holding her shoulder snugly.

As she watched his hand, still caressing hers in her lap, she noticed an inked chain around his left wrist and quickly lifted her left hand to look at her own wrist. Startled, she realized they were the same.

"Billy?"

He turned his head back to look at her.

"You told me women often wear tats, but what do these mean?" She held up her left hand and the exposed the chain design.

He smiled. "Like you told Knife Wednesday night, you have a squeeze. So do I."

"What? We're a couple?" She sat up and stared at him.

He nodded. "We are, unless kissing me back Wednesday night is not how you really feel. I could not take you to the kitchen and let anyone think you were available. And as I told you, they are temporary and can be washed off. But out in the 'hoods, women can't have rings and keep them. Someone would steal them right off their fingers, sometimes fingers and all, so they wear matching tats to mean the same thing. They can't be stolen."

"So these are like rings? Like you've given *me* a ring? Like, we're engaged?" She looked at him and he nodded. She inhaled deeply and slowly let it out as she looked at their wrists again,

We're engaged! No asking...No...What if I didn't want...?

"No asking what I think about it? No—" She stopped and looked at him, surprised as she suddenly realized she was not actually upset with the idea. "Without asking, you just make everyone think we're—What if the women change their minds?

The women that have real tats?"

What if I change my mind? Everyone thinks it's a real tat.

"Do they change the tat or have it removed?"

"One or the other," he said, and turned to face her. "Maybe I should've told you up front, but when you put the Knife down at the serving table, I thought you'd figured it out."

"I hadn't, but it makes sense that everyone should think we were." She looked at him with a thin smile. "Even if you were pretending."

"If you feel uncomfortable with the arrangement, implied or not," Billy said, and squeezed her hand, "just remember the chain can be removed."

She sighed and took a deep breath.

Oh my, what next?

"Thank you again," she finally said, "for thinking of that and again for protecting me, even when I didn't know you were."

He pulled her back against him. "I know I'm being very forward here. Are you okay with me holding you? With everything else?"

She did not respond at first.

"First you ink me and tell the world we're engaged without explaining it to me, then you suddenly kiss me without warning before you drag me into the dark alleys to face a drug dealer, you set me down under a tree on your lap and tell me your secret that you're a homeless person, and now, you think you might be a little forward?" She stared at him. "Is there anything else you're planning to do to me before you tell me first?"

He just smiled, deciding he really should not say what he was thinking he'd like to do *with* her. He gently pulled her back against him instead. "You did kiss me goodnight, twice. But I'll try to remember to tell you first if I plan on anything."

Billie slowly smiled. "In that case, I think I can get used to this, Billy."

"I was hoping you could," Billy said.

She reached to him with her free hand, pulled his head to

her, and kissed him long and tenderly. She turned toward him and slipped her arm behind him, pulling herself tightly against him.

Twenty-Three

Lori and Becky were giggling over something when Billie met them in the Onion and Olive, a lively dance and martini bar on the upper west side. Dressed in her usual fashionable and colorful leggings, thigh-length skirt, and fitted blouse, Billie followed the door attendant through the crowd to their table. She slid onto the bench beside Lori and noticed the looks that followed her into the room.

They sure are watching tonight.

Just ignore them.

What? You've always liked seeing them watch. You dress so they will.

I know, but somehow it doesn't feel right. It's bothering me tonight.

"Are you feeling better?" Lori asked, stifling her previous laughter as Billie glanced back at the nearby tables and the smiling faces she had passed as she sat down. "You still look a little poorly."

"Much better actually," she said, and smiled. "What was so funny?"

"Becky was telling me about Stacy's date last night," Lori said, and looked at Becky.

"It didn't go well, I guess," Becky said, and leaned over the table. "It seems Tom took her out to the Gardens for dinner, steaks, wine and everything."

"And when they were done—" Lori snickered again.

"He'd left his wallet and card at home—" Becky said.

"And couldn't pay," Lori finished with another giggle. "Stacy had to pay the tab."

Lori and Becky's giggles turned into full laughter but the uncomfortable memory of Blake and their similar incident flashed through Billie's mind. She inhaled sharply, remembering that Blake had *planned* his "forgetfulness."

"Knowing Stacy, I bet that didn't go over very well," Billie said, and did not laugh, surmising the concern and conflict Stacy must have felt. "I'm sure he'll pay her back and try to make it up to her."

Lori slowly stopped laughing and looked at Billie. "Are you okay? You're so serious, not your normal self yet."

"Sorry, been there. I know what Stacy had to have felt." She forced another smile and gestured for Becky to pass the menu pad. Billie sighed and realized the resonance was not there tonight.

I should be the happiest woman in the city, and yet I feel strangely depressed. What's wrong with me? I'm engaged! But I can't bring myself to tell them. Billy didn't actually say I couldn't, but they sure wouldn't understand.

Billie took a deep breath. "I guess this week has been more tiring than I thought. With the press of work, trying to get Mr. Boster's jobs done on time, and not feeling well, I guess I'm more stressed out than I thought."

"Well, cheer up and have a drink," Becky said as she pushed the menu pad across the table. "After a couple, you'll feel a lot better."

Good idea.

Yeah. So what can I get that's different? Like me. I'm going to be different!

Billie smiled and scanned the list on the pad, selected one she had not had in a long time, and then inserted her card into the slot. When she pulled the card out, she realized Becky was telling them more about Stacy and her new boyfriend.

"...his father owns a paving company out in Briar's Green," Becky was saying, referring to the suburb southwest of the city, "and from what I can find out, he gives Tom a rather nice monthly allowance. Stacy says he has a position in his father's business with a lot of responsibility, but Tom takes off as often and as much as he likes."

"That must be nice, but who's taking up the slack while he's gone, 'taking off as much time as he likes'?" Billie asked. She kept her outward expression tightly under control, realizing she was comparing Tom's ethics against those she was beginning to see in Billy. "Someone's got to do the work. Just saying."

"He's been off almost every day this past week," Lori admitted, and smiled at Becky. "I wish I had someone that would spend that much time with me." She glanced around at the nearby tables, as if she could see someone that might unexpectedly be available.

"Sooner or later," Becky said, "his father will get tired of carrying him and will probably cut him off. His father can't be so blind that he doesn't see his son's milking him and the business."

"You have that right," Billie agreed. She did not fully understand her new seriousness, but she knew she had to find a balance. Seeing Billy's life was changing all her perceptions, and she realized, like Billy had said, she was suddenly living in a new world: her old world joined with his new-to-her world. Not one or the other.

"I know," Lori admitted, "but I don't think Stacy is thinking that far ahead. Neither of them are, for that matter."

A physically toned waiter served the table behind Billie's side of their booth, and then delivered Billie her drink. He asked Lori and Becky if they needed another and they quickly admitted they did.

As he walked away, Becky leaned toward Billy. "I can't find anything on a Billy Carson," she said softly, and looked at Billie. "Nothing." She spread her palms flat on the table. "Have you seen him recently?" When Billie smiled and nodded, Becky asked, "What does he say?"

"Only what little I've told you," Billie said with a smile that she hoped looked normal.

Stop worrying. Be normal.

Billie straightened her shoulders, picked up her drink, and decided to act like her previous shallow self.

"What's that?" Lori asked, and grabbed Billie's left hand as Billie sipped her drink. "What do you have under your bracelet?"

Becky caught Lori's hand and pulled Billie's hand to the center of the table. "Is that a tattoo?"

"No." Billie smiled. "Just a sketch of what one might look like."

"You're not seriously thinking about getting a tattoo? Are you? One that obvious?" Lori asked, surprise and concern showing on her face.

"I might," Billie replied nonchalantly. "It's distinctive, isn't it?" She smiled, glad they did not know what it meant.

"Well, I'm certain," Becky added, and picked her glass up and drained it, "your parents would not approve."

"I'm sure there are worse things I have done that they would not approve of," she rebutted, and pulled her hand back. "Besides, if they complain too much, I just might get one out of spite."

"You wouldn't dare," Lori said expressively.

"I certainly would dare." Billie smiled and winked at her.

"So, what have you talked about?" Becky asked, turning the subject back.

"My school, education, dance and drama classes, work," Billie said.

"Sounds boring," Lori admitted.

"Well, we have broken the ice," Billie admitted, hoping she was not digging a hole she could not climb out of. "And some things don't take a lot of talking."

"So you've forgotten all about Blake?" Lori asked with a sly look in her eye.

"Dammit, Lori! If you bring him up once more, I swear I will personally show you where you can stick your—" Billie stopped, glaring at Lori when the waiter interrupted, returning with another round of drinks. She took a deep breath and smiled tightly when the waiter left. "What about you, Lori?" Billie looked around at nearby tables. "Can I help you find a future ex? If not, tell us about the drugstore business."

Lori's expression turned to surprise and Billie hoped she would realize she should not keep bringing that subject up. Lori stammered and started explaining the end-of-the-month issues they had and how Old Man Swaggard kept worrying about the timing of shipments and their arrivals, never seeming to understand how on-time deliveries worked.

Becky wisely ignored Billie's rant and talked about the museum and more about their plans for the new exhibits and traveling shows. And after a third round of drinks, Billie checked the time and decided she needed to get some sleep before she started the two-hour drive up to her parents' ranch.

"Gotta call it a night," she said. "I have to be up at Mom and Dad's by around ten. Honestly, it'll take me an hour to pack," she said, knowing that was not completely true.

As they got up and she pulled her jacket on, Becky and Lori slid out of the booth and carried their coats through the crowd to the front door. Billie turned and picked up her bag. She noticed the man in nice but casual clothes at the table beside their booth. Her surprise quickly faded into a smile as she recognized him, nodded, and softly said "Stretch" in greeting. "Didn't expect to see you here."

"Sometimes a beer is nice," he said, tapping his mug with his finger and nodding in reply.

"I guess so. You have a good night." Billie shook her head, trying to remember if she knew which one was Stretch's wife as she turned and followed Lori and Becky out.

-◻-

Instead of crashing when she got back to her apartment, Billie sat on the sofa with one leg pulled up in front of her and the other wrapped around it, sipping a tall glass of iced water and embracing the city lights. Her thoughts wandered from her memories of Wednesday night, the most unusual night she had ever spent, then the afternoon with Billy confiding a small part of his life and his secrets, to seeing Stretch in the club.

I should've known Billy would check on me and make certain that I can be trusted.

Like you trusted him when he scared you out of your mind and took you to the kitchen the first night?

Yeah, she chuckled, *just like that.*

Becky and Lori—and especially Stacy—would simply say he was stalking you.

If they knew why, they would probably be okay with it.

Not Stacy!

You're right. Not Stacy. But they don't know why, and I am not going to tell them it's just Billy protecting himself and the others.

She was pleased she had shown him she was keeping her word.

But I'm surprised Beck couldn't find anything out about him or his family. Surely the wreck would have made the news...but then I couldn't find out anything either.

She sipped her water again.

So much has happened since I met him again. Can it really be only two and a half weeks? It sure feels like more than that. He's changed everything.

Everything?

Yeah. I can't stop thinking about him. That's normal, right?

She looked at her left wrist.

To feel that way about the man I'm engaged to? Engaged! Wow. I am, aren't I?

Seems like you are. Are you okay with it?

I think I am, actually. I know it doesn't feel real yet, but...He feels so familiar. I'm so comfortable when I'm with him. Why is that?

Because you're not rational.

I am too. And I don't know why I feel the way I do, but I do feel that way. And I like it.

She took another sip.

And I like how he's concerned for my safety, my needs, and what I want. He works and gives of his time, and I suspect what money he has.

Good for him.

Do you realize, he's never, not once, asked me for anything—not even money. He's nothing like the other men I've known. Or even some women I've known. Most of the others have only had themselves in mind, to get what they wanted or what I could give them.

There's still time.

She hugged her leg and thought about the long afternoon sitting on Billy's legs under the tree in the park, cuddled securely in his arms, listening to anything he allowed himself to share with her. She cherished every small detail he gave her to remember, each a small glimpse into the past that made him the man she was beginning to respect above all others.

Smiling, she uncoiled her legs and stood up in a fluid motion, took the glass to the kitchen, poured it out, and set it in the dishwasher. As she climbed the spiral stairs, she turned and looked into the city center.

Are you out there tonight? You or Stretch or Mace? Looking for Pink, Knife, or someone else?

She undressed in the dark, thinking about the many things he faced that threatened the tenuous peace in their 'hood. She slipped into her pajamas, then pulled her bed covers back and slid into bed. Billie lay watching the expanse of the city, now fully aware of some of the dangers unseen, masked by the quiet beauty of the city architecture and lights. She pulled a pillow tightly in front of her, and with a mix of concern, worry, and excited anticipation, she wondered if there was a future for her with a mysterious homeless man named Billy.

Twenty-Four

Sunday, May 1

It was nearly dawn, and Billy checked the alley to see if anyone was watching. He always waited before he unlocked the metal door and slipped into the department store, relocking the door behind him. He carried plastic sacks, two in each hand, down the stairs and across the large, empty basement room. At the wide doorway into the room of curtains and divided niches, he stopped, greeted by the soft sounds and stirrings of people sleeping or just waking.

"Anyone up for coffee or a sweet roll?" he asked the quiet room.

Suddenly, every curtained den stirred, and a small girl's smiling face framed in blond curls peeked from under a curtain on his right. "Juice?"

"Certainly, Abby," he said, and smiled at the girl. "And a roll for each of you."

Cat stepped out into the clear aisle, stretched, and yawned. "You know you don't have to do this," she said, and followed him back into the larger room. Her husband, Stretch, hurried quickly behind her, following the smell of fresh coffee.

Billy stopped near the bathrooms, turned, crossed his legs, and sat down on the floor with two sacks on each side of him. When Abby sat down cross-legged beside him, he dug four cartons of juice out of one bag and let her choose. She decided and he handed it to her. "Give the others to the boys," he said as he gave her the sack of juices and handed the two sacks of sweet rolls to Cat.

Cat took one and a napkin, then passed the sacks around as

the rest of the group stumbled out of the sleeping area or came back from the bathrooms.

Billy handed the box of coffee to Mace and the cups to his son, Ernest.

When everyone had settled in front of him and the coffee was making its way around, Billy smiled.

"Some of you saw me and a friend of mine this past week," he began, and saw Cat, Stretch, and Mace nod as he spoke. "I'm sure the rest of you have been told that I'm seeing someone."

The rest nodded and Abby tugged his sleeve. "Is she as pretty as Stretch says she is?"

He smiled and said, "Yes she is."

"Have you known her long?" Abby asked eagerly.

"She came to the restaurant once when she was twelve," he said, reluctant to tell them he had known her as a child. He ruffled Abby's hair and continued. "Now let me talk to the others too. Okay?"

Abby nodded and took a bite of her roll.

Billy took a sweet roll when the sack made it back to him and continued to explain their meeting in the restaurant fifteen years before, their meeting almost three weeks ago, and what had happened since.

"She bought distressed clothes so she could follow me around and find out what I did. From her experience with Lenny at the village and me explaining, she had a sense of how dangerous it was around the kitchen," he said. "Cat, did you notice her when you came to the kitchen to tell me I was needed back here?

"Not really. I saw that you had someone new helping with the bread and fruit," Cat admitted, "but she wasn't anything to speak of."

Billy smiled. "That was Billie. She put Knife down when he tried to make a move on her, threatening to…" He stopped and looked at the four children. "…cut him in a way that would affect his love life, and I think she was serious."

Stretch looked at Mace. "Keeper said she wielded a knife

and backed him up when he confronted Pink."

Mace and the others turned and looked at Stretch, then at Cat's nod. "I watched them from the alley. She was surprising."

Billy nodded at each of them. "She was scared, but she's a bit of a tiger, I must admit. But that's the problem. Right now she can bluff very well, when she can control her nervousness, but she's never had any defensive training."

"That could be bad," Cat said softly.

"That's my dilemma, Cat," Billy said. "She wants to continue going with me to help at the kitchen or anything else I do, and you and I know that sooner than later, someone will put her to the test."

"Can we teach her?" Mace asked, and the woman beside him hugged his arm and smiled.

"I wanted to ask you if you would feel comfortable if I brought her here so I...*we*"—he gestured to the group—"can teach her. I told her a little of my past to see if she can keep a secret or how publicly she checks me out. I also told her she could not tell anyone about what she did Wednesday night, Thursday night, or yesterday. Last night she met with her closest friends. Stretch, did I give you enough to cover dinner?"

Stretch nodded.

"What did you hear?"

"She met her friends about seven," Stretch said, "at a martini bar up in the northwest part of town. They talked about another girlfriend of theirs and a problem she had with her boyfriend, and she got upset with the shorter of her two friends when she brought up Billie's ex-boyfriend." Stretch continued to relate everything Billie and her friends had talked about, including how she had dodged her friend's questions about the partnership tat on her wrist.

"Partnership tat?" Cat asked with a start, and looked at Billy.

Billy held up his left hand and pulled his sleeve up to expose his wrist. "They're temporary, but I had to give her some protection while she was at the kitchen."

"You're still wearing it," Cat said with a gleam in her eye, "and she's still wearing hers? I think there's more than just an alibi here, Keeper."

"Maybe, Cat." He smiled and turned back to Stretch.

Stretch picked up his telling where he had left off when Cat interrupted. When he finished recounting their evening, he looked at Billy and then at Cat.

"I don't know when she saw me and connected a face with the name," he said, looking at Billy. "I was at a table behind her, but when she got up to leave and the others headed for the door, she picked up her purse and saw me. She smiled, nodded, and said hello before she left. She called me by my street name, Billy." Stretch looked at Cat. "I think she has a very sharp mind." Then he looked at Billy and the others. "She didn't say anything that would give anyone a clue as to what you two were up to Wednesday or Thursday night, and nothing about your afternoon in the park yesterday. She didn't say anything about any secrets you might have shared with her. And since she helped you defend the city blocks and wants to learn how to protect herself and help you, Keeper, I'm willing to let you bring her here."

"Thanks, Stretch." Billy looked at the group. "What did you hear, Ferret?"

"About the same, Keeper," Ferret said. "Friday night she met her friends for a light supper and drinks. Only talked about a missing girlfriend, her boyfriend, and her work."

"Thanks, Ferret," Billy said. "I'd like to train her here, but I won't bring her here if any of you think it is unwise or are uncomfortable with it. This is your home."

"It's yours too, Keeper," Mace's woman said.

"Thanks, Pidge. But I'm just a tenant like you," he said, and poured himself a cup of coffee from the box and waited for them to consider their feelings.

After a few minutes, Pigeon turned and talked softly with those around her and then looked at each of the others. With a quick nod, she turned and looked at Billy. "Okay."

"Thanks, Pidge. Everyone," he said, and smiled. "I'll let

you know when she can come and you can all meet her. I think you'll like her."

"Good," Mace said, then changed the subject. "Have we heard anything more concerning the dealers?"

"Not yet, Mace," Billy said seriously. "As I told some of you yesterday in the village, I think Hammersmith's or Westman's businesses are trying to get control, or ownership of this block. Billie works at Hammersmith's and I asked her to let me know if she hears anything as well. So far Hammersmith hasn't mentioned to anyone we know why he's so adamant about that project."

"You sure you can trust her?" Pigeon asked.

"Yes. I certainly am, Pidge."

Mace nodded and then Hammer raised his hand and said, "You said that was why Pink and his two cronies showed up— so it'll look like the area is going downhill. Pink hasn't nosed around here in years."

"That's right, Hammer," Billy said. "I think all of the dealers and peddlers we are seeing are being pushed to get into this area so they can make a few sales and someone can complain that this is a haven for druggies, panhandlers, and loiterers. It will only take one sale for our house of cards to fall. We need to keep a vigil and chase any 'undesirables' out."

"Aren't we the 'undesirables'?" Cathy asked.

"I'm not," Abby said quickly.

"To some, yes we are, Lynx," Billy said, looking at Cathy and ruffling Abby's hair again. "But we have one difference. We have the owner's permission to live here, and as long as the properties do not change ownership, that permission stands."

"Do you think the owner can keep Hammersmith and Westman from getting control of the property?" Mace asked.

"I'd like to say yes, Mace, but there's always a risk of something changing or happening that can mess things up. I'm trying to keep watch. If I see or hear anything, I'll let you all know," Billy said, knowing there was a slim possibility.

Twenty-Five

Billie parked her SUV just off the gravel beside the drive to the garages attached to her parents' house. She got out, pulled her jacket around her, and smiled, slowly looking across the backyard at the training corrals, the fenced paddocks, the feed and horse barns, and the assorted other buildings, letting the fond memories of her childhood flood back and wash over her. She inhaled the scent of the spring grass, the trees, and the earthiness drifting in from the pastures.

Billie reminisced about how much she had enjoyed growing up there and wondered how she would have reacted if the life she knew suddenly went away like Billy's had. Could she simply change and accept losing it and live without needs like he had?

No, she admitted bluntly. *It would've overpowered me and probably driven me to do something I would regret later. Maybe forever. Losing Willum was almost enough to do that.*

She shook her head, smiled at Billy's courage as she took the sacks from the back seat.

Saying hello as she came through the side door into the kitchen, Billie set the bags of things her mother had requested on the counter and gave her a hug. In the foyer past the living room, she hung her jacket up as her father came in from the bedroom wing and followed her back to the kitchen.

"How have you been?" he asked, stopping at the coffee pot. "Want a cup?"

"No thanks," Billie said, and snitched a carrot stick from the tray her mother was fixing. "Been good. Work is very busy, and I see Lori and Becky often."

"Wasn't there another one?" he asked, trying to remember.

"Stacy," her mother said. "You should remember her. Billie

brought her out last fall for the Labor Day weekend."

"Yeah, yeah. I remember," he said, and sipped his cup. "She's the sort of snooty one."

"Now really, Bob," Billie's mother said. "She just wasn't used to life on a ranch."

"Maybe so." Then he turned back to Billie. "How's that boyfriend of yours?" he asked. "Ricky, Brady, or—"

"Really, Dad?" Billie asked, surprised he did not remember. "He's actually ancient history. He was too much of an opportunist and too mean for me. I couldn't trust him. And life has been much less stressful since he's been gone."

I'm sure not going to tell him it took the cops to get rid of him.

She saw her dad smile and she turned back for another carrot stick.

"Who's coming?" Billie asked, looking at her mother. "You're making enough to feed the homeless." She chuckled to herself at her use of the unfamiliar reference.

"Would you believe, leftovers?" her dad asked over the rim of his cup.

She looked at him, cocked her head, and looked back at her mother. "Not again? Who did you invite this time?"

"She invited the Markins," her dad said softly.

"Oh God, no, Mom!" she said, and stomped the floor. "I don't like Jackson! Not that way! He's an uncoordinated, overeducated boor." She glanced at her dad and saw him smiling behind his cup. "You think this is funny?" Her voice pitched at seeing his expression.

"Honey," her mother said. "He's just in his awkward stage—"

"Awkward stages are supposed to be over in your teens, Mom." She glared. "Not when you're twenty-seven or whatever."

"Please, Billie. Just be sociable," her mother said. "I don't even know if Jackson is home this week."

Billie saw her dad roll his eyes.

"Damn, I think I'll just go back home," she said, and started into the living room.

Her dad caught her halfway across the room. "Billie, please. I know she's being pushy, but we only see you about twice every three months or so, and she worries about you being alone in the city."

"Dad, I can take care of myself," she rebutted with her hands on her hips.

That's not entirely true.

Hush! It's close enough.

"I can make my own friends," Billie said, trying to control her rising temper, "and I certainly will not put up with matchmaking, especially not from my own family. Has Mom tried to set Sandy up yet?"

"Billie, don't," he pleaded. "Let's enjoy what we can of the day. I do understand how this makes you feel, and I understand when you have no interest in Jackson, but your mother worries when every boyfriend you've had turns out be another... opportunist, I think you called them."

She stopped and absently studied the western-themed, leather pelt valances over the front window. She inhaled and then looked back at him. "Dad, I can't entertain Jackson or his folks under the pretense that I like him that way. I can't."

"You can't?" he asked, holding his daughter's eyes in question.

"No. I've...sort of found someone. Someone that has very strong principles and cares a lot about the needs of others. Someone that is not an opportunist in any way—not that I can tell."

"You'd know if he was. You always could, even when I disagreed with you. Is it serious?" he asked, still watching her.

"Yeah." She shrugged and shook her head slowly. "We've only been seeing each other for a short time, but our time has been better than I have ever had. He cares about *me*—what I want, what I need."

"Sounds refreshing. Does he have a name?"

"You're going to laugh," she said, and grinned hugely at him.

"I am?"

"He's a Billy."

He did laugh. "Now that is very unusual. A Billie and a Billy and you both get along."

"It's *better* than 'getting along,' Dad," she admitted. "But he doesn't have an upper crust job and doesn't fit with your expectations."

"Ah well, he seems to have caught your interest and maybe even your affections," he said. "You'll have to tell us about him and we'll try to not be too judgmental."

"Thanks, Dad," she said, and hugged him.

"Are we going to get to meet your Billy?"

"Soon, I hope," she said. "He stays pretty busy and it's hard for me to pull him away. But I'll try."

"I guess we should go and let your mother in on the news." He caught her arm as he turned her to the kitchen.

"Maggie," Bob started as they entered the kitchen. "I think Billie has something interesting to tell us,"

"That's good, dear," Maggie said, turning to the door at the sound of a car crunching to a stop on the gravel drive just outside. "Oh, it looks like they're here already."

"Mom?" Billie asked in surprise. "Don't tell me you invited them to come and ride before dinner."

"Why, yes, honey. I thought it would be nice to visit for a while first. You can tell us your news after they've settled in a bit."

Billie looked at her dad, mouthed an apologetic *I'm sorry*, and then turned to the back door.

Before her mother could say anything, she had stormed across the yard and into the stables. In the tack room, she pushed an arm into an old quilt-stitched jacket and grabbed a saddle and a blanket. She was mounted and out the back of the stable before her mother could have finished her pleasantries and greetings.

What are you doing? What—you can't be sociable for a

couple of hours?

Billie took the wooded trail up to the smaller, twenty-two acre lake at a gallop, slowing her mount to a trot as they passed through a narrow stand of trees and then to a slow walk as she followed the shore along the rushes. Billie was thankful for the time to calm herself, when Jackson emerged from the woods about a half an hour later. He had followed her trail around the lake.

Take a deep breath and stop acting like this. You've known Jackson since high school. You were fourteen.

I know, I know.

She took a deep breath, exhaled slowly, and turned to watch him as he drew near.

"Hi, Jackson," she greeted when he pulled up a few feet away from her.

"Mad at me?" he asked.

"No, not you. My mother," she said, and smiled, keeping her voice pleasant. "Sorry."

"I know. Mine too. I think they sit around waiting for us to come home so they can try to fix something up."

"My mom especially," she said with a smirk. "I'm sorry I ran off before you got here, but—"

"Don't apologize, Billie," he said. "I know how it is when I'm not your choice for company and our parents keep trying to throw us together."

"I don't mean to seem that way, Jackson," she admitted. "I don't know why we never clicked, but—"

"Don't," he said with a smile. "We can just enjoy the day."

"Thanks," she said, and stretched her shoulders, pushing against the saddle horn.

"Is that a partnership tat I see?" he asked, seeing the sketch on her wrist.

"Oh, shoot. I..."

He held up his left wrist and showed her a twisted rope design wrapping around it. "Seems strange to see so many popping up around campus—sort of a fad now. But we did some research when Katie asked about using them instead of rings. Katie worked with a lot of people from third-world countries and we found out they are actually a tribal custom originating in northeastern Africa and some countries in that area. Immigrants spread them and brought them and their meaning to America, and they were widely adopted by the less-fortunate people. Most likely a cost thing. So I agreed, sort of honoring a cross-culture, and we each got one. My folks won't understand them when they find out either."

"Really, Jackson? That's great. Is it anyone I know?"

He shook his head. "No. I met Katie in law school and I'm planning on breaking the news to the folks this week. We're hoping for a fall wedding. Do you have a date set?"

"No, not yet." She suddenly felt her cheeks warm. "Mom will die when she finds out he's not of her social ilk, nor does he fit her usual expectations."

"I know the feeling," he said, still smiling. "I'm happy for you, Billie. You always knew what you wanted and I hope you've found it."

"Thanks, Jackson. I hope so too."

"By the way, Billie, everyone calls me Jack. Just simple, plain Jack."

"Okay, Jack," she said, and smiled back. "Maybe we should head back and let our folks know I didn't shoot you on sight."

"Good idea," he said, and reined his mount around to give her room.

-¤-

The visiting before dinner was amenable and pleasant, and both of their mothers refrained from any remarks or gestures they could construe as matchmaking. Billie wondered if her dad had said something to them, but every time she looked at him, he was busy, deep in some discussion with Jack's father. She took the opportunity to visit with Jack and learn a little about him since he had gone off to grad school.

Finally, she asked, "Are you living in the city? Anywhere I might be familiar with?"

"In the 'burbs, out northeast," he answered. "It's not the best part of town, but Katie wants to be close to her mom. She's in bad health and lives alone. Katie's dad died when she was starting college. They had put enough money away for her to get her degree, but he didn't put enough back for themselves. He never expected to die or that her mother would be having a rough time. His small pension and social security aren't really enough."

"I'm sorry to hear that, Jack. Has Katie found work?"

"Yes. She got in with a medical support firm that places nurses in people's homes." He smiled. "It isn't the best pay, but it lets her get some care for her mother while she's helping a lot of underprivileged people. I graduate the end of the month and have a ground-level position with a law firm in the northwest part of the city. Once I'm settled in there, I'll be able to help her care for her mom."

"That's really nice," Billie said. "I hope everything works out for the both of you."

"What about your partner?" he asked, and Billie was about to answer when her mother interrupted and asked her to help bring the food to the table.

"Sorry," she said as she got up. "We'll continue later."

With the food placed, everyone took a seat around the table and Billie decided she did not mind sitting next to Jack. Then her mother glanced her way.

"Billie, please go wash. You have grease or something on your arm."

Billie glanced at Jack and chuckled. "It isn't grease, Mother, and it's clean," she said, and placed her napkin in her lap.

"What is it then?" her mother asked, and Billie saw her father's curious look.

"Well, Mother," she said, and held her arm out. "It's what I was going to tell you about in private earlier. It's a partnership chain."

"Is that a tattoo?" Maggie asked.

"Yes," she lied. "In many countries and in some parts of our own country, a ring on a woman is simply a treasure to be stolen. And a ring only shows you're spoken for, but not to whom. A partnership tat matches only one other tat. It shows *who* your partner is, not just that you have one."

She looked at her dad.

"Sooo...you're engaged?" Maggie asked softly.

"Yes, Mom." Billie was surprised at how nice it felt to say it out loud—out loud to herself and to her parents. To everyone. "It's...it's only our intentions right now. We haven't set a date," she said, trying to not sound too unfeeling, "but when we get married we will still exchange rings."

"I think it's cute," Jack's mother said, and smiled broadly. "I didn't realize what it meant, but Jack's been trying to hide his for weeks and weeks. Honestly, I don't understand why you young folks don't just tell things like they are, straight out."

Billie looked at Jack's stunned expression and started to laugh.

"I didn't think you and Dad would understand," Jack said, looking from one to the other.

"Katie Biggens? Right?" Jack's dad asked.

"Yes," he said slowly. "You remember her?"

"Of course," Jack's mother said. "Met her at the grad school open house. Cute girl. Very intelligent." Then she turned to Billie, glancing at Billie's mother. "Have your folks met your young man?"

"No. Not yet," Billie admitted as Jack passed the platter of ham. "I hope to remedy that very soon. He was tied up today and couldn't come with me."

"We'd love to meet him sometime," Jack's mother said, and took the bowl of vegetables passed to her.

-¤-

After Jack and his family had gone, Billie helped her mother put the leftover food away and rinse the dishes in preparation for the dishwasher.

"I'm sorry, Mom," Billie said as she rinsed the last of the plates. "I wanted to tell you, but the Markins drove up and you wanted me to wait and I got mad and...well, sorry. I should have told you anyway and not run off."

Billie's mother sighed and looked at her. "I thought you just broke up with your old boyfriend, what, a month ago? How long have you known this man you're suddenly engaged to?"

"Not...not very long," Billie said, hesitantly. "I dumped Blake over seven weeks ago—almost two months."

"You have not had very good luck with boyfriends," her mother said, and closed the dishwasher door. "And this one, you decide to marry?"

"I can't explain it well enough for you to understand, Mom," Billie continued. "But we hit it off right away. He's really nice."

"Does this 'really nice man' have a name?" her mother asked stiffly.

"Yes. Of course he does," Billie said, but held her temper as she heard the unmistakable tone in her mother's voice. "He's Billy Carson," she said, and wondered how she was going to describe him and his work as she finished wiping the counter and folded the towel.

"Carson? Bob, do we know any Carsons?" she asked.

Bob rubbed his chin as he stepped into the kitchen from the dining room. "I don't think so, Maggie. Is he from around here?"

"I don't know," Billie said, and turned to lean back against the counter. Then she looked at her mother. "Actually, Mom, you and Sandy did meet him—fifteen years ago when we stopped at the Streetcar Diner and someone spilled their soup and splashed it on my boot. He was the boy that cleaned my boot that day, and remembers that we had gone to the renaissance fair and then were going to the museums that afternoon."

"Fifteen years ago?" Maggie asked, and thought back.

"I remember going to the fair and the museum, but I don't remember how long ago that was, and I don't remember any boy."

"We ate lunch and someone dropped their soup bowl and it broke. Billy cleaned it up and wiped my boots off. You remember, don't you? I followed him around the diner and he put up with my silly questions. You'll remember if you think about it long enough."

"Maybe. I'll think about it and try to remember."

"So, this Billy is the same fellow?" her dad asked, and Billie told them about the repeat of the incident.

"You need to bring him out so we can meet him," her mother said. "We need to get to know him before you set a date."

"I know, Mom," Billie said, trying to keep her exasperation out of her voice. "I know. Like I said, he's very busy, but I will get him to make time."

"That will be nice," her dad said, and glanced at her mother.

"When he told me his parents had died," Billie explained, "I was surprised at how bad it made me feel. I felt like I did when you told me Willum wasn't going to come and visit anymore."

"I'm sorry, sweetheart," Bob said, and reached out to her. "Are you all right with it now?"

"Yeah," she said, and squeezed his hand. "But then I realized that you never told me how Willum, or his parents, died. Was I too young to know, or just too distraught?"

"You were very upset, Billie," Maggie said, and moved closer to her. "I had never seen you so upset, so inconsolable. We couldn't get you calmed down enough to tell you."

"And when you did finally calm down," Bob added, "any mention of the accident set you off again."

"Yeah, I remember." Billie sighed. "Can you tell me now? I promise I won't go running off wailing and lock myself in my bedroom."

Bob smiled. "We never got very many details—just what we got from the few articles that were in the newspapers." He gestured to the dining room. "Do you want to sit down?"

Billie shook her head. "No. I'm going to have to go in a few minutes, so I'll just stand."

"Okay. Well, like I said, there's not much to tell. I know you remember that weekend. You and Sandy and Willum spent all of your time riding and playing around the ranch, and it was late when they left."

Bob poured himself a small glass of water and leaned back against the kitchen counter, and Billie's mother hung her dishtowel on the rod on the side of the refrigerator.

"It was the next day when we heard. The police told the reporters that it appeared Willum's dad fell asleep and missed the curve at the Chestnut Creek Bridge where State Highway Forty-Seven crosses the creek."

Billie swallowed hard.

Shit. I cross that bridge every time I come out from the city and go back. Now I'll think of the wreck every time I cross it.

"Their car was badly damaged and caught fire," Bob continued. "Later the articles in the papers said the fire was so intense, it was hard to identify their bodies. The car's VIN was the only way they could tell the car was theirs, and there was so little left of them, they could only be identified by DNA tests."

"It was that bad?" Billie asked in a disbelieving whisper.

"Yes, honey," Maggie said softly. "It might have been a blessing that you were so distraught and we couldn't tell you what we found out. It was hard for us and Sandy too."

Billie wiped her eyes with the end of the towel she was still holding. Memories of Willum, their many times together, and how she had felt when they told her he had died threatened to overwhelm her again. She felt like her world was closing in around her once more.

"Thanks. I think." She took a deep breath. "I think I'll freshen up and get my coat. I need to start back."

"Are you going to be okay?" her dad asked, and caught her shoulder.

"Yeah. It'll just take a few minutes."

Billie forced a smile, then dropped the towel on the counter as she turned and walked through the living room to the hall bathroom. When she returned to the kitchen, slipping her coat on, she saw that her mother had a small sack of leftovers waiting for her.

"Has your Billy said how long it's been since he lost his parents?" Bob asked.

Billie shook her head. "Actually no, he hasn't. I gather it's been quite a while. He never speaks about them."

Billie glanced around the kitchen, making sure she had everything.

"Thanks for the leftovers, Mom," she said. "I'm off. Looks like it'll be dark before I get home."

She hugged her mom and dad then turned to the side door. "Take care, and I'll see you next week for Mother's Day."

"Drive carefully, Billie," her dad said, and they both stood in the doorway and watched her as she got into the SUV and pulled away.

Damn, Willum. Did you suffer? Were you awake when it happened? Oh God, I can't imagine what you must've gone through.

Billie tortured herself for nearly an hour and a half, worrying about what she imagined might have happened, what he might have felt, whether his death was quick or lingering. She had finally calmed her tears and her anxiety by the time she saw the old truss bridge ahead. The sight of it forced her to change her focus and she slowed, pulling off onto the shoulder.

She studied the slow left curve of the highway as it approached the bridge. Then she got out and walked to the abutment and looked more closely at the ditch. Her headlights shone across it and illuminated the trees on the far side that followed the ditch as it curved to the left, down to the lazily flowing water.

Billie looked back at the road, and without seeing anything obvious, she got back into the SUV thinking maybe he did just fall asleep. She pondered the possibilities concerning the accident the rest of her way home.

Twenty-Six

Her headlights flashed across the front of the parking garage when Billie turned the corner onto Cheyenne; Billy was sitting on the brick planter. She smiled at the plaid shirt, jeans, and the nicer-looking jacket, pleased to see him there and hoping he could lift her flagging spirits.

She pulled into the drive and lowered the passenger window as he stepped up beside the SUV.

"What're you doing here?" she asked, again repeating her greeting.

"Waiting for you," he said, and smiled. "May I talk to you for a little bit?"

"Sure," she said, motioning for him to get in as she punched the parking garage door remote. She pulled a tissue from the console compartment and quickly wiped her eyes, hoping he would not notice that she had been crying on the way home. She parked in her spot and walked him to the elevator.

"How was your visit with your folks?" he asked.

"Okay, I guess," she said. "Mom was her normal self, almost being too much 'mother' again."

Billie opened her apartment door, led him in, and thumbed the dead bolt behind them. She turned and hung her coat on a peg, and was about to ask for his when he hung it on the peg next to hers.

He turned her to him and looked at her face. "Your eyes are red. Why have you been crying? Is something wrong?" He held her shoulders gently in his hands and waited as she stared at the center of his chest.

"No," she said, and shook her head slowly. "I hoped you wouldn't notice, but it's just bad memories." She leaned into him and wrapped her arms around his waist. "I'm glad you're here and I don't have to think about them anymore today." She smiled as he slipped his arms around her and held her close, one hand firmly high on her back and the other just below her waist.

"What bad memories make you so upset that you cry about them?" he asked softly, his chin just brushing the top of her head. "Tell me so they won't bother you anymore."

"Why should I relive them when I have you to think about?"

"I don't know, but it seems you think about them instead."

She slowly nodded, her cheek still pressed firmly against his chest. "I guess I do." She sighed. "All right. When you told me about losing your parents, it reminded me of the death of my close friend when I was ten. I mentioned him before, but I did not elaborate. It's been too painful and the source of years of depression. After I met you again, the pain of that depression has slowly lessened and I've felt better than I have in many years.

"What distressed me was that I never heard what happened to him and his family, other than they died. I asked my dad about it this afternoon and they gave me the few details they know." Billie retold the details as she had heard them. "I was so shocked and overwhelmed that I cried over halfway home."

"So you still don't have enough details to help you put the remorse to bed? Is that what I'm hearing?"

"Probably. I know I was young when we knew each other, and I was young when he died, but he was all I could think about. When he was away, I thought about him, and when he was visiting, I could think of nothing else. I have probably over-embellished my feelings over the years, but his memories have been the only thing I had to brighten my depressing days since he died. His memory was my only source of happiness, and the cause of my depression." She inhaled. "Does that make sense?"

"Yes, in a way," he said, and squeezed her. "But maybe you should just go to the newspaper archives and the police archives and do the research you know how to do. Get the facts so you can stop speculating, so you can put those memories in the right place. So you can be happy with them and they won't depress you."

Billie squeezed him in return. "Okay."

"What else?"

"They saw the partnership chain and I told them what it means. I had to tell them to explain why I was wearing it. I couldn't lie about how I feel about you."

"I figured they would see it," he said softly. "Come with me." He led her into her kitchen, looking at the cabinets for a water glass.

"Left of the sink," she said as she pulled a towel from the rod by the refrigerator and wiped her eyes.

He filled a small glass and handed it to her as he slipped his other arm possessively across her shoulders. "Now tell me how the day went and what happened when they saw the tat," he said, and pulled her up in front of him.

He set her glass on the counter as she slowly explained what had happened from the time she got to her parents' house.

"I told Mom it was a tat because I had told Jack it was at the lake, and that meant they would think it's permanent. I couldn't tell them I had lied to Jack so I had to keep up the ruse."

"Let me try to help you with the ruse," he said.

She started to water up with concern and he daubed her eyes.

"Stretch probably told you," she said, "Lori and Becky noticed the chain, but they don't know what it means."

He nodded and cupped her face in his hands. "Stop talking a minute," he said, and kissed her tenderly, twice. "Now," he said softly, and gently kissed her once more, "go and wash that chain off and clean your wrist the best you can," he said, and gently turned her.

"But I don't want to take it off," she stammered as he pushed her toward the stairs.

"Sssh. Just go," he said. "Trust me."

She looked back at him and slowly trudged up the stairs. "What did I do to make you mad?"

"Just go and clean that scribble off your wrist," he said, and reluctantly she went to her dressing room and slathered a makeup remover over the chain.

"I don't want to take it off. This is making me cry all over again," she told him as the chain paled and tears refilled her eyes. When the remover had done as much as she could stand, she went to the sink and scrubbed the last vestiges of the chain from her skin. "Damn, Billy, I almost feel naked."

"Clean the skin but don't put any lotions or creams on it," he replied. "And please don't come down naked."

She dried her wrist and hands and came back down to her living room, but she found Billy in the kitchen heating a small pan of water.

"What are you doing?" she asked, and looked around him at the pan.

He smiled at her, pulled an envelope from his shirt pocket, and handed it to her. She looked up at him in question when she opened the envelope and took the seven narrow strips of paper out.

"What are these? They look like the chain you drew."

"They are a special temperature-activated wet transfer that won't wash off with water and soap, or any normal detergents. The transfer will normally last months—maybe even three or four—and when the design fades, we can reapply it. I have a special solvent that will remove them when that's necessary, or to help clean up in preparation for another application."

She smiled at him as he dropped one into the hot water and she watched it curl up and then slowly uncurl. "Where did you get these?"

"I have a friend that can make things like this for me," he said, but she watched him; there was more to the story than he was telling. "We trade favors. Ah, looks like this is about ready."

He took the towel she had used earlier and laid it on the counter. "Put your arm on the towel, hand palm down." He lifted the transfer out of the water with a fork and let it cool a minute before he gently positioned it across the back of her wrist. She watched closely as he gently wrapped it around and trimmed the ends to just meet.

Then he tore a paper towel square off its roll and gently pressed the transfer against her skin, slowly drying the paper as he went around her wrist. After diligently working the entire length of the transfer, he turned her hand over and slowly began pulling the paper away. She smiled at the crisp, clean chain design wrapping completely around her wrist as he dropped the paper strip in the trash.

"It looks like a real tat," she said, and twisted her wrist to admire the design. "Did you draw this one too?"

"Certainly," he said, and smiled. "You don't think I'm going to let anyone else ink my Tiger, do you?"

"Your Tiger?" she asked, suddenly looking up into his wide smile. "Like, Keeper and *his* Tiger?"

He nodded and she smiled.

"*My* Tiger," he repeated, and held his wrist, with a matching crisp, clean chain, beside hers. "And *her* Keeper. Now they won't come off or blur when we wash or get sweaty."

"Sweaty?" she asked, and looked at him again.

"My Tiger will get very sweaty in her training," he said. "What nights can you be free?"

"Really?" she asked, her voice pitched with elation as she slipped her arms around his neck again, holding his eyes. "It's okay with the others?"

"Yes it is." He pulled her up in his embrace and kissed her. "They all want to be there to meet you, so I have to tell them ahead of time when you're going to come."

She thought about her schedule for a minute. "The girls will be upset, but I can make excuses and miss Mondays, and I'm usually free Tuesdays and Thursdays, and I may be able to make Saturdays and Sundays available. If I completely stop meeting with them, it'll run up a flag."

"You usually meet them on Monday, Wednesday, Friday,

and Saturday nights. Right?"

"Yeah, but not tomorrow if we can start."

"Then we'll start tomorrow. Skip your meeting and then we'll plan on Tuesday and Thursday. We'll see how your Wednesdays and Fridays work with your friends. Saturdays can be mornings."

"Okay. But do I still get more Saturday afternoons in the Forest?" Billie asked, and he nodded as she led him back to the sofa, sat down, and looked up at him. "Now, what can Tiger do for *her* Keeper?"

"Tonight," he sighed, "*your* Keeper has to make another check of the alleys, a pass through the village, and I must try to get some sleep before another very early start to a hopefully better day."

She took his hand as he reached out and pulled her to him.

"You've brought a light into my life," Billy admitted, "that I hadn't expected to ever see again, and I want to thank you for it. But now I have to slip away and let you have what little of your day is left to you. Walk me out? Before I change my mind and do something we might regret?"

She embraced him tightly, then reluctantly let him go. "Okay, Billy. I don't want you to regret anything we do together."

She took his jacket from the peg and handed it to him. Then she threw hers on as they left the apartment and she locked the door.

"Oh, I forgot to mention that since I told my folks we are engaged, Mom went into her protection mode, like she did when I was in high school. She thinks that since we haven't known each other very long, we're rushing the engagement thing. I told her it was just our intentions right now, but she's in her 'I want to meet him' mode." Billie smiled and looked away for a second. "I will have to take you to meet them, unless we have a big falling out or something."

"I figured that would happen," Billy said, and took her hand. "We'll just have to figure out when we might be able to do that."

"You don't mind?"

"I'd rather spend my time with you, but I will have to meet your parents sometime. Even if we have a big falling out."

She happily held his hand as the elevator descended, pleased that he was amenable.

In the parking garage, he turned, pulled her up, and kissed her again. "Thank you, Billie. Bring sweats and your frumpy clothes. See you in the Forest. You can change in the restrooms there. Six-thirty."

"I hope we can find somewhere warmer to change soon," she admitted, and kissed him before he let her back down on her feet. "Six-thirty."

She let him out through the turnstile, and when he had disappeared into the shadows across the street, she hurried back to her apartment.

-¤-

Billie poured Chardonnay into a stemless wine glass and settled on the three-section sofa with her digital notepad. She smiled and looked at her wrist again.

I was so afraid I had done something to make him mad, but I don't think this is a ruse anymore. A new 'tat'—and he wouldn't have named me 'Tiger' if this wasn't real.

She slowly relaxed, and after a few minutes she thought about his suggestion that she just research Willum's accident and see what she could find out. She had been afraid to look before, but now it made sense that she did.

She flipped the pad's cover open, connected to the internet, and selected the *Beacon's* website. She sipped her wine as the link connected and the newspaper's home page blinked open.

Setting her wine glass aside, Billie toggled for past news articles and entered 'automobile accidents' as a search category. The second search level asked for a range of dates, and after a moment of thinking, she typed a bracket in the search box.

It seemed to take forever before a message popped on

screen noting that her selected range was farther back than the online archives could search. The message directed her to the newspaper's information desk, gave the days and hours they were open, and thanked her for letting the *Beacon* serve her.

Not much service, she said to herself and smiled. *Why did I think they would have ancient history from the dark ages online?* She shook her head, went to the *Herald's* home page, and repeated her request, only to receive a similar reply.

Disappointed, she closed the pad and shut it off, gathered up her wine glass, turned out all of the lights, and went up to her bedroom. She washed and got herself ready for bed, and then sat down cross-legged in the center of her bed. With her wine in hand, she studied the city center buildings and the soft beauty of the city lights.

She was suddenly uneasy, relishing the darkness, the security of her apartment, the comfort of her warm bed in contrast to the very real possibilities Billy faced every night while she slept, like he was now, watching and waiting with the others. Remembering the confrontation with the drug dealers in the village, she worried that Billy might have to face their dangers alone.

Wait a minute. If I hadn't been with you last Wednesday... would you have faced Pink and the others alone? Yes, you would have, unless one of the other men were available.

She took another sip of her wine and sighed.

Well, once you've taught me what I need to know, you won't ever have to face them alone. I'll learn and be the best I can, and that's a promise. I'll always be there to help you.

With a very determined heart, she slid into bed, pulled her pillow up tight in front of her, and prayed for Billy's safety. At least until she was able to help him.

Twenty-Seven

Monday, May 2

Billie ran into a wall of tension when she entered the Boster, Lange and Hammersmith Design offices and, suddenly reluctant, forced herself past the receptionist's desk with a questioning glance. The receptionist shook her head and took a call as Billie followed the right aisle around the central cubicles and entered her office. She hung her jacket on the coatrack behind her door and settled into her chair.

What is going on? She, switched her computer on, and was opening her file drawer when she saw Mr. Boster open his office. He glanced at her, nodded a 'good morning,' and went in.

With the tension permeating the office, Billie remembered her own tense concerns when Billy had told her about the homeless man that said Hammersmith had paid him to kill Billy's parents. Her mind conjured an image of a forlorn homeless man kneeling in a dim alley among the trash bags and dumpsters, with money falling out of his pockets. His expression was a conflict of emotions, from deep contrition for what he had done to earn the money to the unfamiliar elation of suddenly having more money than he knew what to do with. She knew she could never look at Mr. Hammersmith again without thinking that he was someone that would actually pay someone to kill someone else.

They're called 'contracts.'

Billie pulled the project file for her latest assignment from the drawer, laid it on her desk, and opened the folder. She tried to push her thoughts about Hammersmith out of her mind, concentrating instead on better memories as the images of the previous day raced through her mind and slowly came to a stop with her repeated fantasies of possible nights with Billy.

Stop that! Don't count your chickens yet. He hasn't actually asked you to marry him, has he?

No, but wait and see. I expect to have many wonderful nights and days with Billy. Sometime. And maybe he will ask me. Sometime.

She just had to bide her time, learn what he would teach her, and help him with whatever he needed to finish—whatever it was that kept him so preoccupied. After all, he had accepted her offer to help and had named her his Tiger. She smiled, and in a better mood, turned her focus to the folder in front of her.

Almost two hours later, she found an unintelligible phrase in the park project data and stopped to ask Mr. Boster about it.

"It's this one," she said, pointing to the handwritten notes. "I can't make out what's written."

"Oh," he said with a smile, "that's 'ground cover.' It's a new, fire-resistant fiber product."

"Thanks." She smiled and took the folder back. She hesitated before she turned to leave. "Mr. Boster?" she asked. "If I may ask, why is everyone so tense? Everything feels like something's wrong this morning."

He looked up at her concerned expression. "Yes, I guess everyone is feeling it," he said, and his face turned solemn. "The Duckard's Project is on hold, probably canceled."

"Oh, my," she said, sincerely surprised. "That was such a big project. I know you were all looking forward to that one."

"Yes, yes we were," he said. "It seems that ownership glitch you found and pointed out was more of an issue than any of us suspected. Mike says Westman Associates tried to hide the fact that they couldn't secure the properties, and now their window of opportunity has passed—and unless Westman can pull a rabbit out of his hat, the contracts will default."

"I'm so sorry for all of you," she said, and turned to the door.

"Keep your head down, Billie, and keep up the good work," Carl said, stopping her in the doorway. "This will likely affect us all."

She nodded, and decided she needed a cup of tea—strong tea.

Mr. Lange was pouring himself a cup of coffee when she stepped in. "Morning, sir."

"Morning, Billie," he said, and stepped aside to the creamers.

Billie took a cup and poured hot water over two teabags. She was about to leave when he stopped her.

"Did you get a tattoo, Billie?" he asked, pointing to her wrist.

"Yes, sir," she said, smiling. "I got engaged."

He looked at the door and then said softly, "Congratulations, but *do not* let Mr. Hammersmith see that."

"Sir?" she asked, confused. "What—?"

"Just don't, Billie," Robert repeated. "On his best days he does not like tattoos of any kind. He says they remind him of the 'street people' and their deplorable habits, hygiene, and there's something else he always adds that I can't remember. Anyway, as upset as he is today, please don't go anywhere near him. At least for a week or so."

"Oookay," she said, and nodded. "I'll do my best."

"Do better than that," he said with a smile. "Be gone if he should ask or look for you for any reason. I'd hate to lose you due to one of his irrational fits of rage and bad temper. You're an asset here, and I hope we can weather the storm that's coming."

"I don't understand. You're a partner. You'll do fine, I'm sure," she said firmly, as much for herself as for him.

"Thank you, Billie." He smiled again. "But one never knows how Mr. Hammersmith will react to situations like this. Now off with you—get back to your details and keep us out of hot water."

"Yes, sir," she said, and turned, "but I didn't do so well on that ownership issue."

"You pointed it out," he said, and pushed her toward the door. "That was exactly what you were supposed to do."

▯-▯-▯-▯-▯

Wearing his usual white work pants and shirt, Billy was waiting in the little West Side Coffee Shop, enjoying the view of the river, when Walter Gibson entered and stopped beside the tall table where Billy sat.

"Morning, Billy," Walter greeted, and hung his long coat on the back of the chair opposite Billy. He went to the counter and ordered a coffee, and returned to the table and sat down.

"Glad you got my message," Billy said, and took a bite of his bagel. "How's the law 'business' going?"

"Very good. So, what's going on with you?" Walter asked. "I haven't heard from you since sometime in November, I think."

"Personal life is starting to look up," Billy said, and smiled. "But why I called is about a potential issue with the city center blocks. I figured out who's been trying to purchase the Duckard block."

"When I got your message," Walter said, "I ran a check on projects listed with the city, and believe it or not, that one fell through. Canceled Friday, late."

"Yes. That's because they couldn't buy it," Billy said, still serious. "That's why I called you. You and I both know there wasn't any way anyone could buy it, but I put out the bait. Things have been quiet too long, and I was tired of waiting, so in December, just before Christmas, I had a false posting run, showing the Duckard Property in arrears. And from what I found out, Westman fronted Hammersmith and made an Offer to Pay. And now, since the purchase has fallen through, and I've aroused Hammersmith's interest again, I think he'll try something underhanded."

"What do you suspect, Billy?"

"I'm seeing a push to move at least three drug dealers into the area, and I'm certain it's all connected." Billy sipped his coffee. "How difficult would it be for Hammersmith to move some undesirables in and then go to the city and condemn the properties, claiming vagrants and druggies have taken over?"

"He could get away with it," Walter said. "It really wouldn't take much if the city sent someone to check and they found dealers or vagrants just hanging around there. They wouldn't have to actually see a dealer selling anything. You remember he tried that about a year after your folks died?"

"Yeah. We were lucky the city didn't find anything to support his claims. You know everyone that lives there and in the village are clean and have jobs," he said, and Walter nodded. "So we have to keep our yard clean. Somehow, however we can. Is that it?"

"That's about the size of it, Billy," Walter said. "As long as those properties lay dormant, there will be more Hammersmiths and Westmans trying to take them for their own purposes."

Billy set his cup down and thought about Walter's words. "I think you just gave me an idea. Who was that architect that Dad always used? The one in Chicago?"

Walter smiled. "That would certainly change things. I'll give them a call, Billy, as soon as I get back to the office."

◻-◻-◻-◻-◻

"Betty!" Mike Hammersmith shouted into the intercom. "Get Frederick on the phone."

"Calm down, Mike," Robert said as Mike stood back up and paced. "The default clause will cover any losses you might have incurred. And he probably will have to stop one or two of his other projects to pull everything together."

"You don't understand, Robert," Mike said as he continued to pace. "Ruining Frederick isn't what's at stake here. I've been after that property for nearly twenty years, and now, because of him and his over-anxiousness, my reputation is again up for questions."

"You sure you weren't a little over-anxious yourself?" Robert asked, and glanced up at him. "And I don't believe your reputation has been blemished."

"Maybe I was a little over-anxious. But when he called, I checked the tax rolls myself and there it was! A posting for unpaid taxes!" Mike continued to pace. "Unpaid taxes are the only way that property could be bought, but I made arrangements in case he failed..."

"Oh?" Mike had Robert's undivided attention.

"Let me just say the city will not allow the street people to continue marring the city's downtown beauty." Mike turned to Robert, his smile devious. "If I can't buy it or have it bought, I have other ways to get it."

"Why are you so adamant about that piece of property?"

"It's a long story, Robert," Mike said, and stopped for a moment to look at him. "Hawke bought it out from under me nearly twenty-two years ago, and then I heard whispers that he was going to sell it three or four years later, but when I tried to get my hands on it, I found out he had sold it quietly under the table to some holding group I've never heard of. I've tried for years to find out who they are and discuss the properties, but nothing. No one has heard of them. But when we check the titles, two more unknowns show up. I'm not sure who the actual owners are."

"So you think you can cause the land to be condemned and sold at auction?"

"Very possibly," he said, and turned to the intercom and hit the call button again. "Betty! Where's my call?"

"There's no answer, sir. I'm still trying," Betty's voice said.

Twenty-Eight

Billie entered the public restrooms, recognizing the disheveled-looking man reclining under the low boughs of the tree in the northeast corner of the park. When she came out, changed into the woman of meager means with a backpack, she was not surprised Billy had moved and was standing beside the door, waiting for her. She smiled at him as he turned them toward St. Charles Street, noticing when he waved to the woman with the flowers across the street.

"I should introduce you to Maxie sometime," Billy said as they turned down the sidewalk. "She gets the best flowers and always has something special for Mary."

"How's Mary doing?" Billie asked when they crossed Fifth Street West. "I got the feeling from Angie and Julie that she wasn't doing very well."

Billy sighed heavily. "She isn't, but she keeps pushing herself."

"What's wrong?"

"Started as a slow-growing form of Leukemia," he said softly. "She's had it for most of her adult life, but in the past six or eight years, it's been getting worse. These past six months have been the worst."

"I'm sorry, Billy. I know this has to be hard on you."

He forced a smile and caught her hand. "Worse for Sid. He'll be lost without her."

They walked on in silence until they turned a corner and she saw the department store.

"I know this place," she said, and looked at Billy.

"Sure, it's where we met Pink," he said.

"No. I mean I 'know' this place. It's the project I've been

working on," she said, and then turned to him. "Well, *was* working on. Someone called Westman Associated defaulted on it Friday, and the project is all but dead."

"It's the one we talked about," he said, half out loud.

"Yeah."

Without releasing her hand, he led her across the street, down the narrow passage along the south side of the department store, and around the corner into the main alley between the two buildings. She recognized the large dumpster and remembered the large dark shadow they had skirted. Billy stopped at a heavy metal door and took a key out of his boot, quickly unlocked the door, and pushed her in.

Once inside, she looked down the wide staircase as Billy locked the door behind them. "This way to a new adventure, Tiger," he said as he took her hand again and led her down the dim stairwell.

Billie's mouth dropped open when they stopped at the entrance to the huge, dimly lit room, clean and empty except for the number of support pillars arrayed in multiple rows. He gestured to the space as he swung the heavy handle on a breaker panel just past the doorway and a number of overhead lights flickered on.

"Biillyy," a young blond girl squealed as she ran from a room opposite them and collided forcefully with Billy's legs. "Is this your Tiger?"

"Yes, Abby," he said, crouching down beside the girl and smiling up at Billie. "I'd like you to meet Billie, my Tiger. Billie, this is Abby, our seven-year-old wonder."

Billie bent down and extended her hand. "It's very nice to meet you, Abby,"

"Me too," she said, and turned to look back at the room as a number of people came out of the wide doorway in the opposite wall and slowly crossed the room. "Ma, look. It's Billy's Tiger!" Abby shouted, and ran to a woman just walking into the room.

Billy gestured for everyone to crowd around, and he started

making introductions.

"Everyone, this is Billie, known as Tiger," Billy said, and everyone responded with a cheerful "hello." Then Billy turned Billie to face Stretch.

"This is Max. You've seen him around and know we call him Stretch," Billy said, and Max shook her hand. "And his wife Mindy, known as 'Cat.'"

Billie recognized her as the woman she had seen at the soup kitchen.

"And this is Russell and his wife Barbara, and their son Ernest. Russel is called 'Mace' and Barbara is 'Pigeon.'"

"Nice to meet you," Billie said softly, and shook their hands.

"Next is Todd, and Abby's mom Cathy," Billy said as they extended their hands and Billie shook them. "Todd is known as 'Hammer' and Cathy goes by 'Lynx.'"

She's the one that came and got Billy from the diner.

"This is Paul, called 'Ferret,' and his wife Donna, known as 'Mouse,' and their son Richard," Billy said as Billie continued to shake hands.

"Buddy and Jane, known as 'Falcon' and 'Sparrow,' and their son Rusty. Then next is Curt and Judy, 'Cutter' and 'Owl.' They are the oldest in the group, and the first two I sort of met when I first got to the city." Billy chuckled without explaining further, and turned to three younger men standing behind Cutter.

"These guys are the other singles in the group: Josh, known as 'Red,' Randal, known as 'Spear.' and Junior, known as 'Ditto.'"

Billie acknowledged each one again and thanked them for letting her come. Abby stepped up, nudging Billie, and proudly pointed out that she was the oldest of the kids by a year.

When everyone had exchanged greetings, Mindy grabbed Billy's arm and pointed to the two large rolls next to one wall of the big room. "Wiley and Buddy hauled those in about two this morning—said you wanted them delivered before it got light."

"Thanks, Cat," he said, and looked at Max. "Give a hand, will ya, Stretch?"

Billy led the men toward the rolls and Billie, recognizing the rolls, dropped her coat by the doorway and hurried to catch up. She grabbed a corner and pulled along with the rest of them as they unrolled the large wrestling mats and moved them to the middle of the room between four of the support pillars.

Once arranged, Billy asked every one that wanted to watch to sit down around the mats, and Billie looked at him.

"I'm to have an audience?"

"That's the way it works." He smiled. "All of the adults here have had some defense training and fighting experience. The kids are starting. We're all here to help you learn, and criticism will only be constructive."

"Sure," she said, shaking her head and smiling at him. "Okay? Where do we start?"

"Did you bring your sweats?"

"Silly question," she said, and pulled her sweater off over her head and then stepped out of her worn jeans. "They help keep me warm."

He smiled as her sweats top tried to follow the sweater, briefly baring her slender midriff before gently settling back into place.

"Nice," Billy said, and she knew he was thinking of more than the sweats actually allowed him to see. She smiled as he stepped out of his boots, pulled his sweater off as well, stepped out of his frumpy pants, and tossed them against the wall beside hers. In a T-shirt and sweat shorts, he went to the center of the mats and motioned to her to follow.

"We'll start with Knife's reach across the table, like he tried at the kitchen," Billy said, and began by showing her how to evade someone's grabbing and how to unbalance whomever was doing it.

They repeated the moves from various starting positions, each one giving Billie the edge as quickly as possible. They rehearsed the moves until she seemed to be getting them. Then Billy stood up and looked at those around the mats.

"Mace, your turn," he said, and stepped to one side. He

looked at Billie. "I want to see how you react when you can't see your attacker coming."

She watched the taller Russell, easily outweighing her by a hundred pounds, step onto the mats.

Oh shit!

I told you this was not a good idea.

I...have to learn somehow. So be quiet.

"The point of these rounds is to go for the 'kill,' to keep from being pinned on the mat and 'killed' by your opponent." Billy took her to the middle of the mat and she watched him step back, just out of her reach. He looked her in the eyes, keeping her attention on him.

Russell sprang from the side, and when she felt his hand touch her, she froze. He grabbed her, wrapping his arms around her, and rolled sideways onto the mat. When they stopped and she was not resisting, he released her and helped her up. Russell looked at Billy and cocked his head.

"Tiger?" Billy asked softly as he stepped up to her. "When you were a kid, did you ever wrestle with your friend, the one you told me about?"

Slowly she nodded. "Yes."

"Just do like you did then. It's wrestling, but you're supposed to come out on top. Did you ever win as a kid?"

Billie smiled a wide smile, remembering the many times she had come out on top, and only coming out on the bottom when her girly side wanted him on top. She nodded.

"Then let's try it once more," Billy said, and led her back to the center of the mat.

Russel sprang from a different position, and when Billie felt his hand touch her, she ducked in reflex and came up under him, flipping him neatly over and onto his back. She was down on top of him with her knee planted firmly in his groin, her right fist solidly against his neck before his head stopped bouncing.

Billie hesitated, disbelieving that she had just done what she had done. She looked at Billy and saw him smile and nod, and then she sighed, relaxed her rigid stance, and helped a wide-eyed Russell to his feet. Before she could ask if she did all right, Billy said, "Lynx, next." And once again, he positioned her in the middle of the mat and held her attention.

Cathy came straight from behind, hand high, and when Billie sensed Cathy's hand beside her head in mid-grab, she caught Cathy's wrist, spun, and let their weight carry them both to the mat with her on top and her open hand on Cathy's chest, holding her to the mat.

Again, she saw Billy smile as she helped Cathy up. "Are you okay?" Billie asked.

Cathy smiled and nodded.

"Hammer," Billy said, and moved back to the middle of the mat.

She stopped and faced Billy, focusing on his face, his strong, muscular form in the short-sleeved undershirt and sweat shorts, crouched and watching her. He definitely had her attention.

But when she sensed Todd's movement, she spun and pushed him sideways. They both landed on the mat, and she rolled away from him as quickly as she could.

"Tiger." Billy smiled as he helped her up. "Ever ridden a horse?"

She nodded.

"Ridden bareback?"

She nodded again, and he gestured to Hammer as he led her back to the center of the mat.

"Again," he said, and Hammer took another starting position.

This time, when she sensed Todd's movement, she reacted in a blur. She spun and caught Todd's arm and jerked him forward, sweeping his legs out from under him. She leapt in a roll as he fell, seeming to be on his back before he hit the mat.

She pushed herself up and extended her hand as he rolled over and looked at her.

"What in hell did you do?"

"Sorry, Hammer. Are you all right?"

He nodded and she helped pull him up. She turned to a smiling Billy.

"Sit down for a minute, Tiger," Billy said, and held her hands as she crossed her legs and settled onto the mat. "Abby, will you get Tiger a cup of cool water, please?"

Abby was off like a shot, and Billy went over to talk quietly with Russell, Todd, and Cathy.

-¤-

"Where in hell did you find her?" Cathy asked in a whisper. "I swear she knew where I was before I got to her."

"Why did you tell us you haven't been training her?" Russell questioned. "I understand being off the first time, but I've never been surprised in a fight before, but that...that..." He shook his head slightly. "That is a something else."

"Yeah, she is," Billy said softly. "No previous training, Russell. Just Wednesday night and now. She obviously learns very quickly."

"I think you named her well, Billy," Cathy said. "She is a tiger."

Todd nodded. "But can she go through with it if she actually has to cut someone?"

"None of us know if we can until that time comes," Billy said. "But if I were a betting man, I'm betting she would."

-¤-

Abby was back and knelt down beside Billie, watching her while she sipped the water.

"You're pretty good," Abby said. "My mom's the best woman street fighter they've ever had around here. Billy said so once."

"I'm sure you're very proud of her," Billie said.

"Yeah. We all are, but I sure wish we didn't have to fight so much to stay here. We have permus...per..."

211

"Permission?"

"Yup. The owners let us stay here. That's how come we all got keys."

"I see," Billie said, and glanced at the huddled four. "Am I being discussed?"

"Yup. They're taking your measure," Abby continued.

"My measure?"

"Yup. Every little while, the old guys—moms and dads and the other guys—practice, and then they discuss what they did wrong. Measuring each other."

"I see," Billie said as she finished the water and saw Billy turn and start walking back to her. "Thank you, Abby. For the water and the conversation."

"Sure," Abby said, then took the cup and hurried back to her mom.

"Okay, one more lesson before we clean up and head out for the kitchen," Billy said as he took her hands and pulled her up. "Remember what I did when we faced Pink? The crouch, balancing on the balls of my feet? The knife in my right hand?"

She nodded and watched as he handed her a wood dowel about the length of the knife he had given her. She noticed he had one about the length of his knife in his right hand.

"What I know that you didn't was that Pink is right-handed. If he had drawn a knife, he would have had it in his right hand, so I put mine in my right hand." He looked at her. "Always start with your knife in the same hand as your opponent. If your opponent is left-handed, you need to be left-handed." Billy quickly shifted his dowel to his left hand. "Can you use your left hand as well as you do your right?"

"No," she admitted, "but I'll learn how too."

Billy smiled at her and nodded.

"Second," he said, and lowered himself into the same crouch they had used, "always move toward your opponent's knife hand. He can't make as strong of a swipe if you're on his knife side, even if he tries a backhand. His swipe will be shorter, less powerful, while your swipe will have full reach, from your

212

side…" She watched as he demonstrated the movement and touched the center of her chest with the dowel. "…to his body, or wherever you're aiming for. He'll be trying to do the same.

"Remember his lunge? He wasn't expecting both of us to lunge in response. That's where your dance and drama classes give you a real advantage. We were in sync, and he quickly felt you were not an amateur. But now he will expect more, so I'm going to show you how to follow through. Okay?"

She inhaled and nodded.

"Face me," Billy said, and lowered into his crouch. "Balance—always float on the balls of your feet."

She followed him as he moved closer to her right hand and she challenged his stance, crowding his knife hand, then he quickly switched the dowel hand and started back. She switched with him and crowded his knife hand again. But when Billy lunged, she hesitated, stepped back, and feigned to one side.

"Think of it as a stick," he said offhandedly, and she suddenly remembered "sword-fighting" Willum with sticks when they were kids. She smiled, also remembering how she always won as she settled back into her crouch.

When Billy repeated his lunge, she mimicked him with incredible quickness and Billy had to block her with his free hand. The second time she didn't fall for it, and changed her timing when he lunged, touching his chest with the tip of her dowel.

Billy stood up and smiled down at her. Then he dropped back into the fight and she followed as he quickened his pace, lunged and retreated, and then slowed the pace, changing his timing, and each time, she felt the tip of her dowel touch his chest. But four out of five times, he touched her chest with his. She knew she was surprising him, but he stayed focused and kept adjusting his attack, giving her the opportunities to learn.

He suddenly lunged to one side and caught her knife arm, and she almost missed the change. He fell back, trying to pull her down on top of him, but she pushed herself up with her legs and flipped over him. He rolled and stood up, but she was already behind him and caught him with her arm around his neck.

She smiled. "I think I gotcha."

He slowly turned and faced her with the biggest smile she had ever seen from him.

"That was incredible," he said, and hugged her, pulling her up off the floor until she was looking down at him, both of them slowly turning in one place on the mat. "How did you ever come up with that?"

"Dance class, tumbling," she said as he turned her toward the others and lowered her to stand on the mat. He slipped his arm around her shoulders and she smiled, glancing up at him.

"Enough for tonight," he said. "We have about a half an hour to get to the kitchen. Why don't you go wash up and get dressed again. Lynx? Can you be here tomorrow to work with Tiger on defense?"

Cathy nodded with a smile.

-¤-

"I've never seen anyone like her," Barbara said when Billie disappeared into the bathroom with Abby close on her heels. "If you haven't been teaching her any of this before today, I'd say you might have a prodigy."

"She is quick," Cathy said, and smiled at Billy. "She was onto everything you tried, almost before you tried it."

"Thanks for the help," Billy said. "I know she looks like she's done this a hundred times, but she's never had to fight for her turf, so be patient and be critical when you see something that needs to be worked on. This is real important."

"We'll help all we can, Keeper," Russell said, "but you'd better go get cleaned up and dressed yourself."

Twenty Nine

Billie saw Knife enter the serving line and was pleased when he took his bread and fruit and paid her scant attention. Billie felt a difference in the air of the kitchen, wondering if it was because she had done the routines before or maybe because word of Wednesday night had made the rounds. She tried to not concern herself with the why, and was simply pleasant and did her job. Most of the people nodded and gave her a tight smile, while a few quietly took their portion and went off to find a quiet spot to eat.

At eleven, Randy closed the kitchen and Billy led her back toward the city center. As they walked, she noticed he kept glancing around and occasionally looking back behind them.

"Are you expecting something to happen?" she asked as she kept pace with his long strides.

"Always, Billie," he said, and continued looking as they walked. "That's something else you need to practice. Today when you knew something was going to happen, you were very quick to sense it, see it, and respond to that sensation. But at times like this, it's just as important to sense what's around you. Watch for the unexpected, feel for it and expect it. You can't guess correctly all of the time, but you have to be very alert, wary, anticipating that someone is listening, following, or maybe getting ready to do something."

Sounds a lot like paranoia.

They walked a little farther before she spoke.

"Sometimes I can sense things, a little more than just feeling tension like when you walk into a room full of nervous people." She turned and watched a person walking the other way on the opposite side of the street. "But this is so new to me. I've never faced anything like this before and it still scares me a little."

215

"Sure you still want to help?" he asked, and smiled at her. "It might be a lot easier if you went back home and forgot all about me and this mess."

"I don't think I can do that now," she admitted. "Not after meeting you again. Not after finally getting to know you a little and what you stand for. Not after our time together and facing Pink in the alley and Knife in the kitchen." They stopped at the street corner and she looked up at him. "And especially not after getting engaged to you. I have never dreamed of doing the things I'm doing now. Frankly, Billy, you're taking me places I've never been before, making me feel things I've never felt before, helping me believe in myself again."

"You do realize that what I'm showing you in your training isn't just new dance steps?" he asked as they crossed Main Street to the block of buildings east of the department store.

"Yes, I realize that, Billy," she said. "I admit the new moves, the sensations, and the responses are exhilarating, but I know this is for real. And I need this, more than you can possibly know."

"Good," he said, and smiled at her.

"Billy?" she asked as a thought crossed her mind. "If Hammersmith had've gotten the project to renovate the department store, what would've happened to everyone? Those that live in the basement?"

Billy shrugged. "We've been talking about that, but we would obviously have to move. Maybe back to the village. We don't know yet."

"That would be hard," she said softly. "Moving from a place inside, out of the weather, back into the elements. I sure hope you can figure out something better than that."

She looked at him and saw his agreeing smile. "Let's make a walk through the alleys before we go and get you cleaned up."

She followed him, and after a long moment, asked, "Are you ever afraid? Fearful of what might happen if something goes wrong?"

Billy stopped and looked at her. "I never had time to be

afraid, Billie. I've had to act and keep acting, no matter what, to do what I needed to do. Then I met you again, and now, sometimes I am. Mostly I'm afraid of missing something, not training you good enough and you getting hurt."

She looked deep into his eyes for a moment, smiled, and then hugged him as tightly as she could. "Thank you, Keeper. I'll try to listen, learn, and not get hurt."

Tuesday, May 3

Billy and Ned were finishing a table about mid-morning, resetting the napkins and shakers, when Billy looked up and saw the clock over the long counter.

"Ned?" Billy asked. "Can you finish this up? I need to speak to Sid."

"Sure, Billy," Ned said, and continued wiping the chairs.

Billy carried his tub into the kitchen and set it on the dishwasher counter. He turned to Sid. "May I use your office to make that call we talked about?"

"Of course, Billy," Sid said. "You don't have to ask every time you need to use the computer or make a call."

Billy smiled and raised his eyebrows. "Yes, I do, Sid. I'm just a lowly employee, remember? Thanks."

Billy hurried into the office and closed the door behind him. Then he reached up on the shelf and slipped a small-format, thin book out from under a stack of empty CD cases. He flipped the pages and fingered an unidentified phone number in the midst of a column of similar numbers.

He picked up the phone, selected the seldom-used Line 3, and dialed the number.

The phone rang twice and a pleasant woman's recorded voice answered. "Camelot Enterprises. How may I direct your call?"

"Greg Madison, Pastoric, please," Billy said.

"One moment," the woman's voice said, and the connection rang again.

"Greg Madison's office," another synthesized woman's voice said.

"Greg Madison, please."

"Mr. Madison is presently in a meeting. May I have a number so he can return your call?"

"Please tell Greg this is *Dog's Breath*," Billy said, and continued, delivering his specifically worded phrases in a monotone voice. "He has just finished his weekly, private call to John Collier at Circular Reference. He is now available."

"One moment," the woman's voice said, and the line switched to hold.

After a moment, a man answered. "This is Greg Madison. How may I help you?"

"Security phrase, *Cinderella's Mice*," Billy said.

"Billy?" Greg asked, his voice filled with surprise.

"Hello, Greg," Billy said softly.

"My goodness. It's certainly good to hear your voice again," Greg said, his voice full of sincerity and pleasure. "What can I do for you, sir?"

"It's good to hear you as well," Billy admitted, and he explained the current situation with the city center properties. "I want to up the ante, Greg."

"Do you think you have him?" Greg asked, hesitant.

"Getting closer, but I need to push him a little more," Billy said. "A personal push."

"What do you need us to do?"

"You have access to a listing of all of the design and remodeling firms in and around Chesterfield," Billy said.

"Yes, sir. We do."

"I need email addresses for a couple of those companies," Billy said. "And I need the personal emails for their owners and partners. Not just the company emails, but their personal email addresses. Can you get those?"

"I believe so," Greg said. "Which individuals in particular?"

"Obviously Mike Hammersmith, then Carl Boster, Robert Lange, and Frederick Westman, just in case," Billy said.

"Aaah. Of course," Greg said. "How soon do you need them?"

"The sooner the better," Billy said, and smiled to himself. "Tomorrow, if possible. Thursday at the latest. I think things are going to start unraveling very soon, and I need to be ready."

"Yes, sir," Greg said. "I'll put them in your secure FTP site as soon as they are ready. Tonight if possible. Tomorrow night at the latest."

"Thank you, Greg," Billy said.

"Do you still have the FTP site access phrases and codes?"

"Yes," Billy said. "Leave your standard announcement as a message on this number when the information is loaded. No one will answer."

"I understand. Standard announcement," Greg said formally. "It really is good to hear you, sir. Let me know if there is anything more you need."

"Thank you, Greg. I will. Goodbye."

"Goodbye, sir," Greg said, and the line disconnected.

Slowly, Billy placed the hand unit on the hook and smiled. *This could get very interesting.*

¤-¤-¤-¤-¤

Billie was a few minutes late when she arrived at the Forest. Her afternoon had been hectic, dodging Mr. Hammersmith and trying to get the details checked on the new renovation design Mr. Boster had given her. Then, when she had stepped out of the office building after work, the warmer temperature had surprised her and she had driven by the recycled clothing shop to get a lighter jacket and sweater. By the time she got back to her apartment and got everything ready to take, she was running late.

Billy was waiting, and took his usual place by the door while she changed. He smiled at her and her changed look when she came out, and then led the way to the department store. Once inside, before she slipped out of her street clothes, he stopped and turned to face her.

"Make a pocket in the inside of your boot for this," he said, and handed her a large, unmarked key. "I can help if you want, but don't lose it and don't let anyone outside of us know you have it or what it goes to."

"Yes, sir," she said, and smiled into this eyes.

He smiled in return, then quickly turned, stepped back, and tossed his jacket, shirt, and pants into a pile beside the wall.

She put the key into her pants pocket and then stripped down to her sweats.

Billy and Cathy were waiting for her in the middle of the mats, and Abby was as close matside as the grown-ups would allow, with Ernest and the other two boys close beside her.

"I want to start with the same offensive positions we practiced yesterday," Billy said, "but today I want Lynx to focus on how to reach your opponent without him or her reaching you. To show you how to block, feint, and evade. This should tie those first defensive moves you showed us with the moves you've learned using the 'knives.'"

Billie inhaled when he smiled at her, but it was the *way* he looked at her that made her catch her breath.

"Are you ready, Tiger?"

She nodded.

Do your best. Be the Tiger for Billy.

"Show me what I need to learn, Lynx."

-¤-

Billy stepped back, opposite those sitting cross-legged on the floor, and watched as Cathy went through each movement slowly once or twice, and then at speed. It seemed to only take

Billie a couple of tries to master the moves. Cathy kept up the pace, showing Billie one set after another, following the same demonstration-and-trial approach. Each time Billie seemed to grasp the essentials quickly.

Finally, after nearly half an hour, Billy called Hammer to the mat and Billie matched Hammer move for move. He never got a dowel tip on her.

Then Billy called tall and lanky Stretch. Max made a successful advance on Billie the first time, but Billy noticed how she quickly adjusted for his height and the length of his reach. It was obviously a struggle for her, and the matches took more time, but in the end, Stretch's first success was his last.

Billy called the session and told Billie they needed to get cleaned up. Before she stepped off the mat, Abby picked up Billie's backpack and was right beside her, offering compliments and pointers from a seven-year-old's perspective.

-¤-

"All right, Stretch," Billy said as they grouped around him.

"I was sure I could get her with my longer arms"—Max smiled—"but she's slippery. Figured me out in no time." He nodded. "I'd let her back me up anytime, Billy."

Billy looked at Todd and just got a big smile. "Didn't even get a nick. She's learnin' good, Billy."

Then Billy turned to Cathy. "You worked her the longest," he said, implying the question.

"Once she understood the mechanics of what I was showing her, it was like she'd just replay the movements. She has a way of adding a few unexpected twists of her own—sidesteps, squats, feints." Cathy smiled. "That's really good."

"I was hoping she wasn't wearing you down," Billy said, holding his smile back. "You're not old by any means, but she does have a few years on you."

"I'm feelin' it all right," Cathy admitted, wiping her brow again with her towel, "but don't you worry about that."

"Thanks," Billy said. "I've got to get cleaned up too."

He smiled and patted their shoulders as he turned and went to pick up his clothes.

Thirty

Wednesday, May 4

Frederick stormed off the elevator and shoved the glass doors open as he charged into the Boster, Lange and Hammersmith design offices. He barely slowed down as he passed the receptionist and told her to tell Mike "Westman is here to see him." He did not notice the numerous heads that looked up from the low-walled cubicles as he marched down the long aisle, past Carl Boster's and Robert Lange's offices.

"Mike, I want to talk to you," he said as he barged into Mike's office and pushed the door closed, but in his preoccupation, it did not get completely shut.

"Sit down, Frederick," Mike said calmly, and gestured to the chair beside his large desk. "I presume you're here to justify why you did not close on Friday."

"No," Frederick said flatly. "I'm here to find out why you snuck a penalty clause into our contract when you know I filed for the renovation project at your request! I didn't want that project! You did!"

"Now, now, Frederick," Mike said, raising his voice. "I told you it would make you a lot of money—"

"You knew my plate was full," Frederick said. "I told you I didn't have the time or staff to handle it right now, but you insisted! And now you're going to charge me a default payment?"

"Frederick!" Mike shouted, and slammed his fist down on his desk. "You signed the contract! I didn't make you sign it!"

"After all we've been through," Frederick said, lowering his voice as he leaned forward, fists on the desktop. "After all of the deals I've done for you, especially the questionable ones, and you treat me like this?"

"It's business! You should understand that!" Mike shouted.

"Very well," Frederick said with a hard edge in his tone. "If this is what you call 'business,' understand this: neither my firm nor I will ever do business with you again. You can find someone else to do your dirty work! I will not hide any more of your skeletons in my closet!"

"Get out!" Mike shouted, and stood up, pointing at the door. "Get out, Frederick! Don't you ever come around here threatening me again! Get out!"

Frederick slowly stood up, turned to the door, and smiled at Mike as he opened it. "Have a nice day, Mike. I'm very interested in what you do next." He turned and marched back down the aisle, past the receptionist, and out through the glass doors.

-¤-

Billie had stopped in her office doorway, holding her project folder in front of her, when Frederick Westman marched up the far aisle and into Mike Hammersmith's office. She could not make herself move when their conversation spilled out over the cubicles and quickly grew into shouts, ending with the clear demands for Frederick to leave. She was still standing in her doorway, stunned by what she heard, when Frederick marched down the aisle and out of the offices.

Suddenly, Billie could not remember the question she was going to ask Carl when she had gotten up and started to his office.

¤-¤-¤-¤-¤

Billie's head was still spinning when she entered Whiskey's, looking for Becky and the girls. She stopped just inside the entry and saw Becky's wave.

"Man, what a day," Billie said as she slid into the booth beside Becky. "Where's Stacy?"

"She's running late," Lori said, and tapped her entry into the ordering pad.

"You're dressed more casual than usual," Becky said, noting Billie's black slacks, low-topped boots, and her loose-fitting blouse as she took the pad from Lori. "What's up?" Becky scrolled down the list on the screen and made her choice.

"Nothing really," Billie said, glancing around the rustic room, remembering how much she liked the more common feel of Whiskey's compared to the glitzy glass-and-chrome atmosphere that Lori and Becky always gravitated to. But she admitted the variety was good in its own way. "I got comfortable after work and just didn't feel like putting on the glam again."

I decided I didn't want to dress for them this time.

They still noticed.

Too bad.

"You still look nice," Becky admitted as she passed the pad to her. "Just not as flashy as you usually are." Becky thought a moment, then asked, "This wouldn't have anything to do with that new friend of yours, would it?"

Billie smiled and took the pad, selected a brandy martini, one of Becky's rum shots, and an appetizer. She inserted her card.

"What does he have to do with it?" Lori asked, looking confused.

"I think Billie's off the market," Becky said, her eyes dancing.

"Is that true, Billie?" Lori asked, and caught Billie's left hand. "And you *are* still wearing that chain thing on your wrist."

It's an honest question.

Sure is. And we know the answer.

Billie pulled her hand back and smiled. "Maybe. We'll have to wait and see if it's true."

Slowly, Lori's expression turned to a smile and she changed the subject. "So, you had a bad day?"

"I didn't," Billie said as she set the pad down, "but Mr. Hammersmith sure did."

"That could be bad," Lori said, and sat up a little straighter. "Never good when the big boss has a bad day. What happened?"

"He got chewed out by one of his clients," Billie said without going into the details. "They lost a big project last Friday, and I guess there was something in the contracts that the client didn't like. They really went at it."

"How'd you hear about it?" Becky asked.

Billie chuckled. "They didn't close his office door. The whole office heard it—shouts and all."

She stopped when the young waitress arrived with their orders. With a little help, she placed the drinks correctly and then centered the large platter of colorful chips covered with cheese, brown and black beans, ground beef, salsa, and a dollop of sour cream and guacamole on the side. The waitress set a bottle of hot sauce beside the platter and passed three small plates and napkin-wrapped silverware around, asked if they needed anything else, and left when they said they were fine.

Lori and Becky watched in dismay as Billie took the shot and downed it in two quick sips.

"I didn't take time to eat before I came," Billie said. "Dig in if you're hungry." She unrolled her silverware and scooped a serving onto her plate.

¤-¤-¤-¤-¤

"How are you and Sparrow holding up, Falcon?" Billy asked as they walked down Duberry below its junction with Ninth West. "This night after night has to be getting old."

"It is, Keeper," Buddy said, "but we know it's necessary. We can't stop and let these folks get swept under the carpet. Not now that it's obvious someone is trying to upset the cart."

"I really appreciate the dedication," Billy said. "And I'm

looking forward to more peaceful times myself."

"Are you and Tiger going to make a go of it?" Buddy asked.

"I sure hope so," Billy said, and smiled. "In here." He led the way into the alley just north of the Streetcar. "They're still open and I need to check on something."

Billy stopped at the back door, keyed the lock, and entered, pulling Buddy behind him. They stopped in the side room between the bath and the dry room.

"Sid?" Billy called softly and looked into the kitchen.

"Hey, Billy," Sid said, and turned to greet him. "Hey, Falcon. Good to see you."

"I need to check for a message," Billy said. "Can you get Falcon a cup of coffee or something? What would you like?" Billy turned to Buddy for a choice.

"Coffee is fine, Keeper, Sid," Buddy said. "Thanks."

"Anytime, Falcon," Sid said, and turned to the serving counter to get a cup.

Billy was just opening the door to the hallway when Sid smiled and said, "The light's blinking, Billy."

Billy stopped and smiled at Sid in return, then disappeared into the office and closed the door.

Keeper and His Tiger: An Unexpected Complication

Thirty-One

Wednesday, May 5

"Mr. Boster?" Billie asked as she knocked lightly on his office doorjamb. "Do you have a minute?"

"Certainly," he said, and looked up from the file he was reading.

"Is Mr. Hammersmith still angry over yesterday?" she asked. "We couldn't help but overhear him and Mr. Westman."

"I know." He smiled. "But that was yesterday, and today is its own trouble."

"Oh," she said absently.

"Seems that Kelly and Lloyd," he continued, "an architectural firm out of Chicago, has filed for permits to renovate the two Duckard buildings."

"They have?" she said in surprise. "That means the owners have finally decided to do something with those properties?"

And Billy and those in the basement will have to move, sooner than they were expecting.

"It most certainly does, Billie," he said, a sad expression flashing across his face. "And it also means that we will not get any part of the renovation design work."

"That's too bad," she agreed, her mind suddenly jumping from one implication to another.

"And that means Mr. Hammersmith is beside himself today," he said, shaking his head. "He has had his eye on those properties for a long, long time, and now he can't even participate in their revitalization."

◻-◻-◻-◻-◻

Going into the restroom to change, Billie saw Billy waiting in his usual place under the tree in the Forest. He was standing beside the door when she came out.

"I told you about us losing the renovation project," she said when they started walking and were out of earshot of other people enjoying walks in the warmer evenings. "Yesterday, Mr. Westman marched into Mr. Hammersmith's office and they got into a major argument."

"Really?" Billy asked. "They've always been as cozy as two peas." He crossed his fingers to demonstrate.

"Well, yesterday he told Mr. Hammersmith he'd never work with him again and that he'd just have to get someone else to do his dirty work for him."

"Dirty work? He said that?" Billy stopped and looked at her. "You're sure?"

"The whole office heard it. They didn't get the office's door closed and everyone could hear them arguing. Mr. Hammersmith finally started shouting and ordered Mr. Westman to get out."

"Wow," Billy said, and started walking again. "I need to think about this."

"Yeah," Billie agreed. "Especially after Mr. Westman told Mr. Hammersmith that he wasn't going to keep any more of his skeletons in his closet."

"Oh, my. That was a bad thing for him to say to Mike," Billy said, and rubbed his chin.

"That's what I thought," Billie admitted.

"Mike never liked being threatened," Billy said as they stopped at the street corner across from the department store. "And that was about as close to a threat as I've heard in a long time."

When they stepped up onto the curb and started into the

narrow passage between the buildings, Billie started again. "I also heard today that the owners of these building have filed for renovation permits with the city."

"Now that's interesting," Billy said, and smiled. "Looks like things are starting to change."

"I know, but how will that affect you and the others?"

"We'll have to figure something out," Billy said, and stopped beside the heavy metal door.

He looked up and down the alley like he always did, waited a moment, and seeing no one, he unlocked the door and they slipped inside. He relocked the door, and when he turned around Billie threw her arms around his neck and pulled herself up and kissed him fully.

"I've waited almost two days to do that again," she said, and clung to him, feeling his arms tighten around her. "You didn't stop by last night."

"I've missed you too, Tiger," he said, and kissed her again. "Falcon and a few others helped me watch the village, and then Stretch, Cat, and I watched for interlopers until about two."

Billie tightened her hold and kissed him again, long and tenderly.

"I'm glad you feel this way," he said as he slowly lowered her back to the floor. "Because I think you're going to hate me after today's practice. Come on." He took her hand and led her down the stairs.

Everyone was sitting around the mats, and Billie stopped beside a support pillar and slipped out of her sweater and pants. Billy tossed his shirt and street pants in a pile beside hers and stepped to the center of the mats.

When Billie joined him, Max handed them the dowels. She saw Billy point to Cathy and curl his finger, gesturing for her to join them.

"Today is a free-for-all." He looked at Cathy. "Anything we've practiced, goes." Then he looked at Billie.

"Okay," Billie said, and nodded to Cathy.

Okay, Tiger, do your best. Show Billy he named you right.

"Show me what I've missed, Lynx."

Billy watched and let them tangle for a five-minute session before he stopped them and pointed out a few things Billie could do differently to give her a better advantage and to anticipate more than one possible next move. After three more five-minute sessions, Billy called time and asked Abby to bring water for both Tiger and Lynx.

When Abby returned and they had rested a few minutes, Billy asked Billie, "Where did you feel awkward?"

She thought about the sessions and told him where she felt off balance and not quite in control. "When Lynx made that one swipe and tried to grab my knife hand, I almost stumbled when I twisted away. I wasn't sure I could be in position for her next move."

"Lynx," he said. "Your comments?"

"I really like how she crowds and pushes," Cathy said. "I never felt like she was off balance or uncertain. She has a very positive attitude and persistence."

Billy got up and took Billie through the sequences that made her feel off balance, and she followed his changes in how she stepped into the twist, the push, and her recovery footwork. She smiled and repeated the moves, quickly seeing the difference.

"Okay," he said, and motioned for Cathy to join them. "One more session before we move on."

When they finished, Cathy and Billie both admitted it felt much better.

Billy nodded. "Get another drink," he said, and motioned to Max.

Abby recruited Ernest, and together they brought them cups of water.

Billy turned to Billie. "Okay. The bad news. It'd be very unfair of me to let you think street fighting is always nicely matched and fair. It hardly ever is. This time, I want to see how you do defending yourself against two opponents."

When they finished with their drink, he led them to the

center of the mats. "If any of you get touched on your torso with a dowel tip, you're out."

He positioned Cathy and Max in front of Billie and called a start.

In the first session, Cathy got a lucky jab and took Billie out, but in the second session, Billie got Cathy first and then took Max out. The third was almost no contest as Billie took them both in her first lunge and a quick, ducking spin under Stretch's challenging arm.

When Billie straightened up, Cathy stepped forward, extended her hand, and caught Billie's. She pulled Billie close, hugged her, and patted her back.

"I sure don't want to meet you in a dark alley, girl," she said, and smiled hugely.

"Me either," Max said, and extended his hand.

Billie took it and smiled. "Thanks."

She looked at Billy; he was beaming.

◻-◻-◻-◻-◻

"It's Joey, Mr. Hammersmith," the voice on the phone said. "I got a message that said I should call you as soon as I can."

"That's right, Joey," Mike said. "I need for you to arrange a meeting for me."

"If I can, Mr. Hammersmith," Joey said with a little more pride in his voice.

"Who do you know that can help me with a marketing problem in the city center?" Mike asked.

"A marketing problem?" Joey asked, suddenly bewildered.

"Drug sales, you idiot!" Mike shouted. "I need someone to help someone I know. He was chased out and has not been able to do any selling in the city center."

"Oh, I get it," Joey said. "But the city center is a closed 'hood. No one lives there."

233

"Of course they do, and I want to open it up," Mike said, his exasperation showing.

"Okay," Joey said. "I don't get it, but I'll see if I can set up a meeting and I'll call you back with the when and where."

"Very good, Joey," Mike agreed. "Soon."

"Yes, sir. Soon."

Friday, May 6

Anticipating lunch with Becky and Lori, Billie had shut her computer off and was taking her coat from the rack beside her office door when she heard her name called. She looked up and saw Mr. Hammersmith looking at her through his open office door.

Shit! Not now!

She knew she could not avoid him this time.

He beckoned and she saw Mr. Lange turn to see her. She folded her jacket over her left arm and put her head and right arm through her purse's shoulder strap. She walked to his office, careful to keep her coat over her wrist, and saw the disappointment in Mr. Lange's face when she entered.

"Yes, Mr. Hammersmith?" she asked politely, and stopped in the doorway.

"Billie," he said by way of a minimal greeting. "Have you found out anything about the owners of the Duckard Property?"

"Nothing of value, sir," she said, and glanced at Mr. Lange. "I'm not working that project any longer."

"What was the name you found?" he persisted.

"Pas...Pastoric Group," she said. "I don't know what it means, and I did not find anything on them from the internet or any city sources."

"But I believe the titles were in some other names," he said.

"Yes, sir," she admitted. "Tri-Funds and CR Associates. My

suspicion is they are divisions or subsidiaries of Pastoric, but I couldn't find anything to prove it."

She absently made a flat gesture with her right hand to signify finding *nothing*. Her movement inadvertently uncovered her left wrist and Mr. Hammersmith saw the inked chain.

"What's that?" he asked loudly.

"What?" she asked, startled by his sudden change.

"That," he said, and pointed. "That. On your wrist."

"Oh, that," she said, holding her voice calm, remembering what Mr. Lange had told her.

You should've taken that off. Mr. Lange warned you.

I know, but I don't want to take it off.

"It's a partnership chain. I got engaged last week—"

"No one is allowed to wear tattoos in this company!" he shouted.

"That's silly, sir. There's nothing in the policy manual prohibiting them. Many people may have them and may just have them where you can't see them," she said, trying to lighten his mood.

"Well, I see that one and I don't like it," he shouted.

Shit! Really?

"Sir, it's hardly something to get worked up over," she tried again.

"I will not have employees that stoop to the ways and morals of the rubbish in the streets! Either you have that removed or I will have you removed!"

Well, damn! I sure hope Billy will understand where this is going.

"That won't be necessary," she said calmly and squared her shoulders. "I like working here, but I do not have to suffer an irrational tyrant for a boss. I have many friends among the 'rubbish,' as you call them, and they have higher morals and ethical values than some I have had the misfortune to work with."

"Get out, you, you…miscreant! You're fired! I don't ever

want to see your face around here again!"

She looked at Mr. Lange and nodded. "It was very nice working with you, sir. Thank you. Please tell Mr. Boster the same for me." She looked at Hammersmith, and the image of the homeless man with blood money falling out of his pockets instantly came to mind.

Billie turned, and with a slow and measured pace, walked back to her office to box up her personal items.

Damn irrational bastard!

So now what are you going to do? You knew this had to happen!

I did! I wasn't going to take the tat off and Hammersmith wasn't going to like it when he saw it. So I guess I knew it was coming. All right?

She inhaled, taking a deep breath, and held it for a moment.

What are the folks going to say?

Nothing. I see no reason to burden them with this minor setback.

Minor setback?

Yeah. I'm okay financially—the lease is paid up and I can make the utilities. I can train and help Billy more now. Something good has to come out of that. Right?

You ought to sue him! He has no legal leg to stand on for firing you for a tattoo! You could understand if it was a hateful or suggestive tat, but—

Billie smiled at the thought and shook her head as she collected a letter storage box from the supply closet.

I know, but a discrimination lawsuit will just hurt Carl and Robert. They aren't the bad guys here. I'll just have to think of something else.

Back in her office, Billie started collecting the few personal things she had, like the pictures of her folks, her sister, the desk set with her name *Billie Mattis* engraved on it, and a few other odds and ends.

Hah, I know! Mr. Hammersmith has no idea what he's just

done! He's just freed me up to help Billy nail him for his parents' death.

She chuckled.

That's the perfect karma for a man like him.

Keeper and His Tiger continues in

Book 2: *Deadly Undercurrents.*

Glossary

Characters:

-A-

Abby
Daughter of Cathy (Lynx). Seven years old.

-B-

Bennett, Dave
Owner of a well-known and respected paving company located in a Chesterfield suburb, Briar's Green.

Bennett, Tom
Son of Dave Bennett. Stacy's latest boyfriend.

Betty
Mike Hammersmith's secretary at Boster, Lange and Hammersmith Designs.

Billie Mattis
See, Mattis, Billie.

Billy Carson
See Carson, Billy.

Boster, Carl
Partner in Boster, Lange and Hammersmith Renovation and Design Consulting Company.

Butch
An undercover cop helping in the City Center.

Butler, Sid
Owner of The Streetcar Diner.

Butler, Mary
Sid Butler's mother. Sister of Dorothy Hawke.

-C-

Carson, Billy
31 year old homeless man. Has worked as a dishwasher and scullery man at The Streetcar Diner for seventeen years.

Copper
Streetwise drug dealer. Competitor of Pink's. Tries to sell drugs in the city center after Pink died.

-D-

Davis, Lori	26 year old, blonde woman, Accountant for Swaggard's Drugstore at Main and Branch Water Street. Long-time friend of Billie Mattis.
Diner Staff, Streetcar	Sid Butler – Owner and Head Cook
	Billy – General Scullery duties – Sid's background assistant
	Angie – Dining Room Manager and Head Waitress
	Julie – Waitress and Counter Attendant
	Carole – Waitress
	Melony – Order Organizer
	Niles – Assistant Cook
	Kevin – Assistant Cook
	Ned – Assistant Dishwasher
Donna	Frederick Westman's secretary at Westman Associates.

-F-

Filton, Grier	An Executive officer at the First State Bank and Trust. Billy's financial advisor.
Fowler, Gilbert	Sandy's college boyfriend. Medical Grad School student studying Neurological Medicine.

-G-

George, Rebecca	25 year old, brunette woman, the Assistant Curator at the City's Arts and Culture Museum. Friend of Billie Mattis. Aka, Becky or Beck.
Gibson, Walter	Attorney specializing in Business Law. Billy's personal Legal Council.

| GC | General Contractor. The lead contractor on a construction job. Often referred to as the General. |

-H-

Hammersmith, Mike	Principal partner and founder of Boster, Lange and Hammersmith Renovation and Design Consulting Company.
Hawke, William Carson III	Son of W. C. Hawke II and Dorothy (Dottie) Hawke (both mudered).
Herb	One of Mike Hammersmith's henchmen. A mean sort.
Homeless People	Department Store 'Street People' & their '(Street name)'

Billy (Keeper)

Max (Stretch) and Mindy (Cat)

Todd (Hammer)

Cathy** (Lynx), daughter Abby

Russell (Mace) and Barbara (Pigeon), son Ernest

Paul (Ferret*) and Donna (Mouse*), son Richard

Buddy (Falcon) and Jane (Sparrow*), son Rusty

Curt (Cutter) and Judy (Owl)

Josh (Red)

Randal (Spear)

Junior (Ditto)

* have a talent for hearing what's happening on the streets.

** Cathy's maiden name was Nikleson, married to and abandoned by Clark Jefferson.

-J-

Joey — One of Mike Hammersmith's henchmen.

June — Contracts Administrator at Westman Associates.

-K-

Keeper — The street name of a homeless man that has protected a number of blocks and properties in the City Center. Tiger's squeeze.

Kelly, Chase — 32 year old owner of a Medical Supply business. Volunteers at the Crescent Street soup kitchen.

-L-

Lange, Robert — Partner in Boster, Lange and Hammersmith Renovation and Design Consulting Company.

Lawrence, Blake — Billie's recent ex-boyfriend. A con artist with a bad temper.

Leonard, The Knife — Street-wise, self-proclaimed 'exterminator' known for removing two-legged problems for a price.

Lori Davis — See Davis, Lori

-M-

Majors, Stacy — 26 year old brunette woman. Works as a sales clerk and stocker at Pages Bookstore. Friend of Billie Mattis. Dating Tom Bennett.

Markins, Jack — Son of Billie's parent's long-time friends. Fiancé of Katie Biggens

Mattis, Billie	Wilhelmina Georgiana Mattis, a red haired woman, 27 year old daughter of Bob and Maggie Mattis. Works for Boster, Lange and Hammersmith Real Estate Developers and Renovations Consultants. Graduate with Master's degree in Business and Business Law (non-Barred). One older sister, Sandra, living away.
Mattis, Sandy	aka Sandra Mattis. The 30 year old daughter of Bob and Maggie Mattis; Billie's sister. Studying to become a Doctor in Pediatrics.
Mattis, Bob and Maggie	Robert (Bob) and Margaret (Maggs, Maggie), parents of Sandy and Billie. Owners and operators of a viable horse ranching business.
Maxie	Street vendor selling flowers on the north side of St. Charles Street, across from the park nick-named "The Forest."
Mitchell	Frederick Westman's 'go for' person.

-N-

Nolan, Detective	A Chesterfield city police detective. A friend of Billy Carson.

-P-

Pink	Street-wise drug dealer with his eye on the Chesterfield's City Center to expand his area of business.

-Q-

Quinn, Hannah	A local socialite woman, once engaged to Mike Hammersmith in his younger days.

Keeper and His Tiger: An Unexpected Complication

-R-

Rebecca (Becky), George See George, Rebecca

-S-

Simmy Street vendor that has a newsstand business near the west side of City Center.

Stacy Majors See Majors, Stacy

-T-

Tiger Keeper's squeeze.

-W-

Westman, Collin Daughter of Nancy and Frederick Westman. No siblings. Student at Michigan State University, East Lansing, Michigan, studying to become a veterinarian.

Westman, Frederick Real Estate Developer. Daughter Collin. Ex-wife Nancy, divorced sixteen years.

Westman, Nancy Frederick Westman's ex-wife.

Places and Things:

-B-

Baily A small farm town NE of Chesterfield. Mike Hammersmith's sister lives there.

-C-

Chesterfield A middle sized, sprawling mid-west city in the United States. The city had an eighteen block City Center core with high rise buildings, the tallest being fourteen stories. The city is serviced by a regional airport and local and interstate bus services.

CR Associates

Circular Reference, Subsidiary of Pastoric Group – General Manager: John Collier.

Custer's

An eating and drinking establishment located in a strip-mall on the NE corner of Lakota and Fourth Street East.

-D-

Daisy's

A Wine Bar, NW of City Center located at Emmit and Fifth Street West.

Danny's Steakhouse

Distinguished Steak and Beverage Restaurant on Calvin and Duberry. Owned by Danny Willis and his three daughters, Lydia the youngest, Monica in the middle and Nikki (Nicole) the oldest.

Duckard's Department Store   Deserted department store building in a shared block in City Center. Situated at the corner of Second and Baker St

-F-

Forest, The

A city park in west Chesterfield bordered by St. Charles Street on the north, St. Anne on the south, and by Fifth and Sixth Street West on the east and west sides.

-K-

Kelly and Lloyd Architects   Chicago based Architectural Firm specializing in large commercial renovation projects. Owner: Jim Donaldson

Site review architects: Bob Dawson, Joseph, Jane, Lucy

-M-

Marquee Cocktail Lounge	A modern downtown cocktail lounge on the NW corner of Main Street and St. Anne.

-O-

Olive and Onion	A Martini Bar at David and Twelfth Street West.

-P-

Pages Book Store	Book store on Main between St. Anne and Arapaho. Stacy works here.
Pastoric Group	Investment group holding and protecting W. C. Hawke's assets. Controlled by W. C. Hawke III and daily operations managed by Gregory (Greg) Madison.

-S-

Streetcar Diner, The	A shiny, metal-look diner on the west side of City Center. Owner: Sid Butler.
Swaggard's Drug Store	Drug store on Kiowa and 7th Street West. Lori works as an accountant and general clerk / stocker here.

-T-

Tri-Funds	Subsidiary of Pastoric Group.

-W-

Westman Associates	A land development and construction company owned by Frederick Westman.
Whiskey's Bar and Grille	A rustic casual dining bar and grille on the NE corner of Blackfoot and Sixth Street, two blocks south of "The Forest."

Books by Aidan Red:

Keeper and His Tiger
(After living homeless to find his parents murderer...)
Book 1: An Unexpected Complication
Book 2: Deadly Undercurrents
Book 3: The Trap

Paladin Shadows Series
Terran Assignment
Book 1: Things Are Not As They Seem
Book 2: When Luck Is Not Enough
Book 3: Fate Has A Different Idea
Terran Recruits
Book 4: In the Wake of Chaos
Book 5: Terran Talents Join Forces
Book 6: New Rules of Engagement
Operation Retribution
Book 7: The Training Phase
Book 8: Taking the Fight Off-World
Book 9: Luring the Prince Into the Open
Garda Nua
Book 10: The Proliferation of Talent
Book 11: When A Planet Is Stolen
Book 12: Right Does Not Ask Permission
Assignment: Casha-Six
Book 13: No Warning
Book 14: The Best Laid Plans
Book 15: A Change of Heart?

Fearin' the Banshee

More Books by Aidan Red

Eight's Warning
A West's Ghost Ranch Trilogy
(A tale in the world of high octane aviation fuel and restored warbirds)
Book 1: The Past Hunts
Book 2: The Past Attacks
Book 3: The Price of Escape

About the Author

Aidan Red's passion for aviation and aircraft design, engineering, and a deep interest in space and space travel go back many years. An avid reader from an early age, Aidan, with great trepidation, ventured into the world of writing during college. With real world experience in business aviation, Aidan's creative side led him to create an alternate world where the beautiful Riggs Valley was born and Shara's life became chronicled in his epic science fiction series, Paladin Shadows.

Paladin Shadows consists of the five triptychs (three-part works), *Terran Assignment, Terran Recruits, Operation Retribution, Garda Nua* and *Assignment: Casha-Six.* In between the Paladin triptychs, Aidan has penned two, three book series, *Keeper and his Tiger,* and *Eight's Warning,* a West's Ghost Ranch Trilogy, and a novel, *Fearin' the Banshee.*

The unpublished books in his various series are scheduled for release on a regular basis in the coming months.

You can visit

www.RedsInkandQuill.com or

www.AidanRedBooks.com

for more information on books published by Aidan Red books and where to purchase them.